FIRST RESPONSE

A BOYS BEHAVING BADLY ANTHOLOGY BOOK #5

DELILAH DEVLIN   ELLE JAMES   REINA TORRES

AVA CUVAY   PAYTON HARLIE   MEGAN RYDER

N.J. WALTERS   JAAP BOEKESTEIN

KIMBERLY DEAN   TRAY ELLIS   MICHAL SCOTT

M. JAYNE   JANUARY GEORGE

MARGAY LEAH JUSTICE   A.C. DAWN

TWISTED PAGE INC

First Response

A Boys Behaving Badly Anthology
Edited by Delilah Devlin

The stories in this book are works of fiction. The characters, incidents and dialogues are of the authors' imaginations and are not to be construed as real. Any resemblance to actual events or persons, living or dead, is completely coincidental.

EBOOK ISBN: 978-1-62695-317-8

ISBN PRINT: 978-1-62695-318-5

Dedicated to readers for their love of great stories!

Delilah Devlin & Elle James

STORIES INCLUDED

FAR FROM OVER

BY REINA TORRES

S *on of a bitch.*

The PASS alarm was normally a godsend, but blaring in his ears in a tiny space, almost flattened under a pile of debris…? *Who needs eardrums…*

…when you're dead.

And the way the debris was pressing down on him, the lack of viable oxygen in his lungs—it wasn't going to be long.

Arms pinned, one beneath him and the other under debris, a lack of wiggle room meant he was just another piece of debris lying on the floor. And the pile? Well, it just kept getting bigger.

Something exploded above him. Glass, most likely. If it was caused by the heat, he was dead already. Air hot enough to break out a window would fry him. Sear his flesh from the outside in. Then again, it could be water.

As first on the scene, Chief Brewer was probably pummeling the building with water. The man didn't have two brain cells to rub together on a good day, but when the chips were down, the man's brain froze up like the last update on his computer, running in circles until he yanked the plug out of the wall. And given that his uncle was the Center City Fire Commissioner, no one was going to take the reins out of his hands.

Russell knew he'd be toast then.

More water dripped onto his cheek from the debris over his head, held back by luck and the edge of his helmet. Where the water had been a cautious drop, off and on, it was quickly becoming a thin stream of gritty water, and trying to keep it out of his mouth was almost as bad as letting it in.

If they didn't stop hosing down the building, it was a tossup as to whether he would drown first or die, praying for air.

No matter what, unless something changed drastically in the next few minutes, it wouldn't matter either way.

Something shifted in the pile on top of him, pushing the pile a few inches to the side. Not enough to move his head or any whole body part, but it was enough to roll a long stretch through his body, hoping to keep his muscles supplied with enough blood—

For what?

So he'd be a good-looking corpse?

The world above him shifted, and then shifted again.

It was hypoxia.

His brain was as starved as his lungs. His oxygen tank had lasted a few heartbeats past the shattering of his mask. Layers of protection gone in a few heart-breaking moments.

The edges of his vision had lightened, blanching out in spots and flares.

As long as it wasn't a light at the end of a tunnel—

"Hey, I got him!"

The weight on his back moved, lifted.

"Hey. *Hey! Webb!*"

Light hit his face as the debris around his right shoulder fell away.

Russell blinked into the bright light. He couldn't lift his hand up to block the onslaught. "I'm Webb—"

He heard a bark of laughter and saw the downward swing of a Halligan, punctuated with a heavy thud.

Russell didn't even blink. He wasn't afraid of the Halligan. Whoever it was standing beside him knew his job. Each swing and strike lifted a little more of the debris from his back.

When he had full range of motion in his shoulder and managed to pry his arm free, he reached up and pushed at the layers trapping his hips, and more weight lifted free of his other arm and feet.

The heat was like a monsoon in the desert, wet and hot, forming steam in the air and prickling at every inch of exposed skin.

"Come on, Webb!" He felt something slip under his left arm and pull. "All that muscle's got to be good for something."

"Hey," he groaned, "I was dying here!"

Her laughter was warm and smooth.

Her?

"There's time to die later, Webb. If you do it here,

you're going to take me with you, because I'm not leaving without you."

Pushing up from the floor, he turned his head slightly and saw a pair of warm brown eyes through the facemask above him.

Maybe he was dead.

Or having the best hallucination of his life. "Gina?"

"Who else would crawl into a hole on fire to look for your sorry ass?"

He laughed, and somehow found the energy to lift and backpedal toward the light behind him.

She set him down and leaned out of the hole in the wall to call for assistance.

He tried to roll over onto his side and felt every muscle in his body scream in protest. "I can get up. I can."

"Oh, I know you can get it up, Webb, but this isn't a bar, and I'm not one of those girls begging for your attention."

He laid back down, his body aching in protest from the sudden movement. "I'm willing to beg for yours, Gina. You know I am."

"Promises, promises," she ground out the words as she pulled the cradle into the opening before another firefighter stepped into what was left of the room.

"Hey, Rock," she said.

Webb swore under his breath. Rock was on his crew, and the look the older man was giving him promised years of shit.

"You giving the lady trouble, Webb? Why, I oughta

haul you out of here by the scruff of your neck instead of on the cradle."

"Har har, old man."

Rock laughed. "You're lucky I don't want to break in another smoke eater on the crew."

Gina came around to the opposite side, and together, she and Rock grabbed him by his turnout coat and set him down in the cradle so they could remove him from the building.

"You better stop drinking all that beer, Webb," she grumbled. "After I get you out of here, you owe me."

"Anything you want, baby. Anything. It's yours."

She didn't say anything back to him. From that moment on, all he remembered was the jarring descent down the ladder. Somewhere along the way, he drifted out… like a light.

Smokin' Joe's Bar wasn't his normal haunt. It wasn't even a place he'd visit on a lark. Center City was a few hundred feet smaller than Chicago, not that Chi-town let them forget the difference. Still, Center City was big enough to house a handful of bars frequented by firefighters. Beyond that, Joe's was one of two bars owned and run by firefighters.

The front door opened, and a young couple stepped out into the cold. It only took a moment for the woman to give a playful little shiver. The man let go of the door and opened his coat, letting her step into his warmth.

It was a cute little scene, but it didn't interest him. Well, the couple didn't interest him.

Leaning his shoulder against the glass, Russell Webb turned and looked inside the bar. The walls were lined with fading tin signs and neon antiques with most of the letters still legible.

It had probably been a great place to get together a few years ago, but the decorations inside looked like they hadn't changed much since the Marlboro man had been big. And he was still hanging on one of the walls. Things were clean and well kept, but a little shabby and dated. Go to any bar that was packed on a cold night like this, and you'd see why they were packed. Joe's had just gotten stuck in the past.

To prove his point, a handful of guys walked up to the door, took one look inside, then stepped back and continued down the block. It was only when they passed Russell that one of the guys caught on to why he was standing outside on a night cold enough to put frostbite on his balls.

Gina Ferrer.

She was one of the bartenders in Joe's every night she wasn't working at Station Five.

And he wasn't the only one there at Joe's who came precisely to see her. Taking another look at the bar, he saw that almost every inch of the bar on her side was filled. Guys had probably pried open spaces to stand in her section using a well-placed elbow or two.

They were keeping her busy, almost too busy to look up when he opened the door.

Almost.

But she saw him.

And almost smiled.

Russell walked across the empty dance floor and found a seat near the end of the bar. Far enough away from her admirers so he wouldn't get lost in the crowd, and yet close enough to the other bartender that he didn't have to wait for service.

"Good to see you walkin' around, Webb."

"Good to be walking around, Mahony."

The older man leaned forward on the bar. "Should I read somethin' into you comin' over to this side of town? Thought you Station Twenty-Nine folks were loyal to Ciro's."

Russell shrugged. "There's loyal, and then there are other interests, Mahony. Do I need to spell it out to you?"

Mahony pointed a finger at him and added a knowing wink. "No need to spell it out, son. Besides," he leaned back from the bar, "I hear folks at Twenty-Nine don't spell too good."

Ah, the rivalry between houses was alive and well.

"What can I get for you?"

Russel didn't have to turn his head to see Gina at the other end of the bar. The mirror on the wall was mostly foxed with age, but there were reflective spaces enough to show him her stellar backside and the cascade of dark curls around her shoulders.

"Off the menu, Webb." Mahony's smile was a wry twist at the corner of his mouth. "Off the menu."

Tapping his fingers on the worn wooden surface, he gave the older man a pointed look. "Water, please."

Mahony's eyes went dull and his jaw a little slack. "Sorry, I must have misheard you. I thought you said—"

"You heard me, Joe."

Mahony didn't move for a long moment, seemingly frozen in place.

Taking out his wallet, Russell fished out a bill and set it on the bar. A twenty-dollar bill. "And keep them coming."

Moving with a distinctive hitch in his stride, Mahony poured him a tall glass of water and set it before him on the bar. "Best there is, straight from our tap. Enjoy."

GINA FELT like she was working under a microscope.

Every time she looked up from her work, or turned to one of her customers near the middle of the bar, she saw him.

Russell Webb.

Even after spending a good week in the hospital and two more in doctor-ordered physical therapy, he still looked like a marble-hewn god in jeans and a long-sleeved Henley shirt, which did more for his muscles and her libido than anything else ever could.

"Miss? Can I have another beer?"

"Sure." She turned around and put on her best grin. "Not a problem." Reaching into the cooler, she fished out a bottle of his lite beer of choice and wiped off the ice chips clinging to the sides. The chill that crawled up her arms was welcome.

It fought off the worst of her memories. Russell buried under a pile of detritus. Russell's facemask cracked. The sight of him being loaded into the back of an ambulance.

Yeah, those were memories she'd be glad to forget.

The problem was, they'd featured in her nightmares nearly every night since the fire, waking her up in a heart-pounding sweat.

"Miss?" Mister Lite-beer said. "What time do you finish work?"

Gina looked at the clock and spoke to the room. "Last call, folks. So, if you want another one, speak up."

A hand shot up a few empty stools away from Russell, and she started toward the customer, but someone caught her sleeve.

Mister Lite-beer.

Irritated, she kept her expression neutral as she turned to address him. "You needed something, sir?"

"Come on, you can call me Greg." He gave her a big, easy grin. "What can I call you?"

Relaxing her arm, she slid out from under his hand and shook her head. "I don't get personal with customers."

Giving him her best customer service smile, she moved on and served the guy near the middle of the bar, and from there on, it was a rush of patrons closing their tabs.

She couldn't help stealing glances at Russell whenever she could.

He was alive.

And she couldn't help the way she felt, having him so close. Distracted and hyper-aware of his every move, every breath. Ever since she'd realized that it had been

Russell pinned under rubble in the house, she'd been on edge.

MAHONY MAY HAVE BEEN in his seventies, but the man had sharp eyes and a sharper tongue. And both were aimed at Russell. "Are you planning on making your move?"

Russell looked up at the bartender. "And that's your business, how?"

"Because she's like a daughter to me, asshole."

Plainly spoken and from the heart. Russell couldn't argue with that.

But he could ask a question of his own. "If you think I'm an asshole, why would you want me to—uh, make a move, that is?"

Mahony shook his head and mumbled something like "imbecile" before he leaned both hands on the sink below the bar. "I figure the two of you were bound to happen sooner or later."

Picking up his water glass, Russell tipped it back to take a drink.

Mahony kept talking. "Might as well let her get it out of her system before she decides to settle down. Besides, if your attentions are unwelcome, my girl has pepper spray in her purse, and she's ready and willing to knee your nuts into your ribs."

Russell coughed up some of the water in his mouth, and Mahony had a good laugh as he chucked a towel at Russell. "Clean it up. I'm going in back to close. Keep an eye on 'mister slick' down there."

There wasn't a need to point out who he was talking about at the end of the bar. Russell knew the hungry look on the man's face. He'd stared at Gina like that too many times to pretend he didn't understand.

But he wasn't going to let the man try anything. Not while he was around.

GINA SAW Russell out of the corner of her eye. He was still there. And so was the preppy puppy in front of her. Neither of them looked like they were going anywhere.

"If you wouldn't mind…" Tapping on the printed bar tab that she'd set before Greg, she managed a smile. "We're trying to close up."

"I know." He stood and leaned closer. "So, where can I take you to eat around here."

"It's after midnight."

He shrugged. "There's got to a be a café or—"

"She wants you to pay up and leave."

Blowing out a breath, Gina shrugged. It was true, but she could have gotten Greg to pay up without Russell getting involved.

Leaving his water glass behind, Russell moved down the bar, his gaze focused on the other man. "Pay up. Bar's closed."

"Mind your own—"

She'd never seen Russell move that fast before. Not even when they'd been caught in the turnout room at the academy.

One second, he was just standing there, and the next,

he had the guy by the throat, walking him backwards to the door.

"Webb!" she called out.

He didn't stop to listen or answer her. The door opened under their combined weight, and when the door closed again, Russell reached up, locked the door, and closed the bolt at the top of the frame.

When he turned around, she nailed him with a stare. "Thanks."

He had the nerve to smile. "You're welcome."

Gina rolled her eyes. "He didn't pay his tab."

Russell walked back to the bar, and she couldn't help but look him over. The last time she'd seen him, he'd been in a hospital bed unconscious. Now, he was wearing a cream-colored Henley that stretched over his arm muscles in just the right way.

He'd certainly kept up with his PT.

"Uh, hello?"

Something brushed her nose, and she brushed it away. "What the hell, Webb?"

Laughing, he picked up her hand from the bar and put a couple of bills in it. "I'm paying for the jerk and adding a generous tip because you had to put up with the asshole."

"Takes one to know one, Webb?" Looking down at the bills she saw that he had indeed added a tip. A generous one. With an appreciative nod, she looked up into his dark eyes. "Thanks, though." She turned to the cash register and rung up the sale. "Now, I don't have to chase him down and frisk him for the cash."

"Well, if you'd told me that, I would've hidden the cash on me and made you look."

She couldn't exactly tell him that she hated the idea. Turning away, she started to cash out her drawer. It was a rote activity that didn't need more than a handful of brain cells, so she could let her mind wander over his impressive physique. He looked like he'd put on some muscle since the academy, and even back then he'd had an impressive six-pack and forearms that made her wet.

When she was done, she lifted the cash box from the register drawer and turned to walk it into the kitchen.

"Whoa, hey, now."

She heard him hustling to catch up to her and smiled. *Good, let him chase me.*

Before she got to the kitchen door, it swung open. Mahony leaned to the side to look over her shoulder. "Good for you, sweetheart. Make him work for it." Giving her an outrageous wink, he took the box from her. "I'll do the bank deposits tonight."

There went her stall tactic. "I can do it, Joe."

"Nope." He lifted a chin and grinned. "Why don't you let Romeo here take you home."

Gina shook her head. "Why does everyone think Romeo is a romantic hero. The whole story is a tragedy."

Mahony paused to think about her words, and then shrugged. "Then it fits even better. Being with Webb certainly is a tragedy, but you're only young once. So, let the asshole knock your socks off, and then I'll set you up with a keeper. You deserve a little fun."

With that ringing endorsement, Mahony disappeared down the hall.

Gina grumbled under her breath. Mahony knew too much.

And he damn well talked too much.

"You going to let me take you home?"

Yeah, Russell was going to be insufferable now. She kept right on walking, pushing through the kitchen door with a slap.

"Hey," he got ahead of her and stood in front of her, "I came here because you saved me."

At first, Gina just stared at him, running those words around in her head. "So, the reason I haven't seen you since we graduated the academy is because I didn't yank your ass out of a fire sooner?"

"We're assigned to different stations."

"In the same city." She hoped he couldn't hear the ache in her voice.

"Yeah." He shrugged and gave her the smile that had fueled a thousand late-night fantasies. "And I came all the way across town to see you."

She lifted her chin and stared down her nose at him. "Well, I'm impressed. A whole thirty minutes driving to get here."

"Why are you so upset with me?" He stepped closer, and she took a step back. "I came to thank you, but if you're going to shut me out, I don't see how I can do that."

She shook her head and glared at the ground.

It wasn't all his fault. What she'd said to him about not bothering his ass to see her...? She was guilty of the same. Center City wasn't all that big. It was chock-a-block full of people, but it was just a drive. What was her excuse?

"Hey." He touched a finger under her chin.

Rather than fight him, she looked up. For once, the look in his eyes wasn't cocksure. She could see something in those dark brown eyes that felt… real.

That felt… vulnerable.

And if that didn't melt her panties more than his regular self-assured masculine confidence…

Fuck.

"Well," she stepped back and walked around him to the door, "are you going to take me home, or what?"

She didn't have to look back to know that he was following her. She swore she could almost feel the heat rolling off his body as he caught up to her.

Gina pushed open the back door of the bar and ignored his attempt to get her attention, waiting for him to step out after her before she locked the door.

"Hey. My car," he tried again, "is parked on the street."

She shrugged and walked around the fenced-in patio. "They don't tow tomorrow."

"Okay…" He caught up and walked alongside her as she turned another corner. "Are we taking your car?"

She would've laughed if she hadn't been trying to hold herself together. Her heart pounded frantically inside her chest. Nerves. That's all it was.

Setting a hand on the bannister, she gave him a look over her shoulder while letting out a steadying breath before she explained, "I live upstairs."

Gina didn't expect him to say anything. All that mattered was what he did. She took her time walking up the steps, letting her hips take on their natural sway, all the way up to the second floor. There was only one shot at a first time, and she had years of fantasies for him to live up to.

Gone were all her fantasies about planned seductions with a pretty dress and a fancy meal. No, she was wearing a simple blouse and a pair of worn jeans. She didn't even have fancy underwear to put on or take off.

Oh, well.

She managed to pull her key from the front pocket of her jeans and slide it into the door.

His hand closed over hers before she could turn it. "Hey," his voice was a warm caress against her ear and cheek, "we don't have to…"

"Don't have to…what? Weren't you supposed to come up here and fuck me senseless?" She felt her breath still in her lungs as her nipples tightened against her cotton blouse.

"Hey," his lip skimmed the curve of her ear, "I don't think Joe actually thought that we'd—"

"Why not?" She squeezed her eyes shut, wondering if she was assuming too much. "Unless you don't…want what we wanted before. If that's the case, then just say so. I'm a big girl."

One long, heart wrenching moment passed by filled only with the soft swish of the wind moving through the ivy covering the trellis beside the stairs.

And the sound of her heart pounding in her ears.

His hand clenched over hers on the doorknob, while

the other clutched her hip before it slid over her belly. "Oh, I want you, Gina. It's been too damn long since I've touched you, but this isn't about a quick one and done. Make no mistake, I'm here because we started this dance a long time ago, and I want to see where this leads."

Words. So many pretty words.

Words she couldn't believe coming out of his mouth.

Yanking her hand out from under his, she turned, putting her back to the door. Looking up into his eyes in the long shadows of her apartment landing, she said, "I'm not asking you for more, Webb. If you fuck me and you walk away, I'm good. You're right. We started this a long time ago.

"That night in the turnout room? I was ready to jump into the fire feet first 'cause there was that thing between us."

He shifted against her, placed an open-mouthed kiss on the side of her neck, and then tilted his chin up until their faces aligned, cheek to cheek. "Yeah, I felt that, too. You had me so wound up I would've sold my soul just to get balls deep inside you."

"So, what are you waiting for, Webb?" she murmured. "This is your chance."

If he turned around now and walked away, she'd just head back downstairs and finish off that bottle of tequila under the bar, but she really hoped he would stay. She was desperate to know how hot they could burn.

She reached up and took hold of his face. They were

almost the same height. All she had to do was lean into him and slant her lips over his.

He didn't hold back. He didn't even try to move away.

No, Russell Webb met her kiss and returned with more, pressing her against the door until her breasts were crushed up against the wall of his chest. It wasn't comfortable, but she could feel the tight points of her breasts against him, and that felt damn good.

She felt alive.

Gina opened her lips, and he moaned into her mouth, chasing the sound with his tongue. She wasn't going to let him take total control, not like that. Tangling with him, she reveled in the scratch of her tongue against his, lightly closing her teeth against him.

He pulled back and held her still against the hard wood with a hot look. "Don't bite unless you want to be bitten."

She licked her lips and smiled at him. "You don't see me arguing with that logic."

He grabbed at her hips, yanking her forward until her head and shoulders were the only things against the wall and his fingers were pawing at the front of her jeans.

Button undone.

Zipper down.

And then his hand was there, sliding his palm down her belly until his fingers slipped through her curls and gave her clit a hard rub.

Her lips parted on a gasp as her hips pushed closer.

Russell slipped a finger into her heat and leaned

forward until his forehead was on her shoulder. "Fuck me."

His breath fanned over her clothed breast and raised goose bumps on her flesh.

"You're so fucking hot down there."

"It started when you walked in tonight." The confession fell from her lips on a groan as he swirled this thumb over her clit, trapping the over-sensitive flesh.

"I watched you through the window." His voice was dark and hushed, as if he was sharing a secret. "I wanted to kick all of those assholes out of my way."

"Then you'd be just another asshole at the bar, right?"

He curled his fingers inside of her and rubbed at the slick spot on the front wall of her sex, pulling a breathy moan from her lips. "Sure, baby, words don't hurt me. But standing out here, waiting to get inside…your apartment and your body? That's torture."

"Who said we had to go inside?"

In a heartbeat, Russell went silent and still.

And without the friction from his body moving against hers, the chill of the air around her made her shiver.

For a moment, one horrible moment, she thought she'd ruined everything.

He pulled his fingers from her heat. Struggling to understand what was happening, she tried to reach for him, but he was gone.

In the next moment, a cold slap of wind touched her bare ass-cheek, and she almost lost her balance as he tugged down her jeans, lifted her leg, and pulled off her half-boot. The other followed a moment later, dropping down beside the first as he wrestled her jeans off her feet.

She didn't try to stop him. The area was surrounded by businesses, all closed up for the night. Her efficiency apartment above the bar was the only one of its kind on the block. They were all alone in the shadows. As Russell started to stand, she blurted out a protest. "My socks."

"Forget them." Russell continued to stand, his body rising up to block her from the night. When he was standing tall, his gaze watched her. "I left them on," he sucked on the tip of a finger that had been inside her, "because, maybe, I don't want your feet to get cold."

Before her mind could wrap around his words, her gaze lowered, following his hands. He worked his belt open and managed to release the buttons down the front of his jeans in record time.

Gina was left watching him, stunned as he pushed down the front of his jeans along with his boxer briefs. There was little left to the imagination about how much he wanted her, too.

He was hard, thick, and ready, and as he reached into his pocket, she rubbed her lips together to moisten them.

It took Russell no time at all to smooth the latex over his length. Gina flattened her palms against the wall as he lifted her up. He held her before him as he found just the right angle to fit himself inside of her, pressing against her folds, easing the head of his dick into her body.

Russell leaned into her, and she pushed onto him, wrapping her legs around his hips until she could hook her ankles together just above the edge of her socks. Her feet were the only parts of her not wearing a part of him, and when he sank himself balls-deep into her body, she let out a laugh into the night-dark silence.

"You better not be laughing at me, G."

"Not laughing at you." She lifted her hands away from the wall and clutched at his shoulders. "Just thinking that you might be a gentleman for leaving my socks on."

"Gentleman?" He slapped a hand against the wall beside her shoulder and thrust deep inside her. "Ah hell, I just didn't want to spend the time pulling them off."

"Ass," she growled under her breath.

He shifted his hand to give him a better grip on her backside. "I like yours a lot."

"Oh, God," she groaned and rolled her hips, making them both catch their breaths. "Just shut up and fuck me, Webb."

She felt him bend his knees as he stroked into her once, and then again. On the third thrust, he snapped his hips into her with a grunt. "Yes, ma'am."

Her head rolled back as she clamped down on him, making him curse under his breath.

"Don't. Call. Me. Ma'am."

"Bossy."

She'd make him pay for the comment later, but at that moment, with his thick cock pushing through her folds, she was unable to do anything but let her body climb ever higher, reaching for the tipping point.

. . .

HE COULDN'T THINK. Wouldn't. She wanted a good fuck? He was giving her one.

She held him so close with her arms. Squeezed him so tight inside her amazing body.

Outside, she was beauty, sass, and bravado. Inside, oh yes, she was hot, slick, and so fucking tight.

And he needed that.

Needed her.

Somewhere, a siren wailed through the Center City night. Somewhere far away from the shadows that hemmed them in.

He was trapped. Wrapped in her embrace. And every time he pulled back, he was sucked right back into her heat.

Shit.

Yes.

He felt the way she tightened around him, and then she was squeezing the breath out of his lungs, calling out his name as she trembled against him.

He'd never felt like that before.

Triumphant.

Incandescent.

Ah, fuck.

So wound up, his vision dimmed as his every nerve burned like fire.

It wasn't until she collapsed against him, her lips against his neck, that he found his own release. Buried deep within her, he pulsed over and over, feeling the answering draw of her body fluttering around his dick.

When he moved, he stumbled backward, breaking their fall with his forearm against the wall.

Even in the dark, he could see the joy on her face as she leaned back her head and laughed.

"Damn it, Webb." Her voice was a warm river of sound, pulling him under and into the depths. "It was certainly worth the wait."

His heart was still pounding in his chest as her heat worked itself deeper into his body.

She unhooked her legs, but he wasn't going to let her go.

This certainly wasn't going to be a one and done. No, he had plenty of experience with women who wanted his touch and his dick, but Gina was different.

He was different with her.

In her eyes, her laugh, he was a different person. Better, he knew. Gina made him look forward into the future. Made him want so much more than he thought he could have out of life.

"Invite me in, Gina?" he whispered, his hands teasing her tender skin. He trapped her earlobe between his teeth for a quick moment before he released her. "This is far from over."

SHELTERING CHARLOTTE

BY ELLE JAMES

*L*ogan Mitchell stood at the counter in Hellfire, Texas's only diner, his gaze searching for the one person he hoped to see every time he walked in.

Where was she?

"If you're looking for Charlotte, she's helping Al in the kitchen. He got behind with a carryout order for two hundred pancakes."

"Morning, Lola," Logan said. "Wow, two hundred?"

"That's right." Lola Engel sat at the counter, twirling her spoon in her milky cup of coffee. "The football booster club is giving the team a carb feast before the game tonight, hoping it will help them kick their losing streak."

Logan winced. "I understand last year's seniors dominated the field. They're a young team this year. Once they get some size on them, they'll get better."

Lola nodded her head toward the window into the kitchen. "She's gonna say no again."

"I know, but I don't give up easily," he said, lifting his chin. "Especially when it's something this important. She'll come around."

"It'll take an act of God." Lola shook her head. "Some man's done her wrong. Now, she's paintin' all men with the same brush."

He grinned. "At least, it's not just me."

Lola tilted her head. "You really like her, don't you?"

Logan gave her a crooked smile. "I've been in love with Charlotte since she first came to stay the summer with her Aunt Louise fifteen years ago. I was going to ask her to marry me when she returned to her aunt's house after she graduated from high school." He turned away and snorted softly. "She didn't come that summer. She married someone else."

When he glanced toward Lola, he found her studying him.

Lola arched one perfectly penciled eyebrow. "I was surprised to see her back. It's hard to make the transition from big-city living to small-town life."

Logan returned his attention to the window into the kitchen. "I did some digging. She's divorced as of a year ago. He must have been a bastard for her to leave him. I figure he destroyed her trust in men."

"And you think you can restore that?" Lola's eyebrows rose. "Good luck." She leaned over the counter and called out, "Charlotte, you have a customer."

Charlotte backed out of the swinging door to the kitchen carrying a tray loaded with plates of food. "Be right with you," she said without turning and hurried toward a table full of pipeline workers in the corner. She smiled and set the plates on the table.

"When are you going to go out with me, Charlotte?" one of the guys asked.

"Mike, what would Nora have to say about you going out while she's home with your baby girl?"

Another man jabbed Mike with his elbow. "You're married, dumbass. Besides, she's going to go out with me."

Charlotte shook her head. "Sorry, Jim, I don't date customers."

When she turned, Logan experienced that same punch in the gut he always got when she looked his way. She'd pulled her shiny, sable-brown hair up into a messy bun at the back of her head. Soft tendrils had worked their way loose and fell around her cheeks, just begging for Logan to brush them back behind her ears. And her moss-green eyes, fringed in naturally dark lashes, made him want to lose himself in their depths.

Yeah, he was in love with Charlotte.

And she wanted nothing to do with him.

"Good morning, Officer Mitchell," she said, her mouth tightening. "What can I get for you."

"My usual."

She nodded, stepped behind the bar and poured steaming black coffee into a paper cup and snapped a plastic lid over it.

He laid a five-dollar bill on the counter.

Her brow wrinkled, and she pushed the bill back across the counter. "You know the coffee is free for our law enforcement officers."

He nodded. "That's my tip."

She held up her hands. "I can't accept that."

"Then put it in the tip jar to be split amongst the staff." He took the cup from her hand, purposely brushing his fingers across hers. "Charlotte…"

"If you're going to ask to go out with you again," she tucked her hand behind her back and looked at the cup in his hand, "save your breath. The answer is still no."

"If I really thought you didn't have any feelings for me, I'd leave you alone." He bent his head to better see the expression in her eyes. "We had something going."

"That was ten years ago," she said. "People change. *I've* changed." She lifted her chin, her shoulders squaring and her gaze meeting his. "I have no desire to date anyone at this time."

"Fair enough," he said with a nod. "If not a date, how about a drink?"

"No," she said. "Now, if you'll excuse me, I have other customers."

"I don't give up easily. I don't know what your ex did to make you gun-shy with men, but I'm not your ex-husband."

"I know you're not," she said softly. "You're a good guy."

He hadn't expected that comment, or how she said it. All sad-like. "Damn right, I am."

"And you'll respect my decision…" she continued, "my decision not to date."

Damn, she had him there. He sighed. "All right, I won't ask you out again. But I haven't given up. I don't quit on things or people who are important to me."

She stared into his gaze for a long moment, and then sighed. "I really need to get back to work."

"And so do I," he said. "Think about us, Charlotte, before you write us off. I like to think that spark we felt all those years ago is still alive somewhere inside that shell you've build around your heart. Don't worry. I'll find my way in." He nodded to her. "I'm on duty until five, if you need me. And if you need help with renovations, I've done my share of remodeling. I'd be happy to help."

She shook her head. "I'm doing it all myself."

"It's looking good," he said. "Your aunt would've been pleased with the changes."

"She wanted to make changes but never had the extra money."

"I can hold a hammer and help hang drywall. Don't hesitate to call me."

"Thank you." She gave a tired smile, ducked around him and headed for another table, grabbing menus off the counter as she passed.

"Like I said," Lola murmured beside him, "it'll take an act of God."

Logan left the diner, his mind churning. He'd just promised not to ask her out again. That was okay. There were other ways to woo a woman.

Rather than tell her he wanted to be with her, he had to show her his commitment to making her life better. She needed to come to the realization he wasn't going anywhere and that he loved her and wanted to be a part of her forever, making babies and growing old together.

He even had the rocking chairs picked out for their front porch.

As he climbed into his deputy sheriff's service vehicle, a deep rumble made him glance toward the western sky. A storm was brewing, heading their way. He hoped it would hold off until his shift and Charlotte's were over. Charlotte usually walked to work. Logan didn't like the thought of her walking home in a downpour.

He'd keep an eye on the storm and stop by the diner later for another cup of coffee. Just in case.

CHARLOTTE STOOD BY THE WINDOW, watching as Logan walked toward his sheriff's vehicle. The years since they'd kissed out by lake hadn't wiped that memory from her mind. Not that Logan looked anything like the long, lanky teenager he'd been back then. His shoulders had filled out, and his arms and legs were thickly muscled. The eight years he'd been in the military had made a man out of the boy.

And wow. Logan in a deputy's uniform made her heart flutter.

"Why don't you put that poor boy out of his misery and go out with him?" Lola asked.

Charlotte hadn't realized Lola had come to stand beside her. Over the past couple of months since Charlotte had assumed ownership of her late aunt's home next door to Lola's, the two had become friends. Lola had come over several times to help Charlotte move furniture off the floors to allow her to rip up the tile in the kitchen and bathrooms, and to refinish the original hardwood floors in the living and bedrooms.

A rumble of thunder captured Charlotte's attention.

"You got that storm shelter cleaned out?" Lola asked, staring out at the darkening sky.

Charlotte nodded. "Not only did I get it cleaned out, I moved that old iron bed down there and had a new mattress delivered and installed on it. I've been sleeping there for the past week."

Lola grinned. "How is it down there?"

"Blessedly cool in this Texas heat. I figure I'll leave a bed down there for the hottest days of summer. I can save on air conditioning."

Lola snorted. "As long as you chased out all the spiders and scorpions, it should be great."

Charlotte nodded. "I've strengthened the shelves, and now have a good store of pantry staples down there as well."

"What about lights?"

"I added a couple of fixtures, a battery-powered lantern, and the requisite supply of candles and matches."

Lola grinned. "You'll be all set for the zombie apocalypse."

"You never know. My aunt swore the only reason there was a cellar in the house was because her father, who built it, had been in a tornado in the Panhandle when he was a young boy. They lost his father to that storm. He never wanted to lose another loved one because they couldn't afford to put in a storm shelter."

Lola tapped a finger to her chin and frowned. "As far

as I can remember, we've never had a tornado in Hellfire."

Charlotte frowned and pressed a finger to her lips. "Shh…Lola. Now, you've done it."

"What have I done?" the older woman asked.

"You've jinxed us," Charlotte said.

"You think so?" Lola's forehead creased.

Charlotte rolled her eyes. "No. But it's better to have shelter than not. If nothing else, it's great for storage."

"That's what I use mine for," Lola said. "It was the only thing that survived the fire. We just built the new house over it."

Charlotte hugged Lola. "I still can't believe someone tried to burn down your house with you inside."

"I'm lucky Daniel got to me before I went up with the house." She sighed. "He really is more than just a gorgeous body."

Charlotte laughed. "You crack me up. I'm glad you two are together. It gives me hope for the future."

"Speaking of the future, I don't know what your ex-husband did, but he didn't deserve you. Now, you can't go wrong falling for a guy like Logan Mitchell. He's one of the good guys. He's good-looking, dependable, courageous and loyal."

Charlotte's lips twisted. "So is a golden retriever."

Lola leaned close and lowered her voice so the other customers in the diner wouldn't hear. "Yeah, but a man can give you an orgasm."

"Only if he knows what he's doing," Charlotte muttered, her gaze on the dark clouds building to the west. "I'd better get back to work. I'm leaving as soon as the lunch crowd is gone. I've rented a sander to strip the wood floors in the dining room. I want to get a good start on them today."

"I'm headed back to my shop. If the rain comes, I'll close up early. Hope not, though. I got a new order of Jimmy Choos I need to put on display."

Charlotte opened the door for her friend and smiled. She loved that Lola kept the small town of Hellfire, Texas in designer shoes. They might not have designer clothing stores, but they had high-end shoes.

Charlotte worked her way through lunch, taking orders, filling glasses, and bussing tables. By the time the last customers left, the clouds blocked out the sun, but she could make it back to her house before the sky opened up and dumped rain on her.

"I'm headed out," she called out to Al in the kitchen.

"Need a ride?" he asked.

"No, thank you," she said. "I'll hurry."

She looped her purse over her shoulder and set out. Her home was only five blocks from the diner, easy walking distance in good weather. Halfway there, she was beginning to wonder if she'd make it before the sky let loose. She could smell the rain in the air. Wind whipped her hair out of its loose bun and tossed it around her head and face.

The sky held a greenish tinge and smoky gray clouds were quickly approaching Hellfire.

All the way to her house, Charlotte watched the sky and the passing vehicles. The sky for the storm, the vehicles for the one deputy's SUV that Logan drove.

She'd come back to Hellfire with the intention of

starting over, getting her life back, and finding herself. After nine years of marriage to a man who'd mentally abused her, she was finally free. But who was she? Certainly not the teenager who'd married straight out of high school. That girl was gone.

Charlotte had known that coming back to Hellfire would bring back memories of her summers here. Summers spent with Logan Mitchell. Shortly after her whirlwind romance and marriage, Charlotte had learned from her aunt that Logan had left Hellfire to join the military. When her Aunt Louise had died and left her the house in Hellfire, Charlotte hadn't expected to run into him.

But he'd been back in Hellfire for a couple years, working for the sheriff's department as a deputy. With a house and a life to renovate, Charlotte had told herself she wouldn't let herself fall in love again. Not anytime soon.

However, seeing Logan every day, sometimes twice a day, was wearing her down. If she could just hold out until the house was complete, she might have the demons from her past worked out of her system. She'd hoped that, after taking on the task of renovating the house herself, she'd feel stronger and more confident in herself. Other than having an electrician and a plumber bring the house up to code, she was doing the rest of the work herself. And in so doing, rediscovering her own self-worth.

But the temptation of Logan called to her. So much so that her resistance was crumbling.

She unlocked and pushed the door open to her

home and sighed. Her gaze landed on the sanding machine she'd rented to strip the wood floors. After being on her feet since five o'clock that morning, she wasn't looking forward to being on them some more. Having rented the sander for a week, she could get a refund of some of the rental cost if she turned it in early. So, no matter how tired she was, she needed to get started.

Charlotte crossed the bare wood floor to the kitchen and descended into the storm cellar, a concrete bunker built into the ground before the house had been erected sixty years ago. She'd taken her clothes down below, along with any personal belongings she didn't want to get lost in the construction chaos. Not that she had much. She'd left her husband, taking only what she could fit into two suitcases, and filed for divorce from a women's shelter in Chicago. With both parents gone and no siblings to lean on, Charlotte had been alone, scared and desperate.

Not long after her divorce was final, she'd learned of her Aunt Louise's death and that she'd bequeathed the house and what was left of her meager savings to Charlotte.

The news had been both sad and a godsend when Charlotte had been at her lowest, wondering how she would survive when she had no college degree or formal training to support herself. She'd loved her Aunt Louise and missed the idyllic summers she'd spent in Texas. She'd missed Logan.

In the cellar, she changed into old clothes and shoes and wrapped her hair in a bandana. As she climbed the narrow stairs up into the house, she heard the rumble of thunder and was glad this part of the renovation could be accomplished indoors. Charlotte stuffed foam ear protection into her ears and a mask over her mouth and nose before tackling the big machine. She plugged the sander into the wall, gripped the handle like the rental guy had instructed, and held on tight as she flipped the on switch.

Even with the sponge earplugs, the roar of the machine was deafening. To sooth her mind and body, she picked a song her aunt loved and sang to the tune of the sander as it spit dust in the air. No matter how loud she sang or the sander roared, it wasn't loud enough to get Logan out of her mind.

AT THE END of his shift, Logan parked his service vehicle and climbed into his truck. The wind had grown wickedly strong, slapping the trees around. A wall of ominous clouds charged like a freight train from the southwest, spewing bolts of lightning and continuing clashes of thunder.

Logan swung by the diner to offer Charlotte a ride home as the rain started to fall. He parked in front of the building, left his truck running, and ran inside.

"Charlotte?" he called out.

Al stuck his head around the swinging door. "Left an hour ago. Said she wanted to get home to sand her floors. You need anything before I close up? That storm's gonna be a doozy. I want to get home and into my storm cellar before it hits. Weatherman says it's prime condition for twisters. Got a tornado watch for this area."

"Go home. It's getting bad out there," Logan said. "I'll check on Charlotte."

As Logan left the diner, a weather alert sounded on his cellphone. He glanced down at the text.

Tornado on the ground five miles southwest of Hellfire heading northeast at twenty miles per hour. Seek shelter immediately.

Logan's pulse quickened.

If Charlotte was using an electric sander, she wouldn't hear the alert on her cellphone.

Just then the town's tornado siren spun up, blaring its warning to all.

Hell, Charlotte might not hear the siren, either.

Breaking the speed limit, Logan raced down Main Street toward Charlotte's place, just past Lola's. He pulled into the driveway as the wind whipped leaves and branches from the trees. He jumped from his truck and raced up the front porch steps. Over the blare of the tornado siren, he heard another sound that made his blood run cold and his feet move faster.

A heavy roaring sound, accompanied by sideways rain, made him glance toward the end of Main Street.

That's when he saw it. A wide funnel cloud, pounding the earth, spinning everything up in its path, headed straight for Hellfire. Sheets of mangled tin roofing, boards, huge tree branches were caught up in the funnel and flung outward.

With only seconds to spare, Logan burst through the front door of the old house.

Charlotte stood behind a heavy sander, holding tightly to the handles as it ate at the finish on the floor. She'd gone the length of the room several times, with dust making the air murky.

Her back to the door, she hadn't heard him enter.

Logan grabbed the cord to the sander and yanked it out of the electrical socket. The sander spun to a stop.

Charlotte fiddled with the on switch, trying to make it start again.

Logan was halfway across the floor when she finally turned. Her eyes widened. "Logan? What the hell?"

He didn't have time to explain. Having visited the house so many times in his teens, he knew where the storm cellar was. He grabbed Charlotte's hand. "Let's go!"

"What's wrong?" she cried out as he dragged her through the living room into the kitchen. Already, he could hear the wind wailing at the windows and the roof.

"Tornado!" he yelled above the roar of the funnel cloud bearing down on their small town.

Charlotte pulled an earplug out of her ear and ripped the mask off her face. "What?"

"Tornado!" he yelled again as he reached for the heavy metal door of the storm cellar, leading off the back door of the kitchen. He dragged it open and pushed Charlotte toward the stairs. "Go! Go! Go!"

Windows in the house imploded, shooting glass across the room.

Charlotte screamed and raced down into the shelter.

Logan followed, spun to pull the metal door shut,

and struggled with it, the air pressure around the house changing as the twister moved in.

Finally, he slammed the door and locked it in place with the metal bar sliding into the catch. The electric light above the stairs blinked.

Overhead, the rumble of thunder rolled over them. Debris pummeled the metal door, and the wind and changing air pressure shook it, rattling it against its hinges.

Logan backed down the stairs to the bottom of the cement bunker and turned to envelop Charlotte in his embrace.

She went willingly, her body shaking against his.

"Flashlight?" he asked.

She pointed to one hanging on the wall. At that moment, the electric lights blinked out.

Logan reached for the flashlight where he'd seen it last, fumbling to release it from its mount. When he had it firmly in hand, he hit the on switch. Nothing happened. He shook the light, and it flickered on, illuminating the cramped space. Setting it on a shelf, pointing outward, Logan stared down at Charlotte, held in the curve of his arm. "It took a tornado to get you where I wanted you."

She laughed, the sound weak and shaky. "You always were an overachiever."

He tightened his embrace. "Are you okay?"

She nodded. "But I wouldn't have been, if you hadn't come when you did. I can't believe I didn't hear the siren."

"You couldn't, not with that sander going. You

wouldn't have known anything was happening until it was too late."

She leaned her forehead against his chest, her hands curling into his uniform shirt. "Thank you."

The storm raged outside the storm shelter, hammering against the top of the concrete bunker and the metal door.

For the next few minutes, it sounded like a warzone on the other side of the concrete roof and the metal door. Logan held Charlotte, praying the townspeople would be spared.

What felt like hours could only have been minutes when suddenly all sounds ceased.

Logan stood still, listening. Were they in the eye of the storm? Or had it really passed over them and moved on?

After another minute, Charlotte leaned back. "I think it's gone."

"I'll check."

"Are you sure it's safe?" Her fingers dug into his shirt. "You could wait a few more minutes."

"With you in my arms, I could wait forever." He smoothed a hand over her hair.

She melted against him, her arms encircling his waist. "Why?"

"Because I've wanted to be with you since we were kids."

She buried her face in his shirt. "But we're not kids anymore. We've changed."

"You're still the same girl I fell for when I was fourteen."

"No. I'm not. You don't know me anymore." Her voice dropped to a whisper. "I don't know me anymore. I need to know who I am before I bring anyone else into my life."

"What happened to you, Charlotte? Why are you so afraid?"

She shook her head. "I just got out of the marriage from hell. I could never be good enough for Jimmy. I walked on eggshells in fear of angering him."

Logan's hands tightened around her. "Did he hit you?"

"Not with his fists, but with his words. He made me feel…awful, unworthy, stupid."

"You're not unworthy or stupid. You're the most beautiful, smart, and courageous woman I know. You jumped off the cliffs at the lake into the water before I did."

"I was young."

"And fearless," he reminded her.

"I'm neither of those things anymore." She lay her cheek against his chest. "I'm damaged, trying to find my way back to me."

He tipped up her chin and stared down into the green eyes he'd missed so much. "Let me help you. I have nothing but love in my heart for the girl I knew and the one I'm holding now, because deep down, I know they are one and the same."

For a long moment, they stood locked in each other's arms.

Logan murmured against her silky hair, "I'm going to check outside."

She nodded, not moving at first, then finally stepping back to allow him to climb the stairs to the metal door.

He slid the bar loose and pushed on the door. It wouldn't move. He tried again. The door didn't budge. "Charlotte, the door appears to be blocked."

CHARLOTTE CLIMBED UP BEHIND HIM. "Let's both push."

"On three," Logan said, as she stepped beside him on the stairs. "One, two, three."

Together, they pushed on the metal door.

Charlotte strained, putting as much of her weight behind the shove as she could. The heavy metal door didn't even move an inch.

Logan fished his cellphone out of his pocket and stared at the screen. "No reception. We couldn't call out, even if we wanted to."

"So, we're trapped," Charlotte said, the thought not nearly as disturbing as it should be.

Logan nodded. "But only for a while. Most likely, the house is damaged. Some of the debris has to be blocking the door. The sheriff's department and firefighters will be out soon enough checking damaged structures for—"

"—survivors." A chill rippled down Charlotte's spine. "I hope no one was hurt." She pushed on the door again. "We need to get out and check on Lola."

"Sweetheart, we're not going anywhere until they find us. And we don't know how many places received damage. It could be hours before they get to this house."

He looked around. "We might as well relax and get comfortable."

Charlotte turned and descended the steps to the floor. "The good news is that we won't starve. I have all the pantry staples stored in here, to include cans of tuna, pickles, peanut butter, and crackers." She smiled. "Hungry for any of that?"

Logan shook his head as he came down the stairs. "Nope." His gaze met hers. "I'm not hungry for food."

Charlotte backed up as he closed the distance between them. "I'm not ready," she said, fear of failure bringing her hands up in front of her. How many times had Jimmy told her she was horrible in bed? Frigid?

"I'm okay with that. If we do nothing but hold each other and talk, I'd be happy. Hell, if you don't want us to hold each other, I'm okay with that, too. I'm just happy to be alone with you to start the conversation."

She let go of the tension inside and smiled. "Is this alone enough for you?"

Logan held open his arms. "Yes."

The walls she'd erected around her heart dissolved a little. Charlotte stepped into his embrace and let him hold her. He wasn't judging and finding her lacking. He'd known her when she was young, innocent, and happy. Logan could help her find her way back to that version of Charlotte, if she let him.

"We're going to be here a while," Charlotte said. "I can't offer you a chair, but the bed I've been sleeping on is soft and comfortable."

"You've been sleeping down here?" He shook his head, glancing around the small space.

She nodded. "All the furniture upstairs is stacked into one room until I get the floors refinished. It made sense to move down here."

"Sweetheart, I have a feeling the floors are going to be the least of your worries."

Her eyes filled with tears. "This was my aunt's house. I have so many good memories of being here. Memories of her. Memories of you."

"What's important here is that you're alive. We're alive. Whatever happens after this, we'll be alive and okay together." He led her over to the bed and sat on the edge, pulling her down beside him, his arm encircling her waist.

She kicked off her shoes and scooted back until she lay on the pillow. "Like you said, we might as well relax." Charlotte patted the space beside her. "Come tell me what you've been up to all these years."

He lay down beside her, lacing his hands behind his head. "Did you know I went to Chicago after you graduated high school?"

She frowned. "Why didn't you tell me you were coming?"

"I wanted to surprise you. I wanted to see if you still cared about me."

She stilled. "I met Jimmy halfway through my senior year. He was new at my high school. He courted me and made me feel like a princess."

Without saying a word, Logan took her hand in his.

She squeezed it, loving the strength that flowed from his touch. "I thought I was in love," she said. "When he asked me to marry him, I was flattered that

43

the new cute guy wanted me. We married a week after graduation. My folks weren't happy about it, but I was eighteen and could make my own decisions. Even bad ones." She turned on her side to face him. "I thought about you. I figured you'd found a girlfriend and had forgotten about me."

He shook his head. "I got to Chicago the day you got married. I was too late."

She reached out to touch his cheek. "I'm so sorry. Sometimes, I think Jimmy was right. I was stupid. I married him."

Logan lifted her hand and pressed a kiss against her open palm. "You're not stupid. You fell for a guy who wasn't real. You couldn't know that until you'd lived together and discovered the truth."

She nodded. "I was so miserable. I didn't know how to get out of it. I didn't have a job. I couldn't support myself. My parents...I couldn't crawl back home. And then, when they died, I was truly alone. I had no one. Not even you. My aunt told me you'd joined the Army."

Logan pulled her closer.

She nestled in the crook of his arm, inhaling the fresh scent of his aftershave. Even fully clothed, he made her heart beat faster and that place low in her belly ache for more than an embrace.

"I missed you," she whispered. "We were friends for so long...and that last summer..." Charlotte sighed. "It almost didn't feel real at the time. And later...I knew it was the most real experience I'd ever had."

"I counted the days until your graduation," Logan

said softly. "I worked weekends to save money for a car and gas. I went to Chicago to bring you home."

"And I'd married a monster. Afterward, you were so far away." She rested her hand on his chest. "Everything good in my life was gone."

He covered her hand with his then, again, raised it to his mouth, pressing another kiss into her palm. "What's nice about the past being in the past, is that the future is all ours. All we have to do is embrace it." Logan smiled into her eyes. "Like I want to embrace you now." He pulled her into the curve of his arm, his lips hovering over hers. "If this isn't what you want, tell me now."

"I want it," she whispered. "I want you. I'm just afraid of making another mistake...of losing me in the process."

"Darlin', I fell in love with you a long time ago. Not someone I wanted you to be." He touched a finger to her nose. "You."

Charlotte leaned up on her elbow and brushed his lips with hers. "I hope they don't find us too soon."

He cupped the back of her head. "Me either. I've been trying to get you alone since you came back to Hellfire. I want it to last a little longer." He bent and claimed her lips in a kiss that redefined the way she'd been viewing kissing since her marriage to Jimmy.

Logan didn't kiss with the intention of satisfying only his own desires. He brought her with him, showing her how good it could be when the one kissing you cared.

As the connection deepened, Charlotte pressed her

body to his, sliding her calf over his thigh, riding her center over his thick, hard muscles.

Her body was on fire, her blood scorching her veins, as it pushed through her system with every wild beat of her heart.

She'd thought that by waiting to rediscover love, she'd be more in control of her body and soul. But with Logan, she could only ride the wave of her lust like a leaf on the raging surface of a swollen river.

Charlotte reached for the buttons on Logan's uniform shirt and slipped them through their holes, her fingers fumbling as she hurried to get her hands on his skin. She wanted to feel the changes in his body, to run her fingers over the hardness of his muscles, to press her lips to his naked skin and taste him.

After tugging the shirt out of the waistband of his trousers she pushed it over his shoulders. Then she dragged his undershirt up and over his head.

Logan pulled her over to straddle his hips, gripped her T-shirt and whipped it off, sending it flying across the narrow space. He reached behind her and deftly unclipped her bra, smoothing the straps down her shoulders and arms until they slipped over her wrists, falling to the smooth concrete floor.

Charlotte's nipples puckered as the cool air of the bunker chilled her skin.

Logan cupped her breasts in his palms, his gaze capturing hers. "You've gotten even more beautiful in the past ten years. I didn't think it was possible. I've kept an old picture of you with me since that last summer we had together. The one we took out by the lake at sunset. The sun made your hair shine like ebony silk. That picture…you…" He cleared his throat. "It got me through some hard times while I was deployed in Afghanistan."

Her heart swelled. The look in Logan's eyes made her chest constrict. Jimmy had never looked at her like he would lay down his life for her. She'd been a possession. To Logan, she felt like a treasured gift.

She leaned down, pressing her breasts to his naked skin, loving how warm he was. Being that naked and that close only made her want to feel the rest of him. Charlotte scooted back down his hips and reached for his belt. When she unzipped his trousers, his shaft sprang free. The man went commando beneath his uniform trousers.

If she'd thought he was hot in his uniform, knowing he didn't wear anything under it…well, he couldn't have turned her on more. She slid down his body, kissing his cheek, neck and the hard brown nipples on his chest.

"You're making me crazy, woman." He rolled her onto her back and came up on his arms, leaning over her.

"Aren't you worried someone will find us too soon?" she asked as he trailed kisses down her neck and across her collarbone to capture a nipple between his lips.

"Not in the least. We'll hear them."

Charlotte arched her back off the mattress. "Hopefully, it'll be a while." She gasped as he sucked hard. "Oh, sweet heaven. Can we stop talking?" she said, barely able to get air past her vocal cords. He was doing amazing things to her. Things she'd only dreamed of. Things her ex had never bothered with.

She cupped the back of Logan's head, holding him close, reveling in the sensations he evoked.

He stopped, rolled off the bed, and yanked the belt and holster from his uniform trousers. "Hard to focus with my gun digging into my side."

Charlotte giggled. "Was that your gun or are you just happy to see me?" She rose to her knees on the bed and slipped her hands into the back of his trousers, cupping his tight, sexy ass. Oh, yes. The storm could rage on. She was where she wanted to be. Where she needed to be.

His cock pressed against her breasts, straight, thick, and oh so hard. She took it into her mouth, running her tongue around the head, loving the taste of him.

Logan dug his hands into her hair to make her still. "I'm going to get there far too soon."

She smiled up at him. "Is that a problem?"

He drew in a deep breath. "I want to be fully naked with you before we go there." Logan stepped back, stripped out of the remainder of his clothes and shoes, and then helped her out of her jeans and panties. "Wait," he said and fished his wallet out of the pocket of his trousers, then extracted a small square packet and tossed it onto the bed. "No pressure, just didn't want you to think I didn't care." He winked and laid on the bed beside her, bringing her body against his. "I've dreamed of this for so many years."

"I never thought it would happen. I really thought you were lost to me." Charlotte kissed him, pressing her full length against his, loving how good it felt.

He abandoned her lips and traced a path from her mouth down her neck to her breasts. After thoroughly ravaging them, he continued south to the patch of hair at the juncture of her thighs. Parting her folds, he touched her there with his tongue.

Charlotte sucked in a sharp breath, electric charges raced along her nerves, coiling at her center and shooting outward.

He flicked her clit, swirled and licked her, until she dug her heels into the mattress, rising up to him, silently begging him to take all of her. When she rocketed over the precipice, her body shook in pulsing spasms until she finally came back to the bed, to shelter with Logan.

He climbed her body and kissed her. "If you want," he whispered, "we can stop here."

She shook her head. "Oh, hell no." Charlotte sat up and dug in the comforter until she found the condom, tore open the packet and smoothed the latex over his engorged staff. "We're not done yet."

He laughed and positioned himself over her, nudging her entrance. "I hope we won't be done for a very long time."

She guided him into her, taking all of him, loving how he filled her and made her feel whole.

He backed out and thrust in again, settling into a steady pace, until she urged him to go faster, thrust harder. When he finally came, she held him close, wrapping her legs around his back, wanting to stay that way forever. She'd thought she couldn't please a man. Obviously, she'd pleased Logan.

Loud banging and the sound of a chainsaw brought Charlotte back to reality. "Too soon," she moaned.

Logan kissed her once more and slid out of her. "This is not the end of our time together, Charlotte. It's only the beginning." He stood, smacked her bare ass and winked. "Let's find out what we missed and if we can help."

She rolled out of the bed.

They dressed quickly and pulled on their shoes. By the time the heavy metal door opened, they were ready.

"Charlotte? Please, dear God, tell me you're all right," Lola's voice sounded from above.

Flashlights shone down in Charlotte's eyes. "I am." She started up the stairs with Logan following, holding onto her hand.

"Deputy Mitchell, is that you?" the sheriff called out.

"It is," Logan responded.

"Glad to hear it. I was worried when you didn't call to report in. Especially when I saw your truck upside down on the other side of Main Street. And you two were the only people unaccounted for."

As they emerged from the storm shelter, Charlotte gasped. A tree had fallen on her house, crushing the kitchen. One large branch had landed on the door to the shelter, trapping them inside.

Charlotte stood inside the circle of Logan's arm, tears welling in her eyes.

He squeezed her shoulders. "It's okay. This can be fixed."

She nodded. "I know. It's just that...If you hadn't

come when you did…" She turned her face into his shirt. "You saved me when all I did was push you away."

"I love you, Charlotte, and I'm not going anywhere." He chuckled. "And if it takes being trapped in the cellar to get you alone, I'm willing to take that risk."

She wrapped her arms around him. "Will the rescue workers think we're crazy if we go back down?"

"Do you care?" he asked.

She shook her head. "Nope. When I'm with you, I'm the me I was and want to be."

Logan leaned down, his lips hovering over hers. "You've always been Charlotte to me. I wouldn't change a thing."

She took his hand and led him back into the shelter that had saved her life in more ways than one.

THE SIREN'S SONG

BY AVA CUVAY

"*Fuckafitsu.* That drak of a B'aark is stealing from me." Lorlii Atarga cursed her discovery to the bottles of alcohol piled in her back storeroom. Little wonder her out-of-stocks mismatched her inventory data. Her new bar manager was pilfering her expensive booze. Flames of rage seared her brain. Bad enough she'd been pulled away from the front of her bar, The Siren's Song, on a profitable evening for the tedious task of verifying inventory. Now, she'd have to waste the rest of the night building proof of the theft, checking receivables against payables, searching security vids, and squelching the urge to kick Ikahb in whatever dark crevice his species kept their gonads.

Worse than that? She'd miss out on a nightly visit from Roark Trekker—"Raging Roark," Captain of Sigma-9 Spaceport's Fire Force—their local hero saving burning ships and travelers with feats of valor, *lauda, lauda, lauda.* He needed her there to heap verbal abuse on him as only a best friend can. A best friend who was in love with him, although that small detail would never come up in conversation. Wild *zhors* couldn't drag that tidbit out of her. Not when the object of her unrequited love was a total hottie and shameless flirt with a captivating gaze and knowing smirk which incinerated the panties on all women—and some men—in the vicinity.

Everyone in the port worshiped him. Men clamored to be his buddy, and women pounced to be his fuckmate. Lorlii understood the need. She was a woman after all, and a breathing one at that. But she wasn't about to be an ass-kissing sycophant like everyone else. When he stunk like burnt silicon-carbide, she told him so. Then he'd just laugh, wink at her, and order another Tragdon Whiskey on the rocks.

He'd likely stink tonight. According to the live news vids, Roark and his crew had rescued a freighter bleeding a trail of combustible plasma fuel all over the port. The situation had been dire on a butt-pucker level, but Roark had been an avenging angel, wrangling success from a hopeless situation. By her calculations, Roark, crew, and a barrage of fans and drinks-all-around would arrive shortly. She wanted to be at the bar, armed with eye-rolls, unimpressed snorts, and biting put-downs to keep his ego in check. Instead, she was stuck back here counting bottles, plotting revenge against her bar manager, and pining for someone she couldn't have.

While verbal sparring, especially the joking innuendos, with Roark was entertaining, she'd give a bottle of rare Carhind'n Rum to change that into a physical tussle. But how to transition to a more climactic sort of ribbing? She was hornier than a *bayhar* and ready to ignite with little more than a smooch of his full lips. Her sexual drought had lasted several months at this point. No one seemed interested in her, outside of her mixology skills and Twofer Tuesday specials. A little attention from a handsome man that didn't involve anything shaken, stirred, or two fingers neat…

Lorlii swallowed hard at the thought of what Roark could do with a couple of fingers. He'd never know, but he starred in all her masturbation fantasies.

Speaking of which, she was going to have one now—her own special toast to the station's hero. The bar had plenty of product out front, her so-called thieving drak of a bar manager was off tonight, and her bartenders would avoid her like Klutha-9 while she counted inventory.

Nibbling her bottom lip, Lorlii set her inventory datapad on a nearby shelf and sat atop a sturdy stack of cheap well vodka. She propped a stiletto-clad heel on a low shelf and hiked her dark pencil skirt up her thighs. She didn't wear any panties. Why bother? With Roark around, her pussy was always wet. Then she dipped her fingers to moisten them in the ever-present sheen of arousal. Slowly circling along the sensitive folds, she squeezed a breast through her white collared shirt and pinched the tightened nipple.

And pictured Roark in her mind.

Hair as dark as a black hole, always mussed like fingers had run through the silky strands and grabbed them in the throes of ecstasy. His deep gray eyes that usually sparkled with laughter but could be hard and steely as a ship's hull. With the notable exception of his expressive lips, the rest of him was similarly hard. Big. Muscular. Roped and ripped and taut like a stabilizing wire, strong enough to hold an imploding starship immobile by sheer force of will. From his angular jawline to his anti-grav boots, and all the bulges and ridges in between, he was a powerhouse. Built for making his line of work seem like child's play and enticing women to fight like rabid *bahk'u* to fuck him.

He was a sexy beast, but what fanned Lorlii's flame were his large, rugged hands. Hands with strength enough to pop the seal on an outer airlock yet gentle enough to trust with her expensive Dendathan wine stems. Long, thick, capable fingers. A map of veins and tendons extending over his wrists and along his forearms. She pictured them cupping her breasts, his light coloring contrasting with her characteristic *Dohthan* swirls of blues. She imagined them plumping her ass cheeks. Visualized them plunging into her, fucking her with one hand while he fisted the girth of his cock with his other, veins bulging and urgent with building tension. Dicks and digits... Who knew she was such a fan?

She flicked her fingers across her clit, heat and desire prickling her skin and her orgasm into a growing inferno. She moaned. A few more strokes and she'd explode.

"Thinking of me?"

Lorlii screeched at the intruding voice. Shocked from her reverie, she jerked, tugging at her skirt. Bad enough she'd been caught flicking the bean, but the owner of the voice—her soon-to-be-ex bar manager—would never be thought of in that context. Bile rose in her throat; the sight of him doused her fantasy more effectively than the halon foam Roark's crew used.

She stood and let her earlier rage spark back to life, now fueled by sexual frustration.

"You're pretty ballsy, coming here. I know you've been stealing. Don't think I won't have you arrested." Her body tensed for battle as her voice quavered with emotion. Ikahb's lanky Pluruekian frame belied his scrappy underground-fighter demeanor. He was tough and fast. Confronting him while secluded away from everyone might not be the best idea, but she wasn't helpless. She had a storeroom of glass weapons, and she'd bounced enough patrons and hefted enough bottles that she wasn't weak. Still, she beefed up her threat. "In fact, officers should arrive at any moment. The Port PD doesn't tolerate thieves."

Ikahb merely chuckled and leaned against the doorway, unconcerned. He shrugged one shoulder as proof. "You think I'm just five-fingering your product. No, I'm into something even bigger than booze. And you ain't gonna fuck it up for me."

He straightened and took a step toward her, his casual demeanor morphing into vile intent. Lorlii shrank against the case stacks at her back. Ikahb's sneer was cruel. Her heart galloped and fear hollowed her gut. If only those officers were actually on their way.

He laughed, and the sound froze her blood. "From now on, you do what I tell you. And your little do-gooder buddy out there isn't going to save you."

Clammy ice ran through her veins. Lorlii might as well be stranded out in Sector 12 for all the help she would get. She braced a hand against a shelf, feeling around for the box-cutter she'd left there. Its half-inch safety-laser blade wasn't much, but maybe enough to buy her some time. If she screamed loudly, maybe the bar patrons would hear over the sounds of their revelry. If she could stall him, maybe she could gather her wits and devise a plan.

Those were some shaky *maybes* and *ifs*.

Lorlii gathered her flimsy courage around her no-bullshit mouth. "Oh, no, Roark's not going to save me? News flash—so what? I can handle myself. I run my own bar, and no one will take that away." Her fingers touched then wrapped around the cutter. "By the way, you're fired. Don't let the door hit you on the ass."

Ikahb's expression detonated, and his fists clenched. "Mouthy *Dohthan* bitch. I said *you* are going to do what *I* tell you to do."

He flicked a black clump at her. It hit her collarbone before she could flinch, metallic strands shooting out to wrap around her head, pulling the mass to her face as it morphed into a mask, sealing her jaw shut and covering her mouth. She clawed at the mask, scraping her own cheeks raw from the effort, but it didn't budge. She screamed, but the mask suppressed it to a soft murmur. *Sonuvaslehgah,* it was a black-market gag-mask. Where —how—had Ikahb snagged a hi-tech silencer like the police used with criminals known for biting and spitting?

Her heart stuttered. The night had mutated to terrifying faster than a Screaming Nebula shot got you drunk. She'd regret it when he overpowered her, but she had to fight back. Unfortunately, her mouth was her best weapon, and he'd effectively disarmed her.

He attacked, and she flailed in wild desperation, using anything she could grab as a weapon, possibly cutting him because he screamed. But the fight was over in moments with a blow to her jaw, which wrenched her head sideways and into a shelf edge. Stars burst in her vision, and she tripped on fallen bottles, landing in a pained heap on a low stack of cases.

Too stunned to fight, Lorlii inhaled ragged breaths through her nose. She'd bounced plenty of unruly drunks, using muscle and brazen attitude, but the key must have been the *drunk* part of that phrase. Sober and dangerous, Ikahb had bested her. Her heart convulsed in her chest as he loomed over her, his triumphant smirk—so different than Roark's flirty, nipple-tingling one—apparent even through the tears watering her vision. Like he had all the time in the world, he stooped to pick up her cutter where it had fallen. Immune to her frantic kicks and slaps, he leaned his knees against her thighs, trapping them, and sliced her shirt and bra down the center. Lorlii's muffled yelp choked on a gasp as he yanked her top and bra over her shoulders, pinning her arms to her side.

"You're gonna pay for cutting me." He snarled as he seized her breasts, heedless to her muted cries.

"Well, this is interesting."

. . .

ROARK STOOD at the entrance to The Siren's Song store-room, seething with rage. Some creep, who he vaguely remembered was a new employee, had backed Lorlii into a corner and was manhandling her naked breasts. Although Roark's words had been casual enough, he'd really meant, *Get the fuck off my woman!* At least the creep stopped his barbaric squashing of Lorlii and turned.

The move gave Roark a better view of Lorlii, and his anger hit supernova. She wore an incarceration-grade gag-mask, her normally-sleek hair wild and tangled, her shirt and bra stretched around her arms to leave her glorious breasts bare, her nipples the brightest turquoise he'd ever seen, bright like twin beacons begging him to suckle them like he did in his dreams, and, wait, he wasn't here to stare at her amazing tits—

The other man made some dismissive sound, catching Roark's attention, and flicked a hand in Lorlii's direction. "What can I say? She likes it rough."

It was possible. He and Lorlii didn't talk sex, predilections, or experiences. He hadn't wanted her imagining him fucking another woman, and he didn't want to imagine her with another man. Ever. He looked up from her quivering breasts to her usually animated face. A dark bruise marred one side—he ground his teeth at the thought of the skinny creep hitting Lorlii, even if she'd consented—and tears streaked her cheeks. Her eyes blazed with fire, but he couldn't determine whether from desire or anger.

Only one way to know for sure. "Nod your head if

you're here willingly, Lorlii. I'll go back to the bar and leave you two to continue as you were."

The hardest words to ever pass his lips. Every cell in his body cried out against them. He wanted her to choose *him*. Roark had been working for months to transition their relationship out of the friend-zone, although she hadn't taken even his boldest flirtation seriously. That's what he got for wanting such a feisty smartass of a woman. Lorlii was exquisite. Her aquatic *Dohthan* coloring a gentle palette of blues in hypnotic swirls like an oceanic whirlpool sucking him towards nirvana. Where most *Dohthans* were lean, Lorlii had curves his hands and mouth longed to dive into. And her breasts… sweet stars above, her gorgeous breasts…

The creep fisted his hands and shot her a dark look, his tone vibrating with meaning. "Yes, Lorlii. Nod your head so the asshole will leave."

As she glanced at the creep, Roark tensed for battle. Fear flickered in the sapphire depths of her eyes then hardened. She sat straighter and turned her gaze to him. Red washed his vision as she shook her head.

She didn't like it rough.

Creep swung at Roark, but he blocked it and let loose a volley of his own. This guy was street tough, but Roark was fueled by lethal rage to avenge the pain inflicted on Lorlii.

He. Would. Kill. This. Dick.

A tight room filled with glass bottles wasn't conducive to full-out battle, but he wasn't deterred. Roark barely registered Creep's blows through the tsunami of his anger. In return, he bashed the man's face and smashed his head into shelves and support bars, both of them stumbled over the tumbling, rolling bottles and haphazard case stacks. Alcohol fumes filled the air, stinging Roark's eyes and burning inside his nostrils. But he still wailed on Creep, whose return punches soon waned in power and accuracy.

Crack! Roark flinched at the sharp sound. Creep crumpled to the ground, leaving the vision of Lorlii standing with the broken neck of a bottle clasped in both hands. She'd knocked him out, a goddess of war, quivering with fierce anger, breasts pushed together and upward by her outstretched arms, nipples winking at Roark—

He shook his head, unfulfilled fury still coursing through him. "Dammit, Lorlii, that was *my* job."

She just shrugged her shoulders, not sorry.

"Let me get rid of this guy, and I'll be right back," Roark growled. He snatched an arm and dragged the body out of the storeroom and toward the alley. He handled Creep as gently as a bag of trash, and—yes, he was petty, but Roark didn't give a shit—let boxes, doorways, and exposed pipes bash the already-unconscious man. Roark called his police buddy on a private line to request a no-questions-asked pick-up and detention. Then he marched straight back to Lorlii to vent more of his frustration.

Turning the corner, what he saw evaporated his anger and broke his heart.

Lorlii had collapsed to the floor, her body a small, trembling, sobbing mass amidst a war zone of tipped and broken bottles, upended cases, and listing stacks.

The carpet was soaked in alcohol and broken glass, and gaps yawned on the shelves which had recently held product. Roark didn't bother with the math. The cost of the loss was exorbitant.

Little wonder she was sobbing. He was no stranger to overwrought victims and hysterical women, but watching Lorlii cry left him rudderless for how to offer comfort. The fact her breasts were still uncovered was an added distraction.

He knelt and eased her hands away from her face. "Shhh. Sweetheart. It's going to be ok; I promise," he cooed softly, wiping her tears and the silky strands of her navy hair off her wet cheeks. She blinked at him like he spoke an alien language. Given the taunting nature of their usual interaction, she likely worried he'd hit his head. Comforting her would have to wait. He needed action, which was his strong point. "Here, let me get that damn gag off."

With his hands on her bare shoulders, trying without success to ignore her soft skin, he leaned her forward and reached around the gag, feeling with his fingers for a release latch. She rested her forehead on his pectoral with a trusting sigh. He fought the urge to wrap his arms around her and explore the fascinating eddies of her skin. Follow his fingertips with his mouth, licking and nibbling in a collapsing spiral, ending with his face buried in the heat of her pussy.

His cock swelled, and he swallowed back an anticipatory moan. Yes, he'd been dreaming about her for months. Waking, working, jacking off, and sleeping, all with thoughts of her naked and riding him like a pneumatic hammer. That didn't mean she wanted him in return. She'd never touched him other than a chuck on the shoulder or a fist bump. Where every other woman in this port threw themselves at him, he couldn't judge Lorlii's interest level. The fact had kept him hornier than an adolescent boy upon first discovering his dick.

His fingers found the latch to the gag. *Damn!* It had a fingerprint lock. He dropped his hands and pulled back. "I'll be right back, sweetheart."

Grabbing the box cutter, he stormed back to the alley. A growl rumbled low in his throat, and a giddy smile toyed with his lips. He was a sick bastard, but this was gonna be fun. Which finger to choose? There were six options, so he guessed. if one didn't work, he could come back for another. As he sliced the digit off at the second knuckle, a gargled cry rose in the unconscious creep's throat, but Roark simply returned to Lorlii and pressed the pad of the cauterized finger against the lock.

With a flick and soft whir of nanites—bummer that he'd guessed correctly—the mask retracted off her face and into a black chunk which dropped, forgotten, onto the floor.

She launched at him, wrapping her arms around his neck and whispering against his shoulder. "Thank you, thank you, thank you! What if you hadn't shown up when you did? What if you were in the bar and had no idea I needed you to save me? Oh, stars I'm going to vomit."

Despair was a rising tide in her voice, her arms shaking as her breath hitched. She was coming down from her adrenalin surge, suffering its after-effects. Weakness. Trembling. Nausea. He needed to buoy her strength.

He pulled away enough to look at her. "Hold up a tic, sweetheart. You think you needed *me* to save you? I'll take the credit, but the truth is *you're* the badass who fileted the creep's forearm then knocked him out cold with one swing."

She blinked at him, clearly working to be calm. "Huh. Yeah, I did do that, didn't I?" She laughed, a thin laugh with a thread of hysteria, but she was pulling away from the edge. "So, what are you good for?"

This was more like his Lorlii. He slanted her his best bedroom eyes and lowered his voice to a rumble which never failed to work, except on her, "Let me get you naked, sweetheart, and I'll show you exactly what I'm good for."

Now, she would roll her eyes and—Wait, was that...? Had she...? Did she just... look at his lips? Like she wanted to kiss him? Her ensuing snort couldn't undo the moment of raw need he'd seen.

She shook her head. "What I meant was, why are you *here?*"

He smiled. "I'm here because there's this amazing woman who owns the bar. And I'm in love with her."

Fuckafitsu, he hadn't meant to say that out loud. He didn't even say those words in his head. Blame it on blood loss to the brain because his erection still crammed inside his pants. And the fact that her naked breasts were still pressed against his chest. There was only so much a man could take before he got stupid.

She blinked for several heartbeats, her brows knotting in confusion. Her expression was so adorable he had to bite back a laugh. And resist the urge to kiss her.

"I... I thought you came for the drinks."

Not touching her was no longer an option. He cupped her face in his palm, tracing his thumb along the plump bottom half of her deep indigo lips. He'd known she was unlike other women the first time he'd ventured into the port's new bar. At the time, the name had been unsettling. The Siren's Song. A reference to an ancient alien myth about beautiful women enchanting men and luring them to their doom. One look at Lorlii had proved there was some truth to the myth. She had indeed enchanted him. And if being with her killed him, what a wonderful way to go. "Sweetheart, not to discredit your bartending skills, but I can get a drink anywhere. I come to The Siren's Song to be with you."

Her shocked expression slowly evolved, softened, opened. He sensed it more than saw the physical evidence. A lazy smirk curled her lips, and she looked—no missing it this time—at his lips. "Don't think this gets you free drinks."

Her pale pink tongue swiped across her lips. It was the last straw, the final temptation, and it broke him. "Lorlii, tell me now if you don't want me. If you want me half as much as I want you, I'm going to drown in your kisses and fuck you until we both turn into a puddle."

She fisted his hair, tugging his head down. "Roark... You stink. Now, kiss me."

He kissed her with months of pent-up need. The

kiss wasn't tender or particularly artful, but a deluge of desire he'd kept dammed deep inside until the day she might return his attraction. That day had arrived, and he plunged head-first, tomorrow-be-damned. Her needy moans spurred him on. Her fingernails dug into his shoulders, clutching his shirt and pulling him closer.

He tilted her head to kiss and lick his way down her throat, on a desperate mission to suck on her tits. She arched back and speared fingers through his hair, tugging his face exactly where he wanted to be. He palmed her two perfect breasts, full and heavy, her flesh filling his hands. Her areolas, large and puckered bright turquoise buds demanding he suck them. Who was he to say no?

He laved them in turns, pulling their firmness into his mouth, scraping lightly with his teeth, plumping and rolling them in his fingers. Lorlii bucked, arching against his face, her nails digging into his scalp, her moans and mewls creating heady background music. His cock strained against his pants, desperate to be buried in her pussy, throbbing for release.

He'd do that soon and often enough, but he wanted to taste her first.

He trailed his hands around to her back and down, tracing along her spine, pulling off the tatters of her bra and shirt. Ending at her luscious ass, his fingers dipped beneath the waist of her skirt to the silky fabric of her —*Sonuvaslehgah*, she was commando—and shoved it over her hips.

Tearing himself away from her breasts, he grabbed her ass and hauled her against his cock. Hissing at the pleasure-pain, he ground his dick against her. Lorlii panted, meeting his thrusts with her own. Her moans swelled in volume and urgency. She was close to her own climax, but he wanted her to come on his tongue first.

He kissed her hard, thrusting his tongue in time with his hips. Then he pulled away enough to murmur against her lips, "You're so amazing. I have a cosmos of delights in mind for you. But first I'm going to devour your pussy until you scream."

"So far, you've been nothing but empty promises, Trekker." She panted, her gaze unfocused.

He chuckled as he lifted her to a nearby stack, dropping her skirt along the way, and wedged his shoulders between her thighs. In one swift motion, her knees were spread wide, giving him an unobstructed view. It stopped him cold.

At the apex of her thighs was evolutionary perfection. Her outer lips were edged with fleshy distensions, bulges like a hundred tiny clitorises. Rimming her slit were whorls of short tentacles in shades of aqua, tipped bright pink, and slick with her arousal. The tentacles wafted rhythmically as if from underwater currents, beckoning him, waving him forward. Maybe the Siren myth was true, but instead of women leading men to their doom, it was the glorious *Dohthan* pussy drawing men toward heaven.

He inhaled her natural perfume and thanked the stars above for the gift before him. He moaned long and low. "Sweet Nebula."

Lorlii tensed. The tentacles retracted, darting back

inside her body like a shy *muskih*. Her thighs closed around him, and she tried to skootch away, but he stopped her with a firm hand and looked up. Creases of worry marred her face. She tried to cover her crotch, but he gently swatted away her hand.

"What's wrong, Lorlii?" He caressed her thighs, pressing chaste kisses against her skin.

She frowned and worried her lips, fidgeting as if she couldn't get comfortable. "Nothing. It's ok; I understand. Lots of men, well not *lots*, find it a little...scary... down there. It's a bit intimidating and overwhelming and—"

Roark laughed, which stilled her fretting. "Sweetheart, I jump into exploding spacecraft for a living. This is an altar of the gods. And I'm going to worship until you know without a doubt exactly how much I want you. *All* of you."

He didn't wait for her to relax or give him crap about his as-yet-unfulfilled promises, but instead set to licking and kissing her. He lapped at the outer lips, circling the protrusions with his tongue, sucking them into his mouth like they were smooth nipples. Soon, her legs relaxed on his shoulders, and she hummed and moaned above his head. Her fingers caught his hands where they gripped her thighs and traced the lines of his veins and tendons, twining with his fingers. He thrust his tongue deep in her slit, her honey flowing down his throat. The nubby tentacles slowly reemerged, extending and brushing against his cheeks and chin like a lover's caress. He bathed them with his tongue, licking around and between them, tugging and drawing several into his mouth, swishing and flicking them about. Her juices and papillae covered his face, and he was drunk on it, never wanting it to end yet wanting Lorlii to find her release.

At the apex of her undulating tendrils was a swollen bulb. She convulsed and keened as his tongue flicked quickly over it. Roark disentangled a hand from hers and slid a finger into her slit. Then a second. Crooking them to rub her spot while he set to her clitoris in earnest. Laving and sucking until she was writhing and crying out, her thighs clenching against his head and her hips bucking. On a loud, long wail of his name, she let go, clamping his fingers, and tentacles shivering against his face, her thighs shuddering. Her juices poured forth, gushing over his hand and down his forearm.

Lorlii collapsed in a boneless, gasping heap while Roark stood, licking trails of her ejaculate on his arm as far as his tongue could reach. Her eyes were hooded, and a lopsided smile unfurled on her face. He couldn't help his triumphant grin. She looked well and truly fucked, and he hadn't even begun.

"You're still clothed," Lorlii pouted.

Roark' response was a sultry smile. He lifted the hem of his shirt—smirking when she held her breath in anticipation—and flipped it off, tossing it to the ground. Her tongue flicked over her lips, and he groaned. Stars above to have that tongue on his dick, but he'd never last if she did. With a wrist flick and shove, his pants were at his ankles, his throbbing cock pointing at her like a tracking *dohku* to its quarry. Fisting himself, he pumped from base to tip a few times. She moaned as if he was already buried inside her. Licking her lips, she reached for him, but he shook his head.

"Next time, sweetheart. Right now, I'm going balls-deep into paradise."

Aforementioned balls heavy with expectation, he hooked her knees over his arms and cradled her ass, lifting her body against his chest. He turned toward the shelf, pressing her back against a support beam, and braced his hands on either side, trapping her jackknifed body so she slid down his until her hot core tickled the tip of his dripping cock.

"This is gonna be hard and fast. Feel free to scream."

With only that warning, he surged into her, filling and stretching her until she'd taken him to the base. She keened long and low, her eyes rolling back in her head. He thrust quickly, drilling her with each stroke, so the remaining bottles rattled a tinkling accompaniment to their primal grunts and moans. She clawed at his shoulders, her legs bouncing in time over his arms, her breasts crushed against his chest. She was flushed, sweating, panting his name and other choice words in time to his deep dicking.

Then he felt it. Thousands of papillae clutching at his hips and cock, surrounding and stroking him like little sex helpers wanting in on the action. The intensity of sinking his dick in her tight sheath combined with the tickling grip of her hungry tentacles was unlike anything he'd ever experienced. Until the stinging. A thousand pinpricks of shimmering heat, like a million orgasms, centered on his dick and pulsed knee-buckling bliss through his body. As if he'd been zapped by some climax-taser, he throbbed with the intensity of a sizzling gamma-ray burst. Because, apparently, a regular orgasm wasn't amazing enough.

"*Sonuvaslehgah,* what are you doing to me?" The question ripped from a throat tight with his need to hold off his orgasm—all million of them—a little longer.

She shook her head erratically, stuttering between moans, "It's okay… will… explain… later… d-don't stop…"

She was close, thank the Maker, because so was he. He rested his forehead against hers. "Lorlii. Sweetheart. Taste how delicious you are."

He kissed her—desperate, bruising, teeth-clashing kisses—tangling his tongue with hers until he couldn't tell the two apart. Everything tightened around him, and she dropped her head back, screaming and arching as she came, clenching him with her pussy and tentacles. With one last thrust, he came as well, roaring his release to the universe above.

After a lifetime—or maybe a few minutes—gasping for air and shivering from the aftershocks of their love-making, Roark's breathing and pounding heart rate had calmed enough for him to form words. Carefully, he pulled out and eased Lorlii's legs down, keeping her body close in case she was as weak as he felt—and because he hated to let her out of his embrace, now that she was finally there.

She wobbled and leaned against him with a contented sigh. Then she laughed. "This place is a mess.

I'm a mess." She brushed her fingers through her hair, not meeting his gaze.

He tilted her head, forcing her to look in his eyes. "I'll help you clean up the storeroom. But you're perfect. Naked. Satisfied. You should be like this all the time."

She snorted then slid him a shy smile. "There you go again. Making promises you have to keep."

He kissed her with the long-restrained emotion he'd held, sealing the deal. "Let's get started on that promise. My place. Carry out. Cold beer. Both of us naked."

She laughed, interest lighting her eyes. She rested her head on his chest and sighed as if she'd been holding a breath for a lifetime. "Roark Trekker, you're going to be the death of me."

Roark tightened his arms around her, never wanting her to leave. "I'll say the same about you, Lorlii Atarga. But what a wonderful way to go."

FIRE IN THE STORM

BY PAYTON HARLIE

Kevin

Bands of low-hanging clouds race overhead, bringing intermittent downpours. A random flash of lightning is close enough that I flinch. Judging by the increase in wind over the past day, there's one hell of a storm on the way. For the first time in a month, a twinge of doubt about my vacation choice crosses my mind. Alone, on a barrier island off the Florida coast in hurricane season, with no contact to the rest of the world, might not have been my brightest move.

Another glance at the Gulf tells me it's probably too late to make the boat trip back to my truck. Surely someone would've already come out to warn me if it's a hurricane. Right?

I'd made the reservation over the phone with some chick named Kandi, who took my credit card info and told me the key would be in the lock when I arrived. The place was spotless with fresh linens that smelled like sunshine. Surely, she would've sent someone out if I needed to evacuate.

A low whine of wind sends my skiff to beat against the dock in time with the menacing white-topped waves. No, not looking good. If it isn't a hurricane, there's no reason to leave. If it is a hurricane, the rescue workers are busy enough without having to come fish me out of the Gulf. Staying put is the right choice.

I grab a beer and head out to add extra lines to the boat. Yeah, yeah. It's not even lunchtime, but if I'm going down in a hurricane, I'm entitled to some early morning adult beverages.

Halfway to the dock a boat bouncing on the waves catches my eye. Damn crazy person. For a minute, the craft goes airborne then slams down. And that's why taking the boat is the wrong thing to do. Again and again, the hull rises with each swell then lands with a heavy thud.

I wait on the dock, ready to assist the driver. At least, the fool is wearing a life jacket.

"Slow down." The driver looks straight at me although I know she can't hear my words. Like a pro, she adjusts her approach and slides into the berth. The wind makes it tricky, but I secure the line tossed my way. She cuts the engine and drops anchor before joining me on the deck.

The rain is coming down in sheets now, stinging even the smallest bit of exposed flesh. It's almost impossible to open my eyes.

We tie down the boat in silence, leaving enough

slack to accommodate a rise in the tide. My arms are leaden as I secure the last knot.

There's nothing else I can do except chill the fuck out and get us out of the weather. "We've got to get inside."

She picks up two life jackets and grunts. We prop each other up, each step a deliberate effort as our feet sink into the saturated sand. When we reach the cabin, she drops both life jackets on the porch then takes off around the building.

I scramble to catch up with her. "What the hell are you doing?"

She unlatches the door to the shed out back. "We have to shutter the windows."

"Are you crazy?"

"I can't lose the cabins."

Once inside the shed, she takes two metal sticks off a pegboard. "Hold on to these." She shoves them in my hands then fires up an ancient four-wheeler. "Thanks. Go on inside, and I'll be back as soon as I can."

Like I'm actually going to go hunker down while she's out here. "No way, babe. I'm coming with you."

"Listen, *babe*, you're a guest. Now move."

I don't move. "We could barely walk from the dock to here. We're going together." She frowns in response. "You have six cabins to board up. We'll finish faster if we both go."

"All right. Get on."

I ride bitch. My cock perks up as her muscles flex under mine with each turn she makes. If not for the whole getting stabbed with needles of rain and eating grit thing, I'd be a very happy man.

We arrive at the cabin farthest from mine and begin cranking the shutters into position. It goes about as smooth as it can, given the circumstances. By the time we finish and ride to the second cabin, the waves have doubled in height. We repeat the process on the three remaining cabins, and then return to mine.

She parks the four-wheeler in the shed.

I return her crank to the pegboard. "You go on in and get dry. I'll do the rest." She doesn't argue.

When finished, I shake a couple of buckets of wet off my body onto the porch, go inside, and secure the door. The fireman in me wants to object. If anything unexpected happens, there'll be no fast way out. Guess that's the least of our problems. I give the door one last tug and turn.

She's in the kitchen. Still damp honey curls twisting wild atop her tall, lush body. Dressed in my one of my shirts and shorts. And holding out a beer. Fucking beautiful.

I take the bottle.

She smiles and pops the top off a beer for herself. "Kandi Reynolds, retired Marine. Being waterlogged is second nature."

And funny. "Certainly proved that today. Kevin Trask, Shell County Fire Rescue. Running into dangerous situations is a specialty."

I take a long swallow from the bottle. She gives me a small chuckle. "Haven't felt that good a rush in a long time."

My heart thumps a bit. She got a rush from that? "Ah, another adrenaline addict. So, what was so important that you were willing to risk your life coming here?"

"The hurricane that wasn't supposed to seriously impact us took an unexpected turn overnight. I had no other way to reach you." She pauses. "I didn't realize the Gulf would be so intense. Guess there's no going back now."

Damn, she'd been trying to call. That's bad on me. Her fingers are tight around that beer. She's more shaken than she's letting on.

I scrub my hand across my face. "Left my phone in my truck intentionally. I didn't think that through. I'm sorry."

"Don't apologize. Being out of contact is the point of renting on the island. And I would've come out to do the shutters anyway." She stares at the floor. "You're making a puddle. You should get changed."

I want to say more, but talk can wait. There hasn't been any sun today to power the solar panels. Might as well take a warm shower and get comfortable while I still can.

Kandi is working on another beer when I return. The clock says it's almost six.

"What was the weatherman saying about the storm this morning?" I ask.

"Category 1 and intensifying, moving our way around twenty miles per hour. They're putting landfall about thirty miles south this evening, but you know how that goes."

"Judging by what's happening outside, it has to be close. If it stays to the south, the storm surge shouldn't be as bad. Hopefully, we won't get the full brunt of the eye wall." I grab another beer. "Does anyone know you're here?"

"I tried calling the emergency numbers they were posting on the news but couldn't get through."

"Taking that as a no," I say, concern rolling in my gut. "I wish I'd thought to bring a marine radio." Rescue crews won't even know to look for us.

She points at a plastic sandwich bag filled with rice —and a phone—sitting on the counter. "I had my cell. The need for a radio never crossed my mind." She tears a piece off the label on her bottle. "We have life jackets."

The statement hangs in the air.

I get a couple of six-packs from the pantry and place them in the refrigerator. "You ever gone through a hurricane?"

"No, but I've been in the cellar during a tornado up in Ohio and in war zones overseas. You?"

I shake my head. "Only seen the aftermath. I live inland, and we've only had tropical storm winds." No point in telling her the cabin probably doesn't stand a chance if we take a direct hit. And if the wind doesn't do us in, the storm surge could put us underwater. Hell, the whole barrier island could get wiped out. "All we can do is wait. It should be over by this time tomorrow." One way or another.

"True. So, you're here on vacation?"

I nod. "Needed some space from real life." That's not quite the entire truth. More like, I didn't know what else to do with myself. "What about you? You're the owner, right?"

"Yeah. My father was friends with the former owner. We used to come here in the summer when I was a kid. When Mel died, his wife put the place up for sale. I decided to take my twenty years and retire. This is the only unit I've finished renovating. And now..." Her hands go up like an explosion.

"Hey, one disaster at a time. You didn't die out there today."

A smile lights up her face. "You're right. Any day you don't die is a good day."

Don't I know it. "You doing the work yourself?"

"As much as possible. I like feeling my body ache after a hard day's work. Makes sleeping sweeter."

"I know what you mean. Being a beach bum is nice, but I'm not sure I'm cut out for it." My ex would be thrilled to see me being safe and predictable. Well, before the hurricane, that is. Actually, my ex would have hated it here. Her idea of a vacation is shopping at a new mall.

Kandi's head bobs in agreement. "My mother couldn't figure out why I didn't want marry an accountant and settle down. Can you imagine doing nothing but worrying about what's for dinner every day?"

I am stunned. This beautiful woman gets it. "Not at all." My wife never understood. Making sure someone gets out of a bad situation alive doesn't seem like a risk to me. It's simply the job I'm meant to do. What my ex classifies as "dangerous" is what makes me feel alive.

"So, I enlisted. Being a Marine wasn't easy, but it sure wasn't boring."

"This vacation… it wasn't completely my idea…" So much for not oversharing.

Her eyebrows furrow. "What happened?"

"My friends convinced me some time off was in order. I went back into a burning house after we got the people out." The words continue to spew out of my mouth. "I watched the flames devour the structure."

"Why?"

"I was in a bad place. It seemed like a fitting way to go."

"Damn, Kevin."

"Yeah."

"So, what did you decide?"

"Too damn hot and potentially painful as hell."

Instead of making her excuses and walking away, she laughs. "Good to know you made a choice."

I rub the back of my neck. "Not everyone appreciated my decision-making process."

"And?"

I shrug. "Here we are."

"You better now?"

"I'd like to make it out of this hurricane and take you to dinner at a nice restaurant. So, yeah, I'm better. What about you?"

"I was tired of war." She takes her empty, tosses it in the trash container, then turns back around. Her gaze starts somewhere around my ankles and takes the slow scenic route to my face with an appreciative pause at the front of my shorts. "Want to fuck?"

"What?" My cock is so entranced with her sassy blue eyes it takes a second for my brain to process her words. "Wait. No. I mean yes, but that's no way to pick up a guy."

She fucking winks. "Generally works. You'd rather be wined and dined?"

I give her my best straight face. "And I expect flowers. As should you."

Kandi's laugh is deep and generous and grabs me by the balls. Yet, it feels a bit off.

Narrowing my eyes, I say, "Let me show you how this is done."

Her cheek turns a pretty pink as I move in closer then brush my finger along her arm. My own skin warms in response.

I pause as I gently stroke her wrist. "Let me nuke us some food. You like Italian? We'll split a bottle of wine or two and forget about the storm."

"You don't have to do that." She looks up from the spot where my thumb meets her skin.

"A slow learner, aren't you? I'm asking you out on a date. Say yes."

She points to her clothes. "I don't have anything nice to wear."

I lift her hand and replace my thumb with my lips. "You're at the beach. Smelling like my shampoo. Wearing my clothes. Trust me. You look incredible. And I have the only food in town." I lower my voice. "Now, say yes." Brushing a stray hair off her face, I linger along her cheek and repeat, "Say yes."

Her eyes flutter shut. "Yes."

. . .

KANDI

Yes. To whatever Kevin and his growly voice are asking. A smile bubbles up out of my chest.

"Good thoughts?"

The look he's wearing makes me melt. Heat rushes up my neck and I want to look away, but his gaze has mine in its grasp. His lips move closer until they touch mine, briefly, hinting at what's to come.

"I love how you fit next to me." The words caress my ears, lulling me with their sincerity.

I bury my face into his shoulder. "You are damn near a unicorn."

"How so?"

"It's not often that I fit. I'm a quarter inch shy of six feet and towered over all the boys growing up. Still do. Sexy heels are never an option."

He pulls away, his gaze searing along every inch of my body. "You in heels would be amazing."

There's no mistaking the want in his voice. And then…he steps away. "Food first."

What just happened?

His gaze followed the outline of my body. I know that look. Like a man standing at the meat counter choosing his next meal. And I'm the steak to throw on the fire and enjoy, knowing he'll go shopping again tomorrow looking for something different to satisfy his hunger.

In other words, the right kind of man for the kind of distraction I need to get through these next hours.

The rain and possible flooding don't bother me. The wind does. I was five when that tornado came through, but I'll never forget the sound as I huddled in the corner.

The noise outside doesn't seem to rattle Kevin. I like that. And he's tall, and tanned, and built.

It's been months since I've looked at a man. First, I was busy deciding whether to leave the Marines. Next, my focus turned to what to do once I left. Then, there was the stress of closing on the property. Finding someone to go out with was too much trouble.

And that's just all sorts of sad. When did going out with a man become a chore?

"Why don't you open a bottle of red? Check the pantry," he says.

That jars me out of my head. While he rummages through a stack of boxes in the freezer, I find two glasses and uncork a Chianti.

"Here they are. I knew I had lasagna. Nowhere as good as mine, but we'll make do."

Kevin is scorching hot as he tosses the container in the microwave and punches a few buttons. What would it be like to have him puttering in my kitchen? Too bad I'll never find out. Men like him don't stick around with women like me.

"I can box, lift weights, and secure a military base. Cooking, shopping, and flirting, not so much."

He gives me a quick hug. "Good thing I can cook, shop, and flirt for the both of us."

Damn he's good. "You cook?"

"Firefighter, remember? But absolutely, I enjoy

cooking. Plus, Mom insisted if we wanted to eat, we'd better be willing to cook."

A smile tugs at my lips. "Maybe I could learn."

"Maybe I'll teach you." His words are thick with promise.

He's so handsome it hurts to look at him. Sexy as hell. Makes a living saving people. There must be something horribly wrong with him. "Are you married?"

That statement earns me a blank stare. "Don't beat around the bush, do you?"

"Sorry to be blunt, but married men are a hard no for me."

Handing me two plates from the cabinet, he grabs the silverware and takes a seat at the table. "Only in the past. Fifteen years married, divorced three. Two teenagers—we share custody. She's remarried to a bank manager. You?"

"Never married. No kids. I had to be tough if I wanted to be taken seriously, and no man wants a woman tougher than he is."

His eyebrows scrunch down. "You really believe that?"

"Enough men have told me, so yeah, I do. One-night stands are easier." There's that word again.

"So, all you look for is a quick piece of ass?"

I roll my eyes. "Come on, what's wrong with going after what I want? You think only men get to do that?"

"Not at all. I like that you know what you want. But I want a bit more."

I taste the Chianti. Delicious. "You take all your women on these fancy dates, first?"

"All my women. You are funny." He swirls the wine in his glass.

"You don't strike me as the celibate type."

"I'm not. And I've been known to fuck a stranger or two. I don't want that with you."

My heart does a little skip. "Oh."

Leaning over the table, he drops his voice to a whisper. "It won't be enough to fuck you once."

My lips turn up and a flush of heat stings my face.

"God, I love making you blush."

What is it about this man? I haven't blushed since before boot camp. A clap of thunder saves me from embarrassing myself further.

"It's strange not being able to see outside." Not seeing doesn't mean not hearing. The noise from the storm has become relentless while we've been talking.

"Agreed. The shutters are doing their job, though."

"Would be nice to have some weather updates right about now. I was annoyed at them yesterday. All the stations saying the same stuff over and over. I didn't realize not knowing what's happening is worse."

He nods. "I'm a native. I should know better. The idea of getting away from my real life tricked me into a false security. But, nothing to be done about all that now."

The microwave beeps.

"Wish we had some Cuban bread."

"Oh my, yes." He places a large serving on my plate. "This smells delicious, even if it was frozen." I stop midbite. "Thank you for inviting me to dinner."

85

Our gazes lock for a moment. "I'm happy you accepted."

And oh, my God. Once again, he's looking at me as if I'm what's for dinner.

"Is Kandi short for something?"

Why is he talking? We need to finish this meal and get to the "you're what's for dessert" part. "Nope, it's really Kandi. Mom was so excited I was a girl. She had dreams about evening dresses and pageants. I was supposed to be a girly girl like her." Those memories take the moment down a notch.

"Guessing that didn't go as planned."

"Ha. I played baseball with the boys, made the high school football team as the kicker and backup for the quarterback. She was extremely disappointed. What about you?"

"All boy. Played baseball. Still do on a rec team. No surprises for my parents until I graduated high school and decided to be a firefighter. Dad's a lawyer, Mom's a psychologist, so they always imagined I'd go on to earn multiple college degrees. Once they got over the shock, they realized it was a good fit for me. So, you're from Ohio?"

"Yep. My parents brought us here for a week every year. They plan on selling their house and moving to Florida once Dad retires next year. What about you?"

"Born and still live in a little town about thirty or so miles from here."

"When do you go back to work?"

He blinks a few times. "As soon as this storm is over. They'll need everyone on duty."

Disappointment floods in unexpectedly.

"Oh." A tiny frown escapes before I can compose my face. Why is he bothering to say all those nice things when all this can be is a one-night stand? I take another look at the man across the table and make my decision. One night with him will be better than no nights. I'll deal with the disappointment later.

The conversation meanders. We take turns telling stories about ourselves. It surprises me how much we have in common. After dinner, we move on to ice cream and brandy. In a warm state of bliss, I clear the plates while he loads the dishwasher. Between the carbs and the alcohol, we're both pretty damn mellow given the situation outside.

We hold hands, and then he pulls me in tight. Our arms link around each other like teenagers who can't get close enough.

"It's been a really nice night," I whisper.

"It has." He leans me against the counter, cradles my face in his hands, and sends my world into a tumble for the second time in one day.

He. Can. Kiss.

His lips insist I bow to their wishes. I do and am rewarded with a low growl. I run my hands along his chest. He takes them and puts them behind my back, never slowing the assault on my mouth.

Something smashes into the side of the cottage.

I jerk and break the kiss. "What was that?"

"Nothing we can do anything about." His lips work their way along my neck.

"It's getting worse." I hold a breath as he licks the spot under my ear.

"It'll get worse before it gets better. We've done everything we can. We're safe."

The lights flicker as if to argue.

"Are you sure about that?"

"We could've lost one of the solar panels. We're safe."

And he smells so damn good. "That makes sense."

My leg goes around him, searching for friction.

His hands let go of mine and tighten on my ass. All his glorious hardness presses against all my best places.

"Are you sure you want this?" he rasps.

Is he kidding? "I need you to keep me safe tonight. Sex is life affirming."

"Princess, you know you can save yourself. You need a different type of rescue." He takes possession of my mouth again, our tongues hungry for contact. I dig my fingers into his sculptured ass.

"The bed," I gasp.

But he's already kissing me again, so I forget about the bed and kiss him back.

Kevin

There's nothing petite or fragile about her. My cock swells in approval. She's a fucking goddess.

My hand ghosts along her back—under my shirt—while I taste the skin along her shoulder. Sweet and salty. A warm breeze of her breath drifts sweetly across my face as her lips brush against my ear then return to my mouth.

I take a step, then another, walking her backward, never stopping the kiss.

She steadies herself against my chest while her hand drifts south.

My cock weeps as her palm presses along my length then cups my balls. "Fuck. Sit."

"What?"

I fall to my knees and pull her down to the kitchen chair. I undo a shirt button, then another.

"Touch them," she says, sounding breathless.

"Patience woman." They're full, round, and heavy. I brush my thumb across her petal-pink nipple. It hardens, so I taste it with my tongue. "You are a work of art."

She tunnels her fingers through my hair. "So good."

It's like unwrapping a present. "Lift." My shorts are snug on her as I slide them over her hips and down her legs. "You're so beautiful."

I suck hard on her nipple then kiss my way down to her thighs. Spreading her legs wide, I lick long and slow through her folds.

"Do it, now." She tugs on my hair, trying to pull me up. "I can't come that way."

Her eyes tell me differently. She's already close to coming. "I disagree."

"It's more efficient if I tell you how."

"But then how would you discover that you like this?" I slide a lone finger into her wet cunt then run lazy circles around her clit with my thumb.

She moans. "Oh, damn."

"Good?" She tilts her hips. I add a second finger and settle again between her legs. "Lean back."

I prop her leg over my shoulder and let her sounds guide my mouth until she trembles under me.

"Please, Kevin."

I roll my tongue around her clit then suck hard. She comes undone.

Neither of us moves.

She's panting. "I've never. . . Thank you."

"Shh. I love the way you taste." I ease her off the chair and onto my lap. She tries to leave, but I keep her close.

Her gaze drops away. "It's so intimate. Personal. I feel so exposed."

"Does it bother you being wet for me? My mouth on you? The way your thighs pressed hard against my head? The way you came for me? I love the intimacy of it."

Her blush is deep red. "Let me take care of you."

"Nah. I'm good. We'll save that for later."

"The part of you I'm sitting on doesn't agree."

"He'll get over it. That..."

The whole cabin rumbles. I look up and see the roof flex. "Go to the bathroom. Now."

Rain pelts like bullets against the metal shutters.

Kandi snatches her shorts and grabs the life jackets on the way.

I drag the mattress and comforter. "In the tub."

Except no matter how we try, adults our height do not fit.

We make do with the comforter on the floor and the mattress angled over us. If the roof goes, there's a chance we won't be maimed.

She curls up. "I hate being afraid."

I tuck her close beneath me. "In this moment, you are safe." I fuse her lips with mine.

Her pulse races under my touch. The need to comfort her is overwhelming. "In maybe an hour, the worst will be past us. You can hold on for an hour." My words must connect with her. She relaxes in my arms and takes control of our kiss. Her hands are greedy, struggling until she rids me of my clothes.

"See something you like?"

"Don't be smug. You know you're hung." She shifts and takes my cock in her mouth.

Ahhh. So fucking good. But not on my agenda.

I coax her up. "I need to see you."

Her crystal blue gaze latches onto mine. "I want you."

The words are barely audible under the rage of the wind. She grasps hard around my length. "I want you inside me."

"No condoms." Another regret.

A sly smile flashes over her face. "IUD."

"Then do it." I roll on my back. "Ride me."

"I'll crush you."

"Then crush me. Fuck me until we're both in pieces."

One leg on either side of my hips, she stretches herself oh so fucking slowly over every single inch of my cock. Tight, warm, and wet. Then she grinds. Her breasts sway seductively.

My hands are filled with her luscious ass. "Don't hold back. Fuck me." I pull her down while I thrust upward.

"Again. Do that again."

Her inner muscles clench; the rhythm of her movements is erratic.

"Come for me."

Her back arches. An orgasm rolls over her, and I flip her onto her back while she's still coming. Her eyes widen in shock. Oh yeah, sweetheart, I'm strong enough to do that.

"Wrap those gorgeous legs around me." Her ankles lock and pull me down hard. "Ah, fuck. You were built just for me." And I push into her the way I've wanted to since I saw her jump off that damn boat.

"You're so fucking sexy."

"Stop."

"It's the truth." I pull out.

"What are you doing?"

Fuck the storm. Can't think of a better way to go. I push aside the mattress. "Stand up."

We stand, and I turn her so she's facing the mirror above the sink, her back against my front. I bury myself deep inside her and roll my hips. "Look at us."

She turns her head away. "I can't."

"Oh, Kandi. Babe." I take her hands in mine, bringing one up to cup her breast. "Look at us. Look."

Her eyes open and stare at our reflection. I guide the other hand to her clit, and together, we make small circles while I pump hard and slow.

"Don't you want more, Kandi? Don't you get tired of settling? Let go."

Her breaths come out short and quick.

"I want more."

Our gazes lock in the mirror.

"Come for me."

I feel her contract around my cock. Three more frantic thrusts, and I'm coming with her.

Her lids slam shut as if to shut out everything she just saw. Tears roll slowly down her cheeks.

I hold her tight. "I've got you."

She shudders. "Why did you do that? I was fine the way I was. Don't make me want what I can't have."

"Shhhh. You can have whatever you want."

"For one night…"

The words hang between us, and I wish I could reassure her that this is more than one night. But we both know I'll be gone in less than twenty-four hours.

I lay my forehead against hers. "I wish we had more time."

"It's fine." She drops to the floor and curls under the mattress. "The military taught me to never expect more time. We've had all the time there is."

KANDI

I wake to the sound of Kevin's slow, warm breath. The storm has passed. We didn't die. It's a good day.

Careful not to wake him, I slide out from under the mattress and pad to the kitchen. A few flipped switches later, I have the generator running, and the rich aroma of coffee brewing fills the air.

Bracing myself for what might be outside, I roll up the door shutter.

There's a bit of sun peeking out between the still

fast-moving low clouds. No doubt we'll get additional bands of rain.

Kevin was right about losing the solar panels, but the roof is still intact. I go around back to get the four-wheeler. The shed is gone, the bike buried in its remnants.

"Could've been worse." He plants a kiss on the back of my head and hands me a mug.

"Let's check and see if the boats made it."

The boats are still moored but full of water. We rig a siphon from a piece of hose and continue down the shore.

The cabins are there, but there is extensive erosion. The transient nature of a barrier island slams home.

"I never realized this could happen. This whole island could disappear."

He laces his fingers with mine. "It could. But, it's still here, now."

We walk back in silence. Kevin packs his things. I fill a large cooler with the food from the fridge and a tote bag with items from the pantry.

"This wasn't a one-night stand. You understand that?" He has his duffle bag in one hand.

I sigh. "Let it be, Kevin. It was perfect. This will always be a treasured memory." When I'm in the nursing home, I'll still be telling the tale of surviving a hurricane in the arms of a fine ass fireman.

I sling the tote over my shoulder. He takes one handle of the cooler while I take the other.

After locking the door, we trudge to the dock.

"What are you doing next week?"

We set the things down next to his boat. "Repairing solar panels."

He laughs and climbs in. I hand him the bags, and then the cooler. It's over.

I breathe deeply. "Why don't you see if she runs?"

He nods. It takes a few tries, but the motor starts. It's over.

How can I miss someone I barely know? I mentally kick myself. I've never played the "what if" game. I don't plan to start now.

"Thank you for everything." I hold my voice steady.

"Here's the thing…" He climbs out of the boat. "Letting it be doesn't work for me." He sweeps me into his arms. "I've never met a woman like you. I'd be a fool to let you go, and I'm through being a fool." His lips come crashing into mine. "You are a perfect fit for me."

My heart beats frantically. *It's not over…it's not over.*

"I'm scared," I say, lifting my chin.

"You're safe with me."

I bury my head against his chest. "I'm afraid to tell you you're a perfect fit for me, too."

"Good. I have your office number. You have my cell number. I'll call you tonight when I know what's happening at the station. Yes?"

Fireworks shoot off inside me. He likes me. "Yes."

"Now, go start your boat."

I turn the engine over, and we each cast off our lines. He follows me to my berth at the marina then turns toward the ramp where his truck is parked.

Yes, it's a good day.

CLAIMING LYLA

BY MEGAN RYDER

*L*yla Chatham bent over from the stabbing pain in her side, pausing beside the ancient oak tree under whose branches she'd played as a cherished child of her father, the alpha of their pack. Senses heightened, she focused on the sounds around her—especially the running footsteps of the hunters who had spread out through the forest to pursue her. Her breath came in shuddering pants, and she strained to control the sounds, knowing every noise could give her away, could betray her weakness to those who would take that which she valued most.

Her freedom.

Despite the dark of night, she wasn't lost, having grown up here, roamed and hunted, protected and safe, until her father passed a couple of years ago. Now, her brother had taken over the leadership of their pack, and everything had changed.

A howl came from somewhere behind her and slightly to the left. Then an answering one sounded on the right. They were herding her to capture her in order to claim her. *To fuck her*. She knew the forest but, in the darkness, and with her own pack against her, there was no sanctuary. The city might offer protection for a while, muddy her scent, but it was miles away, and the chance of her making it that far was a long shot.

Because she didn't have just one alpha chasing her. Her brother had offered her up to five, with the winner claiming her as mate, provided he kept her silent about her brother's illegal actions.

A Claiming Rite. Rarely done outside of the traditional packs, and mostly in the old country, never in America—at least not in the last hundred years. Not since the wars had ended and pure-blooded shifter females, like her, had become precious. None of the five who chased her were suitors her father had considered suitable mates, but her brother didn't care much about that.

The cramp in her side eased, and she straightened. She wouldn't be trapped among the trees. She'd make her stand in the meadow where she'd changed for the first time. She'd pray to the goddess that she and the ancestors would lend her their strength and support. She took off at a run, refusing to shift, even though she could run faster on four paws than two. An alpha could force her to shift back to human form, and when she shifted, she'd be naked. Lyla didn't want to make anything easier for him.

She paused on the edge of the meadow, where the moonlight shone bright as daylight. The howls had grown fainter, so her false trail had fooled some of the alphas.

She scented the air and didn't detect anything other than remnant odors from the pack's last hunt. Cautiously, she emerged. She'd been secretly trained by her father's second, who'd conveniently been killed in a car accident just before her father's death. She could hold her own. Not forever against five alphas and their seconds, but well enough to maybe hurt them. It might make the claiming worse, but she didn't care anymore. She wouldn't go quietly to her fate, not Lyla Chatham. She would rage at it.

"LOOKING FOR SOMEONE, PRINCESS?"

Duncan Taggart stepped out of the shadows and into the moonlit meadow, silently cursing the fates that brought the current situation down upon them. Although, staring at the slender, dark-haired vision surrounded by pale light, his body had different ideas rather than facing the clusterfuck about to descend on him and the innocent shifter female standing defiantly in the clearing. Lyla Chatham, the pure-blood daughter of the Chatham pack, stared at him, her head tilted a little to match his height, her ice-blue gaze meeting his in a direct challenge. Despite her defiance, he sensed a hint of underlying fear, only natural for a female in an unwanted Claiming Rite, but her resistance was going to make his job more difficult. Howls rose in the distance; the sound that of pursuing alphas having caught her scent. Lyla was running out of time.

He let his gaze run up and down her, noting the torn and dirty white blouse that exposed a flash of lace underneath and the streaks of mud on the fitted denim jeans and sneakers. An outfit that gave her at least a chance to flee. However, facing down five alphas and their seconds, all herding her toward a forced claiming…? No female could best those odds.

His cock stirred, the erection he'd grown accustomed to living with since he'd come to the Georgia Pack a week or so ago under orders to investigate the pack and their alpha, making itself known. The skin around his wrists burned as if scalded by hot water, and yet, if he had looked, he wouldn't see any injuries. But he might see something far more dangerous, and it scared the hell out of him, especially right now with the danger surrounding them. However, the burning could also be their salvation.

Lyla folded her arms in front of her, a defensive gesture, closing herself off from him while plumping up her full breasts so they strained against the lace. "What do you want?"

He cocked his head at the howls growing closer. "You don't have much time, or much of a choice, sweetheart. You either deal with me or them. And trust me, I'm the lesser of your evils."

A laugh broke from her throat, a raw, harsh sound that held no humor. "I'd prefer none of you. Why can't you leave me alone, you bastards? You want me to just roll over and spread my legs like a good little bitch. Well, fuck that."

He winced at her harsh tone and steeled himself. A

breeze picked up her scent and tickled his senses with it, and his cock hardened further, painfully. His wrists burned hotter under the skin, prickling like a thousand fine needles that made him want to scratch an itch. Nothing would appease the sensation, he feared. He cursed under his breath. *Fuck.* Not the best time to find his mate. Not here. Not in this goddamn situation. This night had just gone to shit, and now the bonds were pulling him in even tighter.

He advanced on her until he was just a few feet away, letting her scent wash over him—magnolias and feminine anger, along with an underlying bloom of arousal as he invaded her space. His inner wolf appreciated her strength, her resolve in not backing down, and wanted to roll in her arousal and sate himself in her pussy. But the other side of himself, the more practical one, wished she'd kept running until she'd found an escape, even though he knew she'd never find one. Running excited the inner wolf, and fighting excited the human side. The alphas who were coming were known for their brutality, and she would pay—unless he could convince her to work with him.

Then his real challenge would begin, a personal one. But business first.

"I don't need you to submit. I'm not here at your brother's behest. I'm here for you."

She narrowed her gaze. "So are they."

He loomed over her, anger burning in his belly, his wolf growling low. "I'm not like them."

She cocked her hip and met his gaze without a care for the dominance he knew shone in his eyes. "Prove it."

He stifled a grin. Cocky bitch. "You can't stand against all of them. You need an ally."

She held up her hands and looked around the empty meadow. "I don't see anyone here." She looked him up and down, derisively. "You think you can take on all of them yourself and save little ol' me?"

He smirked at her southern drawl. "From what I hear, you can handle yourself. They have to abide by a few rules for the Claiming Rite. If we enforce those rules, then we might able to get through this."

Suspicion darkened her blue eyes. "What rules?"

"Claiming Rites are illegal without the Council or a Council rep on hand to observe, to ensure the female isn't harmed and accepts the decision."

She snorted. "I'm not willing, and I don't accept. But I don't see the Council giving a damn about me or any pure-blood female."

"I'm here, aren't I?" His quiet voice stopped her, and she tilted her head, staring at him thoughtfully. He nodded.

"You're a Council enforcer?" Again, she looked him up and down, disbelief radiating from every aspect of her expression. "Well, I'm still screwed. Literally and figuratively."

He barked a laugh then turned as the howls grew much closer. "They're almost here, princess. You need to make your decision. Me or them?"

Panic flared in her eyes at the howls that seemed to echo from every side. They were circling the meadow, surrounding them, ensuring no escape. He resisted the urge to throw her over his shoulder and make a break for it. He had to wait. His full backup wouldn't be there for several hours, if then. He only had one wolf as support, not enough.

She swallowed audibly. "What are the rules?"

"No time. Decision. Me or them?"

There was movement in the shadows. They had arrived.

She stepped closer to him, her only safe harbor in the hurricane of her life. "You. Don't disappoint me."

HIS WORDS HAD BEEN SPOKEN like a fervent vow, and yet Lyla wasn't sure she could trust him or any alpha male. Her faith in alphas had been broken in the years since her father's death, after having been subjected to her brother's tightly increasing control and the allies he'd surrounded himself with. Allies like the men slowly emerging from the forest, lust and hunger almost palpable in their scents and in the feverish glints in their eyes. Their lust was almost as strong as their urge to fight.

This night was turning into a catastrophe, with her in the center of it all. If she got out of this battle alive and with minimal injuries, she'd be lucky. More likely, the clearing would be scattered with bodies, and she'd be irreparably damaged in the process. No alpha would kill her as he claimed her—no, she was too valuable. But she would be scarred. Physically, emotionally, mentally.

A low growl brought her attention back to the immediate situation, and she absently rubbed her wrists, feeling the pinpricks of sensation circling them, as if she had already been restrained by the rope dangling from the belt of the Carolina alpha, Robert Hotchkiss. As he approached her, his thin lips were twisted in a cruel smile, and his tongue darted out to wet them as he leered.

"You shouldn't have run, Lyla. I would've been merciful. But now, I'll have to teach you who's boss." The sick glee in his voice told her he was looking forward to it.

Her entire body tensed, and she opened her mouth to respond when a heavy hand settled on her lower back, the heat of a palm burning through the thin layers of her blouse and jeans. The weight settled her, calmed her, reminded her that she wasn't alone, even as sexual awareness bloomed low in her belly and her pussy throbbed.

They might still be outnumbered, but she wasn't completely abandoned. Even if her birth pack hadn't had the balls to stand up for her, this stranger stood next to her, even if it meant his death. She could have tied herself to someone worse. The strength of the wolf standing next to her radiated. A wolf she barely knew made her feel safe for the first time in a long time, and she found herself hoping for a miracle.

DUNCAN STEADIED Lyla with his hand and almost smiled when the tension imperceptibly leeched from her body. She might not be thrilled with his presence, but she already saw him as a better option than those surrounding them, the power of the Mating taking hold whether she realized it or not. Her wolf already recognized him as her mate. Now, he had to make sure the other wolves acknowledged his claim and backed off without any damage to Lyla. Judging by the way they spread out to completely surround them, he and Lyla weren't going to get out of there without bloodshed. And he doubted they'd respect the Council—or a true mating. Which left him no recourse but to fight his way out. *Dammit.*

The Carolina alpha, a man on the Council's watch list for his cruelty to his own pack—never mind the human women whom he'd transitioned against their will—advanced on their position, eyes flashing yellow, aggression spiking in his scent.

Lyla tensed as Robert stopped a few feet away and sniffed the air, a low growl coming from his throat.

Duncan's wolf clawed his way up from within, fighting for dominance, wanting to defend his mate, knowing the stocky man who had let some of his muscle turn to fat would be no match for him in a teeth-to-claw to battle—assuming he fought fair, which was highly unlikely. But Duncan's rational side remained in control, for now.

He narrowed his eyes. "She's claimed, Hotchkiss. It's over."

Robert's lips lifted in a snarl, and his gaze traveled over Lyla in an insulting way. "She doesn't look claimed or mated. She's still fair game for any one of us, especially if we take you out. So, as I see it, we just need to get rid of you."

Lyla sucked in a breath. "I'll never mate with you. I'd

rather die first. If you force me, you'd better sleep with one eye open."

Duncan let a grin spread across his face. Brave bitch. Even if they incited these wolves into a mating frenzy, it would be worth it. Her spirit wouldn't be denied. She'd be a worthy mate for him and a worthy alpha female for his pack. If they survived the next few hours…

A couple of the beta wolves exchanged glances with their alphas, who stepped forward to catch her scent. Their betas backed off, accepting the declaration.

Robert scowled. "There's a scent of claiming, but it's not final. And no mating marks. She's fair game. Besides, you weren't invited to the Claiming Rite. You have no right to be here."

"I was invited by her father prior to his death. Due to my own pack issues and other duties, I have been prevented from coming, until now. True mating takes precedence over claiming, according to our law. Once a mating has begun, we have thirty days to complete it or reject it before another mating or claiming can be attempted."

Robert rolled his shoulders; his fists curled at his sides. "I'm not waiting. I was promised her. Now, I want my payment." The words shot out of Robert, confirming Duncan's suspicions and the reason he'd been sent to Georgia.

Lyla froze, the words sinking in, and she paled in the moonlight.

Robert smirked, seemingly confident his words had hit their intended target. He swaggered as he closed the final steps between them. "You're mine," he snarled, his gaze boring into hers, "and I'm not leaving this clearing without you. So, accept it and your new place. Under me, bitch."

A low rumble started in Duncan's throat, the wolf becoming harder to control; especially, with his mate threatened. But he shouldn't have underestimated her.

She spat in Robert's face and shook the sleeves loose from her wrists, displaying the faint markings displayed there, holding them high for everyone in the clearing to see.

"I will never be yours. I'd rather die first. I'm claimed."

Duncan's wolf preened at her acceptance of the bond, yet the human side suspected she'd only said the words to get out of the tight spot they were in. He would only trust her claim when she was fully mated, bitten, and covered in his scent, not to mention far from this area and safe.

Robert lifted a fist, but before he could land it, Duncan stepped in front of her, catching the man's hand with his own, easily holding it in place. Robert's second advanced a few steps, but Duncan snarled and the beta froze.

"You dare strike a woman, another alpha's mate?" Duncan bit out. "I sanction you and your pack in the name of the Council."

Silence reigned, everyone frozen in shock. Even Robert stiffened, his hand still held inside Duncan's grip. Lyla sucked in a breath behind him but didn't move from the safety of her position. Damn, he hadn't planned on playing the Council card, not until he had more support on the ground, but that could take several hours, even days, and Lyla needed him now.

Robert lifted his chin. "I challenge you for your mate."

The words weren't unexpected, and Duncan had every right to reject him, but he didn't feel like watching his back every day and night for the next several days, or longer. He wanted this over. "To the death. And only between us. Your beta stays out of it."

A sly smile stretched across Robert's face. "My beta ensures you won't cheat. Too bad you don't have one."

"Says the guy who hunted down and terrorized an innocent woman to forcefully mate her. I don't have a lot of faith in your definition of cheating. No claws or fangs. Human only." He looked around the clearing. "And I do have a second. Lyla."

Not only did Robert looked surprised but so did Lyla. She recovered quickly.

Duncan dropped Robert's arm and deliberately turned his back, leading Lyla a few steps away.

"What the hell are you doing? He won't act honorably. He never has," she whispered, even though everyone in the clearing could probably hear her.

He shrugged. "Worried about me, sweetheart?"

"I just don't want to be claimed by that asshole."

He scowled at her lack of faith. "I don't plan to let him win. I have plans for you and me later, and it doesn't involve anyone else in this vicinity. But first, we need to take out any enemies. Who else is a danger?"

She blinked, not expecting him to ask her opinion. Then she quickly scanned the wolves milling about.

Robert and his beta were glaring at them from the opposite side of the meadow, Robert pumping himself up like an overjacked meathead, while the four other alphas were gathered quietly with their betas and speaking amongst themselves.

"Lyla, I need you to watch my back in case anyone else makes a move against me. I'll handle Robert and his beta. But if the others get involved, you run. I have help coming, but they won't be here in time. Get to Atlanta. Find Ryan Cooper. He'll protect you."

She scowled. "No way. You named me your second. We're in this together. And if we're truly mates, then we live or die together. I won't abandon you. So, we start the way we mean to go on. Or do you mean to shuffle me off when I'm not convenient?"

Shit. Not the time to have this fight. He pulled up his sleeves to show the matching mating marks. "I'm in this for the long haul. But there are too many. I want you to survive. By any means."

"I won't survive if you die. We may not have completed the mating, but we're in it together now." She gave him a quick kiss, and the flare of heat that flashed through him reminded him what he was fighting for. "I don't know the others. Robert and his betas are the only ones to worry about, for now. Destroy them, and we'll discuss this whole Council thing later."

He grinned and headed for the circle.

LYLA CLENCHED her fists by her sides and silently cursed her brother, and not for the first time. Of course, he wasn't here to see the damage his insane dictates and reckless actions had caused, not that he would've cared one way or another. Right now, she had bigger issues to worry about, namely her own future and the risks this wolf was taking on her behalf, a wolf who believed he was her mate.

And she was beginning to believe it, too.

She had the same markings developing on her wrists and the burning urge to go to him. When she'd publicly acknowledged the claim, her wolf had settled inside her after pushing wildly at her skin, clawing to get to him the moment he'd come close. Arousal had spiked, overriding fear, and both parts of her had wanted to soften, to launch herself at him and lick him from head to toe. Then a small part of her had reminded herself of the damage an alpha could do a female, and she had resisted. Barely. But now, as he pulled off his T-shirt, revealing a broad chest and strong, defined muscles that begged her to trace them with her fingers, tongue and claws, she could barely remember why she'd waited.

Robert snarled across the clearing, also having pulled off his shirt, only he wasn't as handsome. Or maybe, it was his less than stellar personality reflected on the outside. He had clearly not spent as much time in wolf form because some of his muscle was layered with fat. That didn't mean he wasn't dangerous. He was cruel and sneaky, preferring to take shortcuts and win through nefarious means. She wouldn't put it past him to have more wolves in the woods to back him up in case he lost the claiming and had to eliminate the other alphas in order to win.

Now, Duncan and Robert were circling each other in the center of the meadow, Duncan quiet and watchful while Robert made grand gestures and feinted at Duncan, as if trying to get him to attack first. Duncan remained calm, hands steady, and his gaze never left Robert's face as he waited for an opportunity.

At that moment, Robert sprang into action, his hands shifting into claws, and he swiped at Duncan's left shoulder and downward, while at the same time his other hand punched at Duncan's stomach with something that glinted. A knife! Of course, he'd had no intention of playing fair.

Duncan turned in to the attack, blocking the claws that caught his forearm in a frenzy of motion, four slashes spattering blood on the grass. At the same time, he chopped downward with his other hand, knocking the knife free. Then he turned aside. Momentum carried Robert past Duncan, and Duncan stuck out his foot, tripping the heavier man so that he fell to the ground.

Duncan was on him in an instant. However, before he could get a good grasp on Robert, another man tackled him, knocking him off Robert and pinning him to the ground. Robert rose, fur sprouting along his jawline and his arms, his eyes golden yellow and canines lengthening.

"Let him go," he growled, the words barely audible through the fangs, his control clearly slipping.

Duncan didn't wait for the other man to release him. He punched the beta under the jaw, knocking him back, dazing him. Duncan slowly rose, fury evident in every line of his body, muscles quivering. "What kind of alpha needs another wolf to help him in a claiming challenge?" he said, his voice rising. "The kind who can't control his wolf. The kind who can't defend his mate. The kind who can't defend his pack. You are no alpha."

Robert blinked, the taunts slowly sinking into his rage-filled brain. Then he lost it. He let loose a howl and shifted further before launching himself in half-beast form at Duncan.

Lyla stuffed her hand into her mouth to stop a scream so she wouldn't distract Duncan.

Duncan crouched, his hands held in front as if waiting to catch a football. At the last moment, he stepped to the side, grabbed the tackling wolf by the head, and twisted. The spine gave a sickening crunch, and the body went limp. Duncan dropped the body, and its fur receded.

Robert lay at his feet. Dead.

FEELING A FIERCE SATISFACTION, Duncan kicked the body aside, and it rolled to a stop at the feet of the beta of the Carolina Pack. The beta stared at the body then back at Duncan, his body stinking with fear.

Duncan stalked over to him and fixed his gaze on the other man. The beta tried to hold his gaze but couldn't, dropping his head to acknowledge Duncan's dominance. Duncan let his gaze roam the clearing, settling on each wolf in turn, and they all dropped their gazes, unable to withstand the pressure of the *uber*-alpha dominance he'd finally unleashed after keeping it tightly controlled for the past few weeks. When he'd come, he hadn't expected to do anything more than check out the packs involved, report back to the Council, and let them pass judgment. Instead, he'd taken down a pack alpha and claimed a mate, pissing off another pack in the process. The Council wasn't going to be too happy with him.

His gaze finally settled on Lyla, and the tension that had been riding him all evening shifted from the urge to destroy to an urge to claim. Immediately. His low snarl echoed through the clearing, and every single wolf stiffened. A couple of the lower-ranked ones cowered and bared their throats.

"Leave us," he growled.

They scattered in seconds, leaving him and his mate standing barely ten yards apart. He inhaled deeply, the musky scent of her arousal permeating the air, her unique marker filling his entire being until he felt drunk on it, his wolf wanting nothing more than to roll in her scent, pin her to the forest floor, and make her his own. But he wasn't one of those other alphas, capable of forcing a mating, even though he had the marks to prove he and Lyla were destined for each other. He wanted her willing, not reluctant…a true partner.

So, he throttled back hard on his wolf and regained control through sheer force of will. He held out his hand and waited.

She eyed his hand like it had grown claws and was going to rip off her hand. His wolf growled low inside, angry that his mate should regard him with such suspicion, but he waited.

She met his gaze. "Who exactly are you? First, you're skulking around my brother's pack like one of his conspirators. Then you join in the Claiming Rite. And now, you defend me, killing one of the alphas who would claim me against my will. Yet, at the end, I'm still mated against my will to someone I don't know. So, tell me, who is this man I'm now tied to for the rest of my life?"

He dropped his hand and sighed. "It seems I played my part too well. I told you, I'm an enforcer for the Council and an alpha for my pack in New England. I was tasked with finding out why so many humans— women, specifically—are disappearing close to your pack's lands. I hadn't intended to interfere, wasn't supposed to, but I couldn't resist. Not when my mate was in danger."

She stared at him, shock reflected in her eyes. "So, they know what's going on? They haven't forsaken us after all. Well, that's something."

"You've been helping them, haven't you, mate? The women who've been going missing, trying to rescue them? That's why your brother set up this claiming, isn't it? To control you, to force you into a situation where they'd make sure you couldn't speak or interfere…?"

She blinked back tears and turned away. "I think so. I tried to get the women to safety to prevent them from being turned, from being sold, and now, I know too much."

He growled under his breath, the wolf and man both wanting nothing more than to protect their mate but equally proud of how strong she was to stand up to the bullies in her own pack, including her alpha leader. This only confirmed his earlier thoughts. She'd make a fine alpha female and mate, if she accepted the bond. Because even though she'd accepted the claiming earlier, her vow had been given under duress, and he was too proud to hold her to it.

She dashed tears from her cheeks and faced him, her chin lifting and her bright gaze fixed on him. "What happens now?"

He was disturbed to see a hint of nervousness, maybe even fear, in her eyes. And it pissed him off. He strode forward, invading her space until she was forced to look up at him. "It's really up to you."

He held his wrist next to hers, his bare upper body showing the visible claiming marks against his deeply tanned skin, so there was no doubt as to their meaning. Her sleeves were still pushed up from when she'd shown her marks to the alphas in a failed attempt to head off the challenge. The marks were obvious, only not as dark, indicating she hadn't fully accepted the mating.

Her eyebrows furrowed. "You're still giving me a choice?"

"Fate doesn't offer much choice, but I'll give you time." His gritted his teeth, the adrenaline from the fight shifting to a mating frenzy he was barely keeping at bay.

His wolf growled inside at the delay but subsided. He'd allow her time, even if it gave him the bluest balls a wolf had ever had. Wolves rarely fought their natural instincts for mating because their urges rode them hard. Even now, his cock was pushing against his jeans, trying to punch through the zipper. Need coursed through his body, his blood pounding a staccato beat in time with the throbbing in his cock. Her musk permeated the air, so he knew she was aroused, but he wanted more than her body. He wanted all of her.

Damn, if she didn't make up her mind soon, the mating frenzy would be upon him, and he might take an unforgiveable action, starting their mating off on the wrong foot.

Lyla's panties were drenched as Duncan eased closer, his masculine scent washing over her, drowning out the forest smells and saturating her in his pheromones, calling to her wolf. And her wolf desperately wanted her to answer, especially now that the danger was over. Adrenaline surged through her body, and her hormones screamed at her to grab onto Duncan and take him for a ride. Many female wolves her age had already been active with male wolves, but Lyla had waited, mostly because she'd been afraid of a forced mating and because she'd never felt need like she felt right now.

Duncan held himself rigid, his fists clenched at his sides, and she imagined he wanted to grab her and give in to the mating frenzy. She respected the hell out of him for not pushing her. Could she trust him to treat her with respect after mating? Too many alpha wolves treated their mates like puppy mill bitches, good for nothing more than popping out litters of pups. Could she take the chance? But honestly, did she have a choice?

She rubbed her wrists where the claiming marks burned, matching the burn of the mating frenzy growing deep inside. Soon, she *wouldn't* have a choice. The longer they remained in close contact, the worse she burned, yearned for him to take her. And judging by the gold in his eyes, the banked heat burning between them, he knew it, too.

He opened his mouth to say something, but before he could speak, she launched herself at him, her arms looping around his neck, her legs clinging to his waist. She kissed him.

DUNCAN WAS glad his legs were planted because he certainly hadn't expected Lyla to literally jump him, though he wasn't complaining or pausing to ask any questions. But he'd be damned if he'd let her control this. He was the alpha, and it was high time she was reminded of that fact.

Never breaking their connection, he grabbed her ass and turned until she was pinned against the closest oak tree. He settled between her thighs, his cock pressing close to the place where heaven resided, and yet was still separated by two layers of denim. He ran his hands along her body, tugging up her blouse as he moved them along her torso.

They separated for a second so he could toss her shirt to the side, then he took her mouth again, his tongue sweeping inside to taste her, his hands plunging into her dark hair, fisting it and holding her in place for his claiming kiss. He needed her like nothing ever before, craved her taste, her touch. She was his every-thing. He'd never known that taking a mate would be like this, that he could feel her like the other part of his soul. His father had told him when he'd grown old enough to understand mating that it would be so, but he'd never quite believed it, never understood the bond. Even now, he swore he could feel her inside him—her thoughts, her emotions—that unique part of her living inside his heart, never to be separated.

She met him stroke for stroke, her hands exploring his bare torso, tracing his muscles, digging in her nails as he rubbed his erection against her core, causing her to moan at the contact, the tiny bite of her nails pinching him while her legs squeezed his waist, pulling him closer. She rubbed against him, moaning, begging for more.

He dragged his mouth from hers and kissed his way down her throat to sink his teeth lightly against the place where he would mark her, the place where her shoulder met her neck, that sensitive spot that made her jerk in his arms, almost bucking him off. He partially shifted his finger and used a claw to slice through her bra and pulled it off, releasing her breasts to his gaze, his lips, his touch.

She gave a throaty laugh. "That was my favorite bra."

"I'll buy you a hundred. Later." He nipped at the side of her breast, and she gasped then sighed when he laved the tiny wound, tracing the creamy skin with his tongue then curling it around her nipple, tugging and sucking while his fingers toyed with her other breast.

She panted, her head thrown back, eyes closed as she

arched into his mouth, legs tightening around his waist, holding him against her.

His jeans were going to strangle his cock, and his zipper was about to be permanently imprinted on his skin, if he didn't get out of them soon. He didn't want to claim Lyla in the woods, but the mating frenzy had overcome them both. He flicked open his jeans, freeing his cock.

Lyla lifted her head and shoved at his shoulders, loosening her legs at the same time to lower her feet to the ground.

She followed his hand to his open jeans and reached down to cup him and pull him out of the denim, caressing the tip. She tugged her lower lip between her teeth, looking absolutely adorable. Then she shocked him by dropping to her knees and taking him into her mouth, and then it was his turn to be pinned to the tree, helpless under her assault.

LYLA HAD ONLY HEARD about blow jobs, had never understood the attraction. But now, she reveled in the power she had over a formidable man like Duncan Taggart. He tasted salty and a little musky; the skin felt hard and smooth, pulsing under her tongue. She could barely fit him into her mouth, so she focused her attention on the mushroom head, the slit at the end, and the vee underneath, an action that made him groan. She used her hand to stroke and pump along his length, as her friends had told her men liked, and judging by his sounds and the hands in her hair, Duncan liked it very much.

Duncan pulled her off his cock. "Not this way. I have more I want to do."

He found his discarded shirt and her blouse and laid them on the ground. Then he placed her on them and lowered himself on top of her. "We should wait, but I can't."

She laid a hand on his cheek, finally understanding what other people had told her about mating. "I think I'd kill you if you stopped now. Make me yours. In all ways."

"Are you sure?"

She smiled, her heart warming even further. "The fact that you asked makes me even more sure."

He kissed her again, his hands stroking down her body again, toying with the top of her jeans, tracing the edge and dipping under the material to tease her skin until she was squirming beneath him. Finally, he flicked open the button, tugged down the zipper, and slipped his fingers inside to caress her pussy over her panties.

She sucked in a breath when he dragged a finger over her clit, and she arched into the motion, but he withdrew almost immediately with a chuckle.

"Beast," she panted.

"Guilty as charged," he murmured.

He tugged off her jeans off and slid his own off, too, revealing his cock jutting out proudly toward her. He settled between her legs and spread them, his broad hands on the insides of her thighs, pushing them up and out, so she was spread before his eyes. He broke the tiny string holding her panties together and threw the ruined scrap of fabric over his shoulders. She sucked in a breath and tried to wiggle, but his grip was too strong. His breath fanned her pussy, and then she froze as his tongue stroked up the center of her slit, from her opening moving upward to curl around her clit.

Her mouth opened in a soundless scream, and her back arched. He gave another chuckle and settled in to explore her with his tongue, tracing her folds thoroughly while she sobbed and writhed in his hold, not sure if she was trying to get away or move closer, only certain that she was striving toward something she had never felt before, at least not anything of this magnitude.

A thick finger traced her opening then slipped inside, filling her but not quite enough. He settled his mouth over her clit and sucked and flicked his tongue until she exploded.

Slowly, she came back to awareness to find Duncan above her, his cock nudging at her entrance. She wrapped her legs and arms around him and pulled him closer. He began to enter her and reached the evidence of her virginity, something few wolves had at her age.

He arched his brow in surprise.

"I never found anyone I wanted."

A broad grin crossed his face, and he plunged deeply, the pain lasting only second and replaced quickly by pleasure. He settled deep inside, his balls resting against her, and he held her close while he waited for her to adjust to his girth. His face and body were tense from the effort it took to hold himself back.

She stroked his back and moved her hips. He must have taken that as a sign and started moving, in and out, plunging slowly, deeply, and then faster. She rose, meeting him thrust for thrust. As she reached that pinnacle again, his canines lengthened, and he bit her in that spot where the neck and shoulder met. Pain and pleasure exploded at the same moment, and she orgasmed around him, her nails digging into his back as she screamed into the forest around them.

Several minutes passed, the moment filled with only the sounds of their breaths and the sensation of a cool breeze licking at their sweaty skin.

Holding her hips, Duncan rolled onto his back, bringing her along to drape over him like a blanket.

"So, when can we do that again?" she asked.

He laughed and started to move inside her, still hard. "How about right now, mate?"

OVER THE EDGE

BY N.J. WALTERS

"This cannot be happening." Mariah Mills stared at the large bear about ten yards away, wondering why the heck she'd come on this wilderness retreat.

Not that she'd had a choice. As a lawyer at Rayburn, Putnum, and Lyle, she'd been expected to go on the retreat the senior members of the firm had arranged. Not that they'd bothered to show. This was a "team building" event, filled with survival exercises for those in the firm whose names weren't on the letterhead.

She could've been sipping a margarita on a beach somewhere. *But no.* She was face-to-face with a bear. Maybe a grizzly. She should have watched more nature shows. Then she'd know whether she should run like hell or back slowly away.

This was all her ex's fault.

Because he was the other reason she was here. They'd been separated for a year now, and he still hadn't petitioned for divorce. The time had come.

The cold knot in the pit in her stomach grew. Not all her distress was due to the bear currently watching her.

She hadn't wanted the separation. That had all been Jack's idea. It had seemed like fate when she'd discovered he was one of the owners of the retreat. This weekend, she could face her past, get the papers signed, and move on.

If she managed to avoid being mauled by a bear.

"Nice bear." She kept her voice low and calm. Hadn't she seen that in a YouTube video? She could only hope the bear had seen the same one.

God, she was losing it.

What had started out as a solitary stroll away from the rustic lodge where they were quartered had ended up with her lost and facing possible death or dismemberment.

"You can do this, Mills." It was the same pep talk she'd been giving herself her entire life. Somehow, she'd managed to get through all the things life had thrown at her—being orphaned at sixteen, making it through college and law school, getting a job at a prestigious firm, finding the love of her life.

Okay, so the last one hadn't worked out so well.

Sweat beaded on her forehead and trickled down her face. The bear gave a loud chuff.

Her legs trembled. Her knees felt ready to give away.

She didn't even have her backpack with the attached whistle. That was back in her room—same place she should've been after a long day of being around her coworkers, none of whom were happy to be there.

The bear rose on his hind legs. Oh God, he was

huge. Had to be at least nine feet. She was going to end up as a bear snack.

She took a step away. A twig snapped underfoot. "You don't want to eat me, bear. I'm a lawyer. Bad for your digestion."

The bear's front paws slammed onto the ground, and he gave another of those loud chuffs.

She tried to swallow, but her throat was too dry. Somehow, she made her legs work, when all she wanted to do was fall down and curl up into a little ball.

That's what you did if a bear attacked. Wasn't it?

Primal fear made it almost impossible to think. She'd been afraid before—when her parents had died, during exams, when Jack had left her. But this was a whole new level of terror.

Her top was stuck to her skin beneath her jacket. Her hair was plastered to her head. She hadn't sweated this much…ever. She wasn't a particularly outdoorsy or athletic person. Nope, give her a good book or a movie any day.

How had she and Jack managed to last five years? They were complete opposites.

"Don't think about him. Not now." She kept slowly moving backward without making any real progress as the bear matched his steps to hers.

At that moment, she didn't even know which direction the lodge was. She'd gotten totally turned around. Her sense of direction only applied to urban landscapes with orderly streets and easily identifiable landmarks. Out in the wilderness, where everything looked the same—trees and more trees—she was lost.

The bear gave a short roar and picked up speed.

Forgetting all about staying calm, she turned and fled. Tree branches slapped at her face and arms. The ground thundered behind her. She risked a quick glance over her shoulder.

The bear was gaining on her.

She dug deep and put on a burst of speed.

The ground suddenly disappeared beneath her feet. It was there one second and gone the next.

Mariah plummeted over the edge and into nothingness. Her arms flailed as she dropped. Her scream was cut short when she struck the ground, knocking the breath from her body.

Dirt fell on her from above. The bear! She rolled onto her side and hugged the wall of rock in front of her, barely daring to breathe. After what seemed like forever, she heard trees rustling. The sound got further and further away.

The bear was gone.

She heaved a sigh of relief, but it was short-lived. She might have escaped being dinner for a bear, but she was now stuck on a ledge in the middle of the woods and night was coming soon.

WHERE THE HELL WAS SHE?

Jack Morgan stalked through the forest beyond the lodge. One of her coworkers had seen her heading in this direction.

He'd purposely avoided her all day, waiting for the right time to approach her. Knowing Mariah,

125

she was just waiting to serve him with divorce papers.

It seemed fate had decided it was time for them to deal with their problems. He'd taken it as a sign when he'd seen her name on the guest list for this weekend.

He stopped and listened for anything out of the ordinary. He'd give it ten more minutes. If he hadn't come across her by then, he'd alert the staff that they had a missing guest.

His gut clenched. Nothing could happen to her.

"Stay calm." This was no time for him to lose it. He was a former search and rescue operator. He'd trained for situations like this, had handled more rescues than he cared to remember.

"Mariah!" How far could she have wandered? She was more of a stroller than a hiker. He rubbed a hand across the back of his neck and released a breath. The woman had no sense of direction. The few times he'd taken her camping, he'd had to keep a close eye on her.

He scanned the area, looking for any sign she'd been there. Up ahead, a branch was cracked, and the break was fresh. He headed in that direction, stopping every minute to call her name.

The clock was ticking down.

If something had happened to her, he'd never forgive himself.

"Mariah, you fucking answer me," he yelled.

A low voice came from the right. "Jack?"

"Mariah." He raced toward the sound. "Talk to me, honey. Let me know where you are." Because he couldn't see her.

"Be careful. I fell."

Shit, he hoped she wasn't badly injured. A flash of another rescue scene, blood and broken bodies scattered around like garbage, almost paralyzed him.

"Not now." He couldn't afford to lose himself. He'd worked too damn hard this past year to get back to being the man he'd been before his SAR work had just about swallowed him whole. "I'm coming, honey."

"I'm here, Jack."

He saw the bear tracks first. Then the churned-up dirt. "Shit." He threw himself down on the ground and peered over the edge of the cliff.

Dirt marred her cheek and forehead, twigs were lodged in her short, lush brown hair, and her porcelain skin was unnaturally pale, but Mariah was still the most beautiful woman he'd ever seen.

"Are you hurt?" The drop wasn't too bad. Only about fifteen feet. And the ground was mossy, not rocky.

"I'm bruised, but nothing's broken. I think. My right ankle hurts."

"Okay, honey. I'm coming down."

"No! It's not safe."

Ignoring her, he removed his backpack. It had been second nature to grab it on his way out the door, a habit so ingrained he hadn't even thought about it. He might not have his climbing gear, but he could rescue her.

He uncoiled a long rope and anchored it to a sturdy tree before pulling his pack back on. "I'm coming down. Move as close to the inside as you can." He wrapped the rope around his waist and eased over the edge. Letting out the rope a bit at a time, he made his way down the rock face.

Mariah was hunched against the inside, as instructed. As soon as his boots hit the ledge, she launched into him. "Have you lost your mind?"

"I did." He released the rope and cupped her precious face in his hands. "But I found it again." Then he kissed her.

IT SHOULD HAVE BEEN impossible for him to find her, but then she'd always thought of him as almost superhuman. In his former job, he'd gone into situations most people ran from. He'd saved many lives.

Sometimes, he'd been too late.

However he'd come to be here, his lips were pressed to hers now. The emotional and physical distance of the past year dissolved in a heartbeat. Their ever-present passion flared to life.

This was her Jack, the man she'd fallen hard and fast for, the man she'd married after only knowing him six months, the man she'd lived with for five years.

The man who still haunted her dreams.

His tongue slipped past her lips and claimed her mouth. His hands were gentle as he held her face close. A tear slipped out of the corner of her eye and rolled down her cheek, coming to rest on the corner of her lips.

As soon as he tasted the saltiness, he pulled away. "You're hurt."

She wanted to pull him back, but distance was

better. He'd left her. The reminder was painful, but it also steadied her.

"I was so scared." It slipped out before she could stop it. She'd planned to be brave. She couldn't lean on him. Not anymore. But old habits died hard.

And Jack, damn him, looked better than he had when he'd left. The last year of their marriage, he'd had trouble sleeping, had started drinking more, and had emotionally pulled away.

His black hair was a bit longer, the back just grazing the collar of his thick flannel shirt. His eyes were still the clearest blue she'd ever seen. A light scruff covered his jaw, as though he hadn't shaved in day or two. His lips were compressed into a hard line.

Now, that was familiar. He wasn't happy.

She closed her eyes and took a deep breath. "So, how do we get out of here?"

He settled his long, lean body beside her and removed a pack from his back. "What happened?" He pulled a water bottle from the bag and handed it to her. "Sip slowly," he cautioned.

The water tasted so good. In real time, she hadn't been gone all that long. It just seemed like forever. "I went for a stroll."

The corners of his lips twitched. He'd always teased her about her sense of direction, or rather, lack of it.

"You didn't stay on the path." He pulled a first aid kit out of the bag and opened it.

She shrugged, wincing slightly when her shoulder complained. "I saw a bunny and wanted a picture." It sounded so stupid when she said it aloud. She was a city girl, born and raised, and bunnies hopping through the forest were rare and interesting.

"Did you get the shot?" He swiped a wet wipe over her forehead.

"Yeah." Her phone was safely stashed in her pocket. "I hope my phone didn't break in the fall."

"You're lucky *you* didn't break in the fall," he muttered. His words were brisk, but his hands were gentle as he cleaned dirt and grime from her face.

He touched her then, not with romantic intent. No, he was all business as he worked his way from her neck to her feet, carefully manipulating her limbs and asking her questions.

"I told you; it's just my ankle."

"I don't want to remove your boot until I get you out of here." He packed up his gear and stood, slinging the pack on his back.

Jack was the quintessential outdoorsman with his dark jeans, scuffed boots, and flannel shirt. There wasn't an ounce of fat on his six-four frame.

"Can you stand?"

She nodded, more than ready to get out of there. "I would've been fine if it hadn't been for the bear."

He froze, his blue gaze pinning her in place. "Bear?"

She shivered and glanced up at the ledge. "Yeah, I kept talking to him and backing away, but he followed. I had to make a run for it. I wasn't paying as much attention to what was ahead of me as to what was coming behind me."

He pulled her into his arms. She pressed her face against his broad chest, drawing warmth and comfort.

"You could've been killed."

"Believe me, I know." Even now, she could hear the loud thumps of the bear's paws on the ground; practically feel its breath on her neck.

He closed his eyes and inhaled deeply several times.

"You okay?" He was pale, his skin clammy.

"I will be." He started to wrap the ends of the rope around her, creating a makeshift sling. Having him so close, having his hands brushing parts of her body, awakened needs that had been dormant for a year.

"Ah, is this safe? Maybe you should go for help." Being alone with Jack wasn't good for either of them. They'd taken their shot and lost. She still had no idea why he'd really left. All he'd ever said was that he had to go.

"I wouldn't do it if it wasn't safe."

Anger, fear, and confusion welled up inside her. She wanted to yell and cry, wanted to demand answers. Instead, she kept quiet. He was right. The faster she got out of there the better. The papers were waiting in her suitcase.

Her stomach lurched, and she swallowed back tears. The divorce was necessary, even if it ripped out her heart.

"I'm going to go first, and then pull you up." He wrapped her hands around the rope. "All you have to do is hold on. I'll do all the work."

She nodded. "Okay."

He seemed like he wanted to say more, but dropped a quick, hard kiss on her lips and scaled the rock like he was part mountain goat. God, she envied him his confidence and skill.

Back at the top, he peered down at her. "Ready?"

Was she? There really was no choice. "Do it."

JACK BREATHED a sigh of relief when Mariah was on the ground beside him. The rope was coiled and back in his pack, and they were ready to go.

He held out his hand. "It's getting dark. We need to get a move on."

"Sure." She bit her bottom lip as she pushed herself up. He wrapped his arm around her waist and pulled her close. Her head only came up to his chin, but they'd always fit together perfectly.

This past year seemed like another nightmare that he'd finally woken from.

"Come on." He guided her back toward the path.

"Is it far?" She was breathing heavily, her voice tight with pain and exhaustion.

He stopped and brushed a lock of hair away from her face. "Not too far." He put one hand behind her back and the other behind her legs and lifted.

"Put me down. You can't carry me."

The hell he couldn't. "You don't weigh all that much, honey." If anything, she was thinner than she'd been. "How's work?"

She shrugged, her thick hair brushing against his cheek. "It's work."

"You don't sound happy." His footsteps were sure as

he corrected his direction. The sun was dipping lower in the sky.

"It is what it is."

The acceptance and defeat in her voice was not the Mariah he'd known. She'd wanted to make a difference in the world, in people's lives. But then, they'd both changed.

"I'm sorry you're not happier."

"Are you? Are you really?" She raised her head from his shoulder and glared at him. "If you mean that, then tell me why you left. And not some bullshit vague 'because I had to' thing."

They broke through the edge of the forest, and a small cabin came into view. It blended with its surroundings.

"This isn't the lodge." Her hand fisted in his shirt. "Where are we?" He wondered if she'd punch him when she learned the truth. Anticipation rose inside him.

"This is my home. We're home."

She wasn't going to read anything into his "we're home" comment. It was his place, not hers. They weren't a couple anymore.

"You're taking me back to the lodge, right?" She leaned forward as they got closer, curiosity aroused.

"No." He opened the door, which wasn't even locked, and stepped inside. The space was rustic but cozy. A rock fireplace dominated one wall in the living and dining area. A compact and efficient kitchen was off to the left of the dining table. A short hallway led away from them. Likely to the bedroom and bathroom.

"You do have a bathroom, right?"

His lips twitched. "Yeah, honey, I have a bathroom. You need to go?"

"Yes." Her cheeks were hot, and she knew she was blushing. "I was out there for a while."

He took her into the small room. Like the rest of the place, there was no wasted space. "I'll call and let them know you're safe." He brushed a kiss over the top of her head and left.

Mariah stared at her reflection in the mirror that hung over the vanity. She looked surprisingly normal considering her ordeal. She used the toilet, and then gazed longingly at the shower. She was dirty and sweaty. Not how she'd wanted to face Jack.

To hell with it. She stripped out of her clothes. The muscles in her back and arms protested. Hot water would do them good.

Her right ankle hurt when she removed her boot, but it was only slightly swollen. She'd see if Jack had a bandage she could use to wrap it.

She turned on the water, grateful it was hot. Not knowing how long it would last, she ducked beneath the spray. She refused to feel guilty about using his soap and shampoo. If he hadn't wanted her to use it, he could have taken her back to the lodge. After all, her firm was paying a lot of money for her and the rest of them to be there.

She was rinsing the last of the lather from her head when a cool breeze brushed over her skin. "Go away,

Jack." Even before she saw his outline on the other side of the thin shower curtain, she knew it was him. Something subtle in the air always seemed to change when he was near.

He'd removed his boots and flannel shirt, leaving him in jeans and a black T-shirt that molded to his muscular torso.

"You should've asked me for help."

"And why would I do that? You haven't been around for me to depend on." A low blow, but she didn't care, not even when he winced.

Being naked around Jack was dangerous. Even now, her entire body hummed with desire.

She cranked off the tap, pulled back the curtain, and grabbed a towel from the rod. It was partially wrapped around her when he caught the end and pulled. They played tug-of-war until the fabric ripped, and she was left with a piece too small to do any good.

"That was childish." Ignoring him as best as she could, she reached for her dirty clothes, since they were all she had.

"I've seen you naked before. Besides, I need to check you out and make sure you're really okay." He scooped her into his arms and carried her from the room.

"We're separated, about to be divorced," she reminded him.

"No." They were both wet when he laid her on his bed. The blanket was soft against her back. She yanked part of it over her.

"You left," she reminded him.

"I had to."

Enough was enough. "Why? You owe me that much, Jack."

He sat on the edge of the bed and closed his eyes, pain etched on his rugged face. "I lost myself."

In spite of the pain and distance, she still cared, would always care. She sat up and placed her hand on his shoulder. "How did you lose yourself?"

He opened his eyes and stared up at the ceiling. "I saw too much. I couldn't leave it at work anymore. It came home with me, followed me into sleep."

Her heart skipped a beat, and then began to pound. "Why didn't you tell me? We could have gotten you help." It hurt her that he'd dealt with this on his own. "You didn't trust me."

He swiveled around and caught her face in his hands. "Never that. I was afraid I might hurt you some night, caught up in a flashback. I fell into a dark hole and couldn't seem to climb my way out."

"I married you for better or worse. You were the one who left when the worst happened."

"I know." He swallowed heavily. "I knew I'd made a mistake almost as soon as I'd left."

"Why didn't you come back?"

He smoothed his thumbs over her cheeks. "I couldn't. Not until I'd gotten help, not until I could prove to myself, and to you, that I can be the man you need and deserve."

Sorrow threatened to choke her. "Jack…"

He shook his head. "It's not too late. Tell me it's not too late."

· · ·

JACK WAS FIGHTING for his life, for their life. He kissed her, letting her taste all the lonely nights he'd yearned for her. No other woman had ever felt right in his arms.

He took her down to the bed, his lips never leaving hers. Afraid that if they did, she'd tell him they were through.

Her hands clutched at his shoulders. Not to push him away but to pull him closer. Her nails dug into his shirt, reminding him he was still mostly clothed.

He pulled away long enough to shuck his clothes and was back before she had time to catch her breath. Her body was even sexier than he'd remembered: her legs long and lean, her breasts a neat handful. The scent of his soap wafted up from her skin. He'd almost swallowed his tongue when he'd seen her naked in his shower.

Now, he had to taste her.

He placed a row of kisses along her jaw and down her neck. He licked along her collarbone, catching a stray bead of water. Her nipples were tight buds, puckered and red and ripe for the plucking.

He covered one breast with his palm, savoring the weight, rubbing his thumb across the tip. The other, he captured between his lips and sucked. Her groan vibrated through him.

"Jack."

"Say it again," he demanded.

"Jack."

Goose bumps raced down his back. This was real and right. He wasn't letting her go again. He'd chase her this time, grovel if he had to. Whatever it took to make it right.

A small bruise marred her shoulder. He kissed it. Then another on her upper arm. "You got off easy. It could have been so much worse."

"I know." Her calm acceptance rattled him. He found and kissed every mark he could find before returning to her breasts.

He teased both mounds, going back and forth between them until she was moaning, her breath coming hard. She tangled her fingers in his hair and alternated between pulling him closer and pushing him away.

He licked and kissed a path down her stomach, taking the time to nip at her hip bone. When he hit the right spot, she laughed.

"Stop. You know I'm ticklish."

"I love your laugh." He wanted to hear it every day for the rest of his life. For all the dreams and fantasies he'd had these past months, none of them compared to the reality.

The scent of her arousal teased him. He made a place between her thighs and looked up at her.

She was sprawled across his bed, her skin flushed, her nipples hard and tight. Her lips were moist from his kisses. When she licked them, he groaned.

When her legs parted slightly, he felt as though he'd won a huge victory. He nuzzled the neat covering of hair on her mound and kissed her inner thighs. She squirmed beneath him.

She'd always been impatient.

He licked at the slick folds of her sex.

"Yes," she rasped, the word drawn out. She tasted sweet and spicy. God, he'd missed this.

He inserted one finger into her opening. Her inner muscles clenched around him. "You're tight."

"It's been a long time."

He closed his eyes and swallowed. He'd hoped she'd been faithful but hadn't expected it. After all, he'd left her. "I'm so sorry, babe."

"Not now. Later."

She was right. He flicked the tip of his tongue over her clit, stroking it just the way she liked. Her hips jerked up, and she whimpered. "Don't stop."

"Never," he promised. He licked and sucked and fingered her until she was writhing beneath him. The telltale signs warned she was close. "I want you."

She gave a jerky nod. He heaved himself up and over her. His cock was close to bursting. His balls were so tight they were about to split. He'd managed to distract himself from his own physical discomfort while he'd been pleasuring her, but his need came roaring back, demanding to be relieved.

Her fingers closed around him. Her touch was so familiar, so perfect, the top almost blew off his head. He reached down and captured her hand. "Keep that up, and I'll be done before I start."

She gave one final squeeze before releasing him.

He fitted his cockhead to her opening and slowly pushed inward. Closing his eyes, he threw back his head. This was what heaven must be like, this feeling of completeness, of coming home.

. . .

MARIAH'S BODY—NO her entire being—was on fire. Everywhere he'd touched her tingled. Her core throbbed, her breasts ached. It had been one hell of a long, barren year. And her vibrator didn't hold a candle to the real thing.

Jack knew just how to touch her, where to touch her, to have her ready to blow.

When he slid home, the doubts, the anger, the regrets all fell silent.

She ran her hands over his broad shoulders, loving the strength in them. But even strong men needed help sometimes, and he'd left rather than share his problems with her.

The cords of his neck rippled. A muscle in his jaw clenched.

"Fuck, you feel good." He looked at her, sincerity glowing in his eyes. "I'm sorry." He brushed a soft kiss across her lips. It was such a contrast to the pounding pulse of his shaft inside her. "I need you." He kissed her again. "I want you." And again. "I love you."

Tears threatened, but she blinked them back. She could have died today. There was no telling what the future held. They were as intimately linked as two people could be. There was only room for honesty between them. "I never stopped."

"Oh fuck, Mariah." He flexed his hips, pushing deep before withdrawing and doing it again.

Like a man possessed, he fucked her hard and fast. He buried his face in the curve of her neck and drove into her over and over. She gripped his biceps, his back, loving the way the thick muscles surged under her hands. His skin was hot and slick.

Her sex clenched around him. She angled up so his pelvis brushed against her clit.

"Yes, yes," she chanted. Fireworks exploded, radiating outward from her core. He thrust twice more, flooding her with his release, calling her name as he came.

He collapsed on top of her, but she didn't mind. He was like her own personal blanket. Only he wasn't, not anymore. Their lives had taken divergent paths.

He lifted up, supporting his weight on his forearms. The move drove his shaft deep, making them both moan.

"I want us to be a couple again."

She thought about the papers in her suitcase. "Your job is here, and mine is in the city."

"I'll leave it behind. I'll find something to do. I've learned I can live with a lot, but I don't want to live without you." He withdrew, rolled onto his back, and pulled her into his arms. "I won't lie. It won't be easy. I'm still learning how to cope with the memories and stress, but I'm doing better."

"All I ever wanted was to help you."

"I know." He kissed her forehead. "I was an idiot."

"Yes, you were." But was she really going to hold that against him when all she'd wanted this past year was for them to be together? "You won't shut me out again. I'm not sure I could get past that a second time."

"I promise." The finality of those two simple words sealed it for her. Jack always kept his word.

"Then I want to give it another go. But not in the city," she added.

He sat up and lifted her onto his lap. "Why not?"

"I've done a lot of thinking this past year. I want to start my own law practice in a small community."

"Whatever you want. Closest town is only twenty minutes away. What do you say? Take a chance on me? On us?"

She pressed her hand to his face, smiled, and willingly walked off the emotional ledge. "For us." Then she kissed him to close the deal.

SAVE ME TWICE

BY JAAP BOEKESTEIN

Okay, it all started out as a joke. Tuesday, the package arrived by courier with Rosa O'dalisk's next new novel in the Dark Satin series. And they, Neon Dog Tales, New York's hippest on-the-edge agency, were going to market it, just like they'd done with the previous four volumes. But this time was different. When Jeannie the intern opened the package, she let out a small yelp, which made all heads in the small office turn.

On her desk sat the manuscript and the cover of the novel. Nothing out of the ordinary. But dangling on a pencil, like she was afraid to touch them, were a pair of gleaming steel handcuffs. "Look at what the publisher sent!"

They looked like the real deal—not some cheap Chinese sheet metal set with pink fur, but sturdy stainless-steel ones. Those cuffs meant business. In addition, a key was taped to the steel.

Some "Wows!" and some giggling followed.

Everyone gathered around Jeannie's desk. There was a note inside the box from the author: *Can we do something with this? A free giveaway promotion action? Just thinking. Pleasure to all, Rosa.*

Of course, over the next few days, everyone had fun with those handcuffs. Chairs were cuffed to desks, the door of the supply room was chained shut, people were cuffed to their chairs—and to each other. Hey, it was fun all around. Office humor. Fun. They were that kind of agency. Small, and quirky, and playful. Exactly the right agency to market and promote things like a series of soft S&M books, or novelty umbrellas with a built-in navigation system, or the opening of a new art gallery/bring your cat cafe.

Fun. A joke.

Friday, it was Amanda's turn to become part of the joke. The entire week she'd managed to avoid those things, those *handcuffs*. Of course, she'd smiled when the pranks were played, but she hadn't commented on or joked about any of it. Amanda had stayed in the background. *Sure, I'm part of the team, this is all fun, but I really need to work on that campaign for those handbags made from recycled plastic collected by community centers. That Rosa O'dalisk and her Dark Satin books aren't my account, thank you very much.*

"Come on, Manda. Time to pay the piper."

Beth sat on the edge of Amanda's desk. She was British, a perky red-head, and a scandalous flirt. The handcuffs were draped over her upper leg, which was covered by a rather short pencil skirt.

Amanda looked up. "Ah, no, thank you. That joke is getting old."

"Manda, dear. Come on, it's time to pop that Fifty Shades cherry of yours. You're the only one who hasn't been cuffed to anything or *anyone* yet. We've all been there, except you."

Everyone was looking at her. Amanda knew escape was impossible. They were a team, and if she wanted to stay part of the team, she had to wear those handcuffs. If only once. It was utterly ridiculous, but she didn't have a choice.

She looked at steel contraption resting on Beth's shapely leg. Somehow, it looked... evil. Criminals wore handcuffs, *bad* people. Oh, and well... *those* people. The whole *Fifty Shades of Grey* crowd. Back then, she'd lied about reading the books because everyone seemed to have read them or watched the movies. Why? Well, she didn't want to be branded a prude. But those things the book described, like being tied up and under the control of someone else, or being...being *spanked*? *No! A thousand times, no!* She didn't even want to think about it.

But now…these handcuffs. She didn't have a choice. If she didn't want to be exposed as boring and an old-fashioned prude. Someone who didn't fit in the team or even the whole marketing business.

To her own surprise, Amanda managed to sound bored. "If you insist. This is so childish. I haven't used those in ages."

All lies, but it got her a few whistles and giggles.

Nonchalantly, she took the cuffs from Beth's leg. She put one of them around her right wrist and closed it. An audible click, metal teeth locking inside the whole damned thing. The shiny steel was heavy and warm on her skin. No doubt due to the heat from Beth's body.

It could have been a heavy bracelet, some piece of industrial gothic metal jewelry, but it wasn't. It was a handcuff. Very much so.

I'm imprisoned now, a little voice said in the back of her mind.

Such a strange thing. It shouldn't mean anything. It certainly didn't mean anything, surely? But why was her throat suddenly so dry, and her heart pounding in her chest? She wanted to rip the metal snake off her wrist and throw it across the room. It felt... it felt... Well, *wrong*. Uh, yeah, wrong. Something like that. She didn't deserve to be chained up because she wasn't a criminal. She wasn't! She hadn't done anything wrong. She...

Amanda forced the thundering train of her thoughts to stop before they completely derailed. *I can't back away now. I have to play it cool.*

She raised her eyebrows, looked around at all the eager faces of her co-workers, and locked the other cuff around the heavy metal bar which was part of the designer desk.

Click. Now, she was cuffed to the desk.

Like a criminal. A bad girl.

She felt lightheaded, and the world seemed to swim. *She was chained to a desk!* It felt so weird.

With her free hand, Amanda waved. "Tada!" She laughed. It even sounded convincing. No undertone of hysteria.

Everyone laughed. A few jeered.

I'm one of them. I've passed the test.

Somehow, she couldn't resist, and she pulled. Yes, she was captured, the steel wouldn't release her hand. She was really cuffed to the office desk.

She had the urge to cross her legs but didn't. *Play it cool, play it cool.*

There were some minor jokes, of course. "Call the cops, we finally got her," and "For our next act, Lady Houdini will escape!"

Amanda jested with them. All part of her cover. All to be part of the team.

I need to use the bathroom. Am I sweating? I feel hot. Oh, I hope nobody notices.

Finally, after enough time had passed, she looked at Beth. "Okay, unlock these things. I need to get back to work. Or maybe put you in these. No doubt you've deserved it."

"Ha! If you only knew! Meow!"

More laughter. Beth turned her head. "Hey Jamal, can I have the key?"

Jamal shook his head. "No, I don't have it. Fleur?"

"No, not me."

Amanda suppressed the sense of urgency that threatened to overwhelm her. *Don't break your cool now.* "Come on, guys. I can't work like this. Who has the key?"

Yes. Who had the key?

Nobody had the key.

"Stop joking, people. Let's have that key," Chloe, the first among equals, said. They didn't really have managers at Neon Dog Tales, but Chloe was the owner and had the final word.

Nobody had the key.

Yesterday, it had been around somewhere. Now, it was nowhere to be found. Not on desks, not in jackets, not on the floor, or anywhere else.

Amanda sat at her desk, chained, and watched her co-workers' antics with a sinking feeling. Her throat felt dry, and for a moment she wanted to curse out loud, which she would never do, of course. The metal bar she was chained to was an integral part of the desk and couldn't be lifted or screwed loose. It was just as efficient as the bar of a prison cell.

She tried the cuffs one more time.

No, there was no way she could slip out of them.

I'm imprisoned. I can't go anywhere.

"I'm so sorry, Amanda. I didn't mean... If I had known," apologized Beth. She sat next to the desk and held Amanda's cuffed hand. Beth was really sorry.

By now, Amanda felt strangely calm. Like the eye of a storm. *This can't be happening. This is so bizarre!*

She moved her hand once more. The metal scraped over the desk, held her flesh. It was no nightmare. She really was handcuffed to a desk on a Friday afternoon at the office. It was really, really stupid. But still, she sat on her chair like nothing had happened. What else could she do?

Her co-workers weren't that calm. They blurted out suggestions. "Maybe if we use soap", which was daft, and "I've seen a movie where they opened handcuffs with a hairpin," which was just ridiculous. "If we get some bolt-cutters…" "Maybe we should call the fire department or a locksmith."

The Fire Department, a lock smith? What will they think of me? My God, why did this happen?

"I'll get Xander," Chloe said. "I'll be back in a minute. Don't go— Oh, don't worry, Amanda."

The boss of Neon Dogs Tales took off.

"Who's Xander?" Amanda whispered to Beth. "Is he the janitor?"

The red-head shook her head. "You know, Xander. The artist in the studio down the hall. He creates those huge edgy metal sculptures with those spikes and rusty lawnmower blades. You must have seen him; he's pretty hot. And he's got lots of equipment."

It took a second before Amanda was sure Beth meant real equipment, not that *other* kind. With Beth, you were never sure.

Okay, Xander. She couldn't recall ever meeting him, but apparently, he was their neighbor and might have the tools to free her. Was that better than the fire department or a lock smith? Amanda wasn't sure. But what could they actually do? Saw through the steel cuffs? She didn't know much about steel, but these handcuffs looked solid. What if he slipped with some power tool and cut her?

Well, I don't have much choice. If he can get me out these cuffs, fine by me.

It took less than a minute before Chloe returned with Xander.

He was tall. Six feet and a lot. Thick unruly blond hair, ice-blue eyes and stubbles of a two-day-old beard.

A black wifebeater under an old lumberjack shirt, jeans, boots. Part of a huge tattoo was just visible on his chest. He clearly worked out or did heavy manual labor. He was lean, with big shoulders and strong hands.

Xander.

Wow.

His gaze found her, and Amanda felt her ears burn.

Oh God, here I am. He must think I'm some dumb office drone who got herself in trouble. Some bimbo who was stupid enough to lock herself to a desk.

Before she could react, he walked over and sat down next to her.

"Hi, I'm Xander. I see you're chained up by accident. Are you okay, Amanda?" He had a warm, slow voice with a hint of a foreign accent Amanda couldn't place.

"I… Hello. Yes, I'm okay. Except for…" She raised her right hand as far as she could. Somehow, she couldn't look away from those eyes. "Chloe thought you might be able to help…?"

"I can and I will, but first, I want to know if you're all right. You're not hurting? Is there anything you need?"

"I just want to get rid of these!" she blurted.

He looked at the handcuffs. He took her hand and studied the metal contraption.

Warm, strong hands. Hers almost disappeared inside his. He was close enough to smell, and Amanda got whiff of machine oil, dust, and metal. What had Beth said, again? Xander created big metal sculptures. *He smells like it.*

"Hm, yes. I see."

"Can… Can you free me? Can you cut them?" Amanda asked.

"Cut? No. I can cut the chain, but for this bit," he said, touching the cuffs themselves, "I'll need a blow-torch. I have one in my studio, but I'm not going to use it on you. Much too dangerous."

Amanda looked at him. "So, you're going to keep me captive?" She smiled. "Come down here and feed me every day?" *Why am I saying this? Ah, just a little joke to release the tension.*

"Well, only if you want me to."

He looked at her once more. His eyes seemed to ask, *Well, would you?*

Amanda was saved from answering by Beth. "But if you can't cut those cuffs, how are we going to free her? Do we need a locksmith?"

Xander looked at Beth for a second but turned towards Amanda once more while he shook his head. "No, that's not necessary. You want me to release you, Amanda?"

"Yes, sure," she said. *What will he do if I say "no"?*

"I will, but I want to ask you something afterwards. Just a minute." He reached for his pocket and got out a chain with a collection of keys. He searched the bunch and finally selected one. "Let's see."

Between his fingers Xander held a very small key.

Is that…?

Click. He had unlocked the handcuffs.

The metal fell from her wrist. She was free!

While everyone cheered, Amanda looked amazed at

her hand, and then back to Xander. "You had the key to those handcuffs all the time? How is that possible?"

He smiled broadly, but it was a warm smile. "No, I didn't have the key to these handcuffs. But almost all commercial models use the same kind of key. Police handcuffs are different, but these things can usually be unlocked by a standard key."

Massaging her wrist, which wasn't sore at all, Amanda looked at him. "How come you walk around with a handcuff-key on your chain?"

His smile turned into a grin. "That's a very good question. Are you sure you want me to answer it?"

What does he mean? Ohhh... It dawned on Amanda which people used handcuffs.

Amanda looked at Xander. *He is one of those? That's...interesting.*

He didn't look like a perv.

He took her silence for a denial. Or maybe he read it in her eyes. No, she didn't dare to ask any further. Even if she wanted. Which she didn't. Of course not. No.

"How are you now?" he wanted to know. "You want something to drink? Some coffee, or tea? A soda, maybe?"

"I'm fine, thank you. You said you wanted to ask me something?"

"Ah, yes." His smile was boyish. "Can I take you to dinner, tonight? To recover from your *ordeal.*" Somehow, he made the last word sound like a joke. *Did you really suffer that much?*

"I... uh." Amanda didn't know how to reply. This guy was asking her out for dinner? She'd only known him for a couple of minutes, and he carried keys for handcuffs, and... and...

Behind Xander's back, Chloe and Beth were nodding like crazy and mouthing silently, *Yes! Do it!*

"Yes," Amanda blurted out to her own amazement. *Did I really say "yes", just now?*

Chloe and Beth cheered and applauded in silence.

"Ah, great. The office usually closes at six, doesn't it? I'll meet you in the hall. If that's okay with you…?"

Actually, she had planned to work on the plastic handbag account a few more hours this evening, but she said, "That's great. Six o'clock."

He winked and rose. "Great, see you at six. Oh, wait." From his wallet, he took out a card. "To be sure, here's my phone number, in case you can't make it or something."

She took the card, almost immediately dropping it on her desk. She felt lightheaded, and her fingers trembled a little.

Wuhhh. "Yes. Thank you. Six."

He didn't wear a leather jacket as she'd somehow expected. Instead, he'd cleaned himself up and wore a pretty decent shirt and a denim jacket.

Oh, here I am in my plain office garb. Well, it will have to do.

"Great to see you. How are you doing?" he asked. "No ill effects?"

"Hi, no, no. I'm fine." Actually, it was a little bit of a lie. Sure, she was fine, but she'd been distracted the entire afternoon. Her gaze had wandered again and again to the pair of handcuffs that lay on the shelf with all the other discarded stuff a marketing agency tended to collect: gadgets, knickknacks, whatever. Somehow, she could still feel the steel around her wrist. Such a strange feeling! To have no choice, to be forced to sit there and wait for things to happen. To be at the mercy of strangers. That afternoon the plastic handbag campaign got nowhere. She would make up for it that weekend. Not that she had any other plans.

"Have you ever tried Indonesian?" he asked. "I know a great little place, just down the block. An authentic *toko*."

"Indonesian? No, never. Sounds good. Is it anything like Thai?"

"You'll see. It's spicy, if you choose."

Basically, it was a shop with all kinds of herbs and foodstuffs, and with two little tables in the back. The owners, a tiny Asian woman and her son, clearly knew Xander.

"I don't think I know any of these dishes," Amanda confessed looking at the menu, which was written with chalk on a board.

"Ah, allow me." Xander explained the different dishes and how spicy they were.

"You eat here a lot?" Amanda asked when the soup, *opor ayam*, arrived.

"I do, but I knew Indonesian food before I came here to the States. I'm Dutch, and we have a lot of Indonesian food in our country. It used to be one of our colonies, and after their independence, lots of Indonesians moved to the Netherlands, bringing their food with them."

Dutch? That explains the accent. "Are all Dutch as tall as you?"

Xander laughed. "I'm quite average! I've got a nephew, he's only eighteen, but he's a full head taller than me. We are a land of giants. That's because we have to look over our dykes to see if the water rises or not."

It took Amanda a heartbeat to understand he was joking. "You have a very *dry* sense of humor."

"Thank God, we have. If we had a *wet* sense of humor, we would be in trouble. Most of Holland lies under sea level."

She grinned. "I knew that. You reclaimed land from the sea."

"I'm honored you know my country, fair American lady."

Their conversation went back and forth, only stopping when new dishes arrived.

He was a smart guy, and his sense of humor clicked wonderfully with hers. Most people didn't get her sense of irony, but Xander did.

After finishing dinner, he took her to a small basement club where they played the blues. Amanda had never been in a blues club before, but she enjoyed it tremendously.

Amanda caught Xander looking at her, right after a number had finished and the band announced they would take a break.

"What?" she asked.

"You want to ask me something. You've wanted to ask it all evening; I can feel it."

Amanda looked down. Was she so transparent? But did she have the guts to ask her question?

She glanced up again. Yes, she would.

He nodded encouragingly.

Drawing a deep breath, she blurted, "Why do you carry a key for handcuffs? I want to know." Instinctively, she braced herself. She wasn't sure she was going to like the answer. Xander was a wonderful guy and absolutely gorgeous, but... If... What if he...

"I have a spare key on my chain because, sometimes, I have to unlock someone in a hurry, and keys have the tendency to get lost. And yes, it is what you think. Sometimes, during sex, I chain up the lady. I'm into BD…uh, into S&M. Fifty Shades, and such. Although it's far more and rather different from the books and movies."

Well, I knew the Dutch were blunt. And I asked.

He watched her intensely. Not predatory, but like a concerned lover. "What do you think? Does it disgust you?"

Amanda finally found her breath. "I… I don't know. I always imagined…you know, that those people were perverts. Like really obnoxious alpha males or utter slimy creeps."

Xander chuckled. "Some are, believe me. But I hope you don't think me an obnoxious alpha male or an utter slimy creep."

"No. Not you."

"Pfew! I'm relieved. But I *am* into the BDSM lifestyle. I'm what you call a top or Dominant. A nice one, not a nasty one, I might add. For me, it's not about pain or fear or obedience. It's about pleasure and fun and love. Currently, I'm not seeing anyone, but occasionally, I play with friends. Actually, a good friend, Rosa O'dalisk, is one of your clients. You promote her books. What she writes is pretty authentic. I believe she once even based a minor character on me. Well, at least that's what she claims."

Amanda swallowed. Her throat was dry; her hands were wet. "I'm not sure I want to know all that."

He kept looking at her with those deep blue eyes. "Are you telling yourself the truth, Amanda? When I saw you this afternoon, chained to that desk…it did something to you, didn't it?"

In one second, her face was all hot. Amanda rose. "I have to go. I can't!"

She'd clearly surprised him. He was up on his feet the next moment, but she was already making her escape.

"Amanda!"

No, no, no! Blind panic took control of her. *She wasn't… She couldn't… He…*

She made it to the stairs before he caught up with her.

"Amanda, don't run. I'm not going to harm you."

You want to put me in chains and… and… Tears sprung from her eyes. Such things were impossible, *bad*. She *never…*

She only shook her head and hurried up the stairs.

This time he didn't go after her.

. . .

THE OFFICE WAS her nearest refuge. It was Friday night. Everyone had gone home to his or her partner, spouse, cat, whatever. Amanda had no one.

Shaking, she sat down at her desk. Her tears had dried up, but she still felt miserable. What had happened? *He scared me.*

That was a lie. Xander hadn't scared her.

She'd scared herself.

He had only told the truth. Being caught in the handcuffs had moved her. In a weird, dark, and dirty, but also a good, very good, way. She'd felt complete, and excited, and at peace, all at once.

Which was bad. She shouldn't have felt that. Handcuffs and being tied up, surrendering to someone, to have no choice but to endure whatever the other bestowed on her... That was plain *wrong. Perverted.* Normal people didn't do that, didn't feel that. And she was normal!

But then, why did I run when Xander told me this? Why didn't I laugh in his face? Why am I not sure?

The questions were like loaded guns, and Amanda didn't want to touch them.

It took her fifteen minutes to compose herself. She drank some water from the cooler and sat once more at her desk. Now that she was here, she might as well work on the plastic handbag account. It wasn't due for a week, but she liked to finish projects early, in case something else cropped up.

Amanda started to work.

After twenty seconds, she caught herself looking at the pair of handcuffs on the shelf.

Quickly, she looked away. *No!*

Ten seconds later, she found herself staring at those damned things, again.

Angry, Amanda pushed up from her desk. She would put the handcuffs out of sight, so she could finally get some work done.

The manuscript was on Beth's desk. She hadn't taken it home. Rosa O'dalisk's next new novel in the Dark Satin series. Authentic novels, like what S&M really meant, according to Xander.

It's smut. It's dirty. It must be.

Amanda shook her head. She shouldn't judge; she hadn't read the manuscript. She'd never read anything in that genre.

After a moment of doubt, she picked up the manuscript and walked back to her desk. No doubt it would be terrible and dirty, with people in rubber suits doing horrible things to each other, but at least she would have the right to judge if she finally knew what it was all about.

She started to read.

At two after midnight, the building was almost completely deserted. Amanda tiptoed down the hallway and listened at the door of the studio. Little flashes of blue light escaped from under the door, and resting her ear against the wood, she could discern the sound of heavy machinery. Someone was working.

Quiet as a cat, Amanda walked back to the office of Neon Dog Tales. She left the door ajar.

The manuscript was back on Beth's desk. Out of harm's way.

Like in a dream, Amanda took the handcuffs from the shelf.

Click, click. Now, both her wrists were caught in steel. She hung over her desk, her butt in the air, the handcuffs around the metal bar of the desk.

She was caught.

Amanda phoned the number of the little card she'd received that afternoon.

Three, four times, it rang—just as many times as her heart skipped beats.

"Hi," said Amanda, her throat dry as the desert, her body shivering.

I want this. I really, really want this.

"Hello, this is Amanda. I'm in the office. Please, help me. I-I need you." Unable to speak any further, she disconnected. What had she done? There was no going back now...

After an endless minute she heard someone entering the office.

A man.

"Hello, Amanda?" It was Xander.

"Over here." It was more a whisper than a cry, but still, he heard her.

She watched him approach. He was back in his jeans and black wifebeater. No lumberjack shirt, though. Broad shoulders, muscled arms, powerful hands used to working with metal and heavy tools.

Amanda didn't feel strong at all. Her knees were wobbly, her head light. She felt hot like she had a fever.

He didn't say anything, just looked at her.

He knows what I've done. Why I've done it.

Did she blush? Well, sure, somewhere in her body the blood was pumping. A little red-hot coal, down *there*.

Dear Lord, I'm such a slut to do this. To let this... No, to want this.

Well, she didn't care. She wanted it. Yes, she wanted it as badly as life itself.

Xander moved over to her. His hand caught her face, tenderly.

Long, strong fingers. The smell of metal, rust, oil. Xander-smell.

Amanda sniffed him, almost licked his hand.

No! I wouldn't dare! I...

She looked up at him. "I've been stupid. And bad. I want you... I... I want you to punish me. Please."

Am I saying this? Am I really asking this? I must be mad!

She was mad. Damned mad. With lust and desire. She had never been so sure of herself.

Please, please, please. Don't laugh. Don't turn away.

"You're sure, Amanda?"

She nodded.

He kept looking at her.

Finally, she said, "I'm sure."

"And do you trust me?"

"Yes."

He nodded. "Okay. Remember you can ask me to stop at any moment. If you're uncomfortable or it feels wrong, just say so. I won't go any further than you're ready for."

"Thank...thank you," Amanda whispered. "I'm sure. Please, punish me. I'm yours. I want this."

He bowed towards her, held her head with both hands, and kissed her.

Lips, tongue. *Nice.*

Xander left Amanda panting, her body hanging over the desk, both her hands cuffed. His strong hands glided downwards over her neck and shoulders, her back and tush, down the line of her skirt.

Amanda shivered.

She didn't want to...

Suddenly, there was no doubt, no hesitation. Yes, she did. She certainly did want this.

Fingers touched the backside of her knees—tickling! *Oh!*—closing around the hem of her skirt.

Amanda sighed deeply while he pulled up her skirt, all the way up, exposing her ass.

Her bum was up in the air, covered by her pink no-nonsense panties. It was Friday. She hadn't expected someone to see her underwear. This wasn't any seductive lingerie, just ordinary panties.

Won't he find me a prude? I guess he's used to real kinky outfits and—

His thumbs pushed on the back of her panties, revealing most of her ass. He kissed both halves. "You're beautiful."

Wuuuuuuh.

"Beautiful, bad girl."

She got weak in her knees and felt a knot in her

tummy.

Without saying anything else, he took her neck with one hand.

Amanda sighed. She was in his power. Completely.

Yes.

His hand smacked her bottom.

Shock rattled through her. It wasn't the pain. Not really, because he didn't hit her hard. It was the fact that someone had struck her. Hit her on that intimate spot! And that she was completely powerless, unable to escape, to fight.

It took a few seconds before Amanda remembered to breathe again.

I can say "no". I can call "stop!". I can.

But she wouldn't. No, she wouldn't. Not in a thousand years. She felt peaceful and hyped at the same time. It felt so good. *Soooooo gooooood*.

He didn't ask her, not out loud, but Amanda knew Xander was waiting for her response. Watching her, observing her.

She grunted, only a little, wanted to raise her head to nod.

His left hand kept her down, but he understood. He understood her completely. With his right hand, he smacked her again.

And again.

And again.

Slaps fell down on her bum like raindrops. Really hard, stinging raindrops. Her skin was on fire; the slaps vibrated through her body.

She clenched her teeth.

Ohhh. Yes! I'm a bad girl. I deserved this, Amanda thought, without shame, without any doubts. A wild joy filled her heart. Blood pounded in her ears. The little red-hot spot between her legs was growing and growing.

I'm a bad girl, spank me. Please!

I know, my sweet, she imagined him saying with his deep voice.

Smack!

Smack!

Uhhhhhhwwwwyesss.

Amanda felt a calmness descending on her. She had wanted this. She had wanted it all her life. She needed it so badly. If felt so good.

Her breathing got deeper; she wiggled and presented her bum to receive more slaps.

Xander didn't stop. He kept on spanking her.

On and on.

And on.

Yesssssss.

Pain? She didn't feel pain. Okay, she rationally knew she was feeling pain, but her mind told her something different. She felt a warm, sweet haze. A feeling of being cared for, being loved, being held by him.

Amanda loved it. She loved it so much.

It took a few seconds before she realized the spanking had stopped. She was floating, so happy. And instinctively, she knew what was coming now.

He let her rest for a moment, her face flat on the desk, her ass up in the air.

She was drooling, a little.

Xander pulled down her panties. They were soaked.

Her ass was burning.

He bowed, his face a mere few inches from hers. "I want to make love to you, Amanda. I'll do it safely."

"Yes. Do it," she slurred.

His face disappeared. Xander unzipped his trousers, was busy for a handful of seconds, and then took her from behind.

So good. So damn good.

The big Dutch guy fucked her. Carefully, but still hard and deep, slowly increasing the speed of thrusts,

Moaning Amanda moved against his strokes, pushing his dick deeper.

He grabbed her, pounded her. Harder. Harder. It was a bit like spanking, but now she felt his delicious dick deep inside her.

She moaned when lust flooded her, the first time.

He kept fucking her.

Amanda screamed when she came for the second time.

He still kept fucking her.

"Mer...mercy!" she begged. She was fighting for breath, cross-eyed. Her entire universe was flesh and heat.

He was Xander, her nice sadistic lover. He was strict. And sometimes, a bit cruel.

So, he fucked her, until she came a third time.

Ohhgggggggggod!!!!!

He pulled out of her.

Two, three steps.

Xander grabbed her hair. His dick was dripping with her cum. He peeled off the rubber.

Amanda opened her mouth.

Yes.

She took his cock and started to suck the big hot thing.

He came almost immediately, blowing his hot seed in her mouth.

She swallowed, sucked, waited for it.

A second load came like an afterthought.

Finally, he was finished. Xander sat down, in one of the office chairs, panting.

Amanda looked at him, blinking away the sweat, licking her lips. "Thank you."

He stroked her hair. "Thank *you*." He kissed her once more. Long, sweet.

An endless, endless kiss.

He dug for his keyring and unlocked the handcuffs.

Dizzily, Amanda got up, and he caught her in his big, strong arms. He carried her to the office couch, and she curled up in his lap.

Amanda smiled and closed her eyes. He had unlocked her chains, twice, but she knew she would never be free again.

And that made her utterly happy.

SAVING TIME

BY KIMBERLY DEAN

*E*verly curled her toes inside her boots to fight off the chill as she waited for the line of workers ahead of her to pass through the security checkpoint. Impatient, she glanced at the heavy sky overhead. More clouds than smog today. She wanted to be inside before the acid rain began.

Huddling deeper into her jacket, she concentrated on the idea that had come to her overnight, the one that might help her break through the roadblock in her research. The line lurched, and she shuffled forward another step.

She was eager to test out the concept, *if* she could ever get inside.

The red numbers on the clock above the checkpoint glowed, standing out against the gray of the weather. Finally, she pushed through the turnstile that detected the chip implanted in her hip. She hurried across campus to her laboratory, making it inside just as the clock ticked to 8:00.

Time was of utmost importance around here.

She glanced around to see if anyone had noticed her nearly-late arrival. The staff allowed into the high-security lab was small: five researchers and—her gaze settled on Sgt. Devlin—two time enforcers.

His back was to her as he walked his rounds, but warmth ran through her all the way to her chilled toes. That predatory stride of his got to her every time. He glanced at the clock on the wall before he took up his post beside the time portal, his steel-gray gaze looking everywhere but at her.

He'd noticed.

She hurried to swap her coat for her lab jacket. The back of her neck tingled as if he was looking at her now. Time scientists and enforcers weren't allowed to interact or even converse. Enforcers were here for her protection and the technology's. Oh, who was she kidding? If push came to shove, she knew what enforcers like Devlin would ultimately protect—the technology that made time travel possible.

She forced her shoulders to relax. Daydreaming about a sexy enforcer would get her nowhere. Focusing instead on her digital lab book, she swiped through her notes.

Time travel was tricky. The first successful jump had taken place almost ten years ago, but the technology wasn't mature by any means. Just look at the portal. It still took up half the room and sucked up the energy of a small city. Her advances in nanotechnology would help with that. She'd solved the power problem, but recently, she'd been more curious about the effect of magnetics.

She drummed her fingers against her desktop. If she tweaked the direction of the micro-electrical coils, would that help stabilize the resultant wormhole? Maybe.

She signaled to Sgt. Devlin's partner that she wanted to access the mobile device she'd been developing. Blond and stocky, he was relatively new in the lab. She didn't know his name, but all she needed was his half of the code. Together, they opened the storage compartment.

She took the device back to her bench, lined up her magnifying glass, and began adjusting the electrical coil. The theory worked out, but the device hadn't yet achieved the repeatable successes they wanted. The wormholes it opened tended to collapse a few seconds after establishment.

She reached into the pocket of her lab jacket for her electromagnetic field detector but hesitated when she touched something unfamiliar. She opened her pocket to look inside. Was that… *chocolate*?

Quickly, she grabbed her EMF detector and fiddled with it.

Chocolate was in short supply these days and expensive—but it wasn't the first treat or comfort that had unexpectedly come her way. Like the day the heating function on her chair had been fixed without her reporting it…or the afternoon there had been the scent of roses at her desk… At least, she thought it was roses. She'd never smelled or even seen one in real life.

She glanced at the researcher beside her. She hoped it wasn't him. Nice guy, but she felt nothing more for him than friendship. And only work friendship, at that.

She trailed her fingers around the foil-covered square in her pocket. Who could have—

A pained cry interrupted her thoughts, and she spun towards the blond enforcer who'd just helped her. His eyes were squeezed tight, and his jaw muscles were knotted. A jolt went through his body, and he reached for the back of his neck.

Oh, no. Not another seizure.

"Help!" Everly called as she moved towards the man.

Devlin had the same reflex. He caught the enforcer as his knees buckled, but the man was already toppling. Another shout of excruciating pain filled the room. Everly tried to steady the enforcer's head as Devlin lowered him to the floor, but the man's heavy weight bumped into her, and she stumbled backwards. She reached out blindly for something to break her fall, and her hand clanged against her bench top. What she caught wasn't substantial. The room spun, and time seemed to slow, but she ended up flat on her butt.

"*Ow.*" The landing wasn't as hard as it could have been, but she shook her head anyway. She was dizzy and a little nauseous. The room had stopped spinning, but there was a light glaring in her eyes, and the floor felt prickly.

Prickly?

She looked away from the blinding light as she spread her fingers through the... *grass?*

Her head snapped up so quickly her neck gave a

twinge. Bringing up one hand, she shielded her eyes from the blinding light. Was that the sun?

Her heart began pounding so loudly it drowned out everything else in her ears. Colors besieged her. Bright colors everywhere. And scents. The grass, not metallic air. And roses. She looked at a bright bushy plant near her. That was definitely what roses smelled like.

Her stomach knotted. She wasn't in the lab anymore. Where was she? Suddenly, she realized she was holding something in her hand to shield her eyes. She swallowed hard when she realized what it was.

Maybe the question should be: *When was she?*

She scrambled to her feet when a car rumbled by, right in front of her. An actual, fossil-fuels-burning car with rubber tires. She coughed, spitting away that all-too-familiar nasty scent and backed up until she hit something. A building—but not her laboratory. And that wasn't her street. The hypertrain line was gone. Everything looked new but old-fashioned at the same time.

Her heart beat fast. She looked off to the distance. Buildings and landscaping could be altered, but topography changed much more slowly. Tears pricked at her eyes when she saw Sunrise Ridge off to the east.

Holy crap. She'd done it. She'd created a mobile time travel unit.

She watched people going about their normal day. She wanted to explore. She wanted to experience things.

But she needed to go back. *Now.*

She'd crossed time without running any calculations. She could have inserted herself in the middle of that rose bush or in front of that car.

Legs shaking, she moved back to the patch of grass. She knew the date, time, and conditions she'd left. If she went directly back, she shouldn't collide with anything or cause any undue effects. She programmed in her destination. Steeling herself against the disorientation, she engaged the unit.

Her stomach dropped when nothing happened.

"Oh, no. Come on, baby."

Another try had the same result.

She shook the device, although that was probably what had caused the problem in the first place. She'd banged her hand so hard against the table when she'd fallen, she knew it would be black and blue tomorrow.

Tomorrow.

She looked up slowly. What did that even mean anymore?

Heaven help her. She was trapped in the past.

DEVLIN NEARLY DROPPED his partner when the pretty time scientist disappeared right in front of his eyes. He lowered the enforcer to the floor and bellowed, "Get a medic in here."

There was nothing he could do for the pain ricocheting through the other man's head like a wrecking ball. He knew. He'd tried.

"Watch over him," he said to a researcher who came to help. He pushed himself to his feet. "Where did the female researcher go?"

"She just vanished." The lead scientist pointed at the open storage box. "My goodness, could she have gotten the portable unit working?"

Gasps went up across the room as nervous excitement charged the air, but Devlin broke out in a cold sweat. If anyone could, she could. He'd watched her day in and day out, whenever he'd been assigned to her area. She was as sharp as a tack.

"When?" he asked. "When did she go?"

He strode around the fallen enforcer to her lab bench. Medics had arrived. There was nothing he could do to help, but that wasn't his priority anymore.

They'd had a breach of the time continuum.

"What year were you looking at?" he bit out. "What date was set as a destination?"

The researcher who sat next to her kept flapping his mouth like a flounder. He knew nothing.

Devlin curled his fingers into his palms. Time travel was outlawed. More importantly, it was dangerous. He needed to go after her, but where in the timeline should he insert himself? The chips implanted in all residents' hips allowed him to track location, but he needed to be in the same time period as the person for the technology to work.

He looked over her things. The mobile doohickey was gone. Had she accidentally activated the device when she'd fallen—or had she taken advantage of an unfortunate opportunity? His training taught him to assume the worst.

Her e-notebook.

He quickly scanned through her notes. Lucky for

him, she was thorough.

He shoved the notebook under the lead researcher's nose. "Set up the portal," he ordered. "I'm going to prep."

DEVLIN MATERIALIZED IN THE PAST, bracing himself for anything. It had taken the scientists an excruciatingly long time to run the calculations. He'd tried to make them just program in her numbers, but they'd been insistent. He pulled out his tracker, ready to move.

Ready to hunt.

It started beeping, and when he looked up, he spotted a woman sitting at a bus stop half a block down. Everly. His knees gave an unexpected wobble. She'd made the jump safely.

He quickly strode down the sidewalk. She hadn't gone far. She'd known that if she wanted to get back, staying in place reduced the risk of being missed. She didn't have the data or computing power with her to calculate a safe jump back from a different location.

He crossed the street. She hadn't spotted him yet, so he took the time to study her full-on. For so long, he'd been limited to quick glances and peripheral looks. Her face was lowered, but he drank in the sight of her brown hair pulled back in a ponytail. Wavy strands had escaped, brushing the back of her neck and her cheekbones as she toyed with the object in her hands. He stiffened when he realized what she was doing. "Do *not* activate that device."

Her head snapped up, and she sprang to her feet. "Sergeant! You found me."

She rushed out into the street to meet him, lab jacket billowing, and Devlin caught her by the waist. He ushered her right back into the glass box of the bus stop. "Are you okay? Did you arrive without incident?"

She let out a nervous laugh, one that made his fingers tighten. "A car passed in front of me, but I'm fine."

A car? Don't tell me that. "Did anyone notice the breach?"

"Breach?" She quickly looked around them. "No, I don't think so."

"Good." He caught her hand. "We need to get out of sight."

Centering his thoughts, Devlin led her down the sidewalk and into a gap between two buildings. They didn't have much time. Reaching for his belt, he caught the handle of his knife and pulled it out of its sheath.

Her eyes widened when she saw the weapon. "What are you— *It was an accident.*" She lurched away. "I didn't mean to make an unsanctioned jump."

Hell. He'd gotten ahead of himself. He hadn't meant to frighten her. "I know."

"You saw what happened," she said, biting her lip.

"I know," he repeated. She was shaking so hard he was afraid she'd drop that precious device—or trigger it, again.

"This doesn't have to be an incident." She paled. "Oh, God. It's already an incident, isn't it?"

"*Everly.*"

Her gaze finally snapped away from the knife to his face.

Devlin moved fast and trapped her against the wall. He quickly disarmed her of the mobile device and stowed it in a pocket in his cargo pants.

"Listen to me." He looked deep into her eyes. Their bodies were pressed so tightly together he could feel her trembling. "I can take you back—or I can set you free."

She went still when he slid his hand down to her hip. "It's up to you."

ADRENALINE RAGED through Everly's system. Devlin was here, all six hard feet of him, bearing down on her. That knife. That hand. That big, warm palm on her hip.

Her hip… The chip in her hip.

Set her free?

Her thoughts came to a screeching halt. No, she'd misunderstood. He was a time enforcer. It was his job to stop time jumpers, not help them flee. This had to be a trick. A test.

But his gray gaze was steely and hot.

"Why would you do that?" she whispered.

She flinched when he reached into the open pocket of her lab coat… but then he pulled out the square of chocolate.

"This is why."

Everly sucked in a sharp breath. "That was you?"

Their gazes locked, and recognition suddenly passed back and forth.

"That was me."

Time slowed down…but then he closed the distance fast.

Everly's entire body pulsed when he pressed his mouth to hers. The kiss was fiery, intimate, and more than a little desperate. Oh, God. Her secret crush.

Fantasy melted under the heat of reality, and she wrapped her arms around him. He felt big and tough against her. Like an avenging soldier, ready to go to battle for her.

With that long blade in his other hand, he just might be.

She wasn't ready when he broke the kiss.

"You need to make your up mind quickly," he said gruffly, lifting the knife again. "They'll send another time enforcer soon."

Everly's mind was awhirl, but she finally understood what he was saying. With blinding clarity.

Life in their time was bleak and authoritarian. Without her chip, nobody could follow her. She could escape into the past. He was offering her a new life. A completely different life, here, away from everything and everyone she'd ever known. But was that a bad thing? She had no family left. Polluted air and poor nutrition had shortened lifespans. She enjoyed her work, but look where it had led. Everyone wanted out.

She'd never get this chance again.

Her hands shook as she pushed down the waistband of her pants, baring the swath of tender skin on her hip where she knew the chip lay. "Get it out of me."

Devlin gave her a hard stare before going back into first responder mode. "I didn't have time to gather many things before I followed you. This will help, but you're still going to feel pressure."

He rubbed a numbing agent over the spot, and Everly's cheeks heated. It wasn't like she'd stripped bare, but she was wearing pink panties, and the skin she'd exposed wasn't normally something others saw. Especially Devlin. He stood so close she could feel his heat.

He prodded the soft flesh of her hip until he found a hard bump. When he began sterilizing that hunting knife, she got woozy. He caught her hand and lifted it back to his shoulder. "Look away."

Her nails bit into his muscles when she felt the pressure of his blade.

"I'd never hurt you," he whispered into her ear, "but this has to go."

Perspiration dampened her upper lip as he dug out the chip. She couldn't help but look at it, fresh blood and all, when he tossed it onto the ground.

"Easy," he said as he pulled out a bio-stitcher.

Her skin tugged and heated. The healing process was as uncomfortable as the wound.

Finally, he wrapped his hand over her hip, protectively covering the pinkened flesh. "It's done. You're free."

Everly's heart jumped. *Freedom.* She hadn't realized how much she'd craved it. And he'd given it to her—this hard, quiet man who'd terrified her as much as he'd intrigued her. She caught his handsome face in both hands. When she went on tiptoe and pressed her lips against his, a gravelly sound left the back of his throat. Their tongues tangled, and his hand tightened on her hip.

It was only the sound of a car horn that pulled them

apart. Devlin slapped the wall. "We need to move." He tugged up her pants. "They can still track me, but you're going off their radar screen."

"No!" Everly cried when he lifted his foot.

It was too late. With a vicious heel strike, he squashed her tracking chip under his boot.

He looked at her, brows lowered. "It had to be done."

"I know, but I want to study that technology." Kneeling, she picked up the broken chip and slipped it into her pocket.

He looked her up and down. "We need to change your appearance."

She took off her lab coat and folded it over her arm. She owned absolutely nothing else. When he took the band out of her hair, she tucked it into her pocket.

He ran his fingers through the strands until they brushed against her shoulders. "Do you trust me?" he asked.

She nodded. She'd better, because there was no going back, now.

"How did you find me?" Everly asked later that day as she followed Devlin into a motel room. They'd been all over town getting food and provisions. "How did you know the year I'd targeted?"

He reached into his saddlebag. "From this."

"My lab book!" She eagerly scooped it up, but then her eyes widened. "You snuck it out?"

"You needed it."

But it had been a risk. A huge one. "Devlin," she said softly.

His gray eyes flared, but then he winced. He took a seat at the table by the door and rubbed the back of his neck. "We need to figure out our next steps."

The move was subtle, almost a habit, but Everly knew better. Enforcers had tracking chips, too, but they were implanted at the bases of their skulls. She moved to stand behind him.

She reached for him, hesitated, but then put her hands on him. They'd kissed—hell, she'd pulled down her pants for him—but the intimacy still felt foreign. Like breaking long-established rules. She started rubbing his neck, trying to ease the stiffness she felt there.

He tensed for a moment, but then relaxed under her touch.

She had to squeeze her thighs together to fight her reaction. It was a simple act of kindness, but touching him made her feel her freedom more than anything. He was warm to the touch, and his skin felt smooth. Addictive.

Trying to keep a clear head, she nodded towards the bag. "Want to catch me up first? That's quite the stash of money you've got there."

"Yup."

They'd gone to a bank, and a man had given him a pile of bills. Paper money. She'd only seen pictures of it in history classes. "Is that standard operating procedure for time enforcers?"

"Not exactly." Devlin leaned more heavily against

her. "Do you know I've made more time jumps than any other enforcer?"

"I know you're always the one they suit up." There were still people out there with illicit technology who took the risk, and then there were those who accidentally got caught up in wormholes. Time enforcers were the ones who brought them back.

But all that time jumping apparently took its toll.

She stroked her fingers over the knots in his neck. The technology in enforcers' chips was more complex, allowing them to be tracked across time and space. It was why the government allowed him to jump across years. They always knew how to get their enforcers back. Unfortunately, the advanced technology and human physiology weren't quite compatible. Not yet.

"I went back to 1930 once," he said, "and I happened to pass by a bank."

Everly stopped with her fingers in his hair.

He shifted. "It occurred to me that the money I'd been supplied with was more than people made in six months back then, so I decided to open an account and deposit it. I did it again the next time I jumped—and the next. Compound interest took over from there."

Everly bit her lip. "But that's how our world got into the situation it's in. Rich men and politicians did the same thing. People went back in time to make money, change outcomes, affect lives… and look how things turned out. The butterfly effect is killing our world."

"You're right, I know. But the money was protection."

And probably his due. She slid her fingers deeper

into his hair and found what she was looking for. His chip. They wouldn't be able to just cut it out. Anger swelled within her. The government had used him as a lab rat, risking his life repeatedly as part of his job.

"You've been planning this," she whispered. "You had everything in place, ready to go."

He shrugged. "I just needed to work out some things."

But he was still chipped. "Why put it into action, now?"

"You know why." He stood in a fluid motion and turned around to face her.

He was so close, so tall, Everly's breath caught. The rules that had kept them separated were gone. The restraints had been loosened, and the fantasy was no longer forbidden. "But we barely know each other."

"You don't have to talk to a person to know them." He slid his hands under her top, and she trembled when his thumbs moved over her stomach. "We've been in the same lab for the past year. I know you're soft-hearted, principled, a little spacey, and—after today—freaking brilliant."

She blinked. "I'm not spacey."

A smile slowly rose on his face. "When you start thinking about something, everything else goes away."

Her pants nearly melted off. She'd never seen him smile. Ever. "That's not spacey; that's focused."

"Yeah?" He nudged her to the bed. "Well, I need that focus. Badly."

Everly shuddered. She needed it, too.

She lifted her arms when he worked her top up her

body and over her head. His hands were on her breasts before the garment hit the floor. Her nipples poked hard into his palms as he kissed her again. He lowered her to the bed and stripped off her shoes and pants, but her belly really sucked in when he pulled off his black T-shirt.

She could definitely focus on him.

She spread her hands wide on his chest, trying to touch all of him at once. He was honed like the weapon he was. She stroked her hands over the slabs of his pecs, and then down his ribcage. He groaned low under his breath and pressed a kiss between her breasts, right over her pounding heart. She arched when he began working his way down her body.

"This better not scar," he said as he cupped her hip protectively and kissed the small pink healing line.

Everly's pussy clenched. "It's okay if it does. It'll remind me of the day you rescued me."

His hold on her tightened, and then he was pulling down her panties. She flushed with heat as he bared her on the bed and skimmed his hands up her legs. He spread them open, and his mouth landed again on her hip.

"Ahhh!" she cried when he cupped his hand between her thighs. He licked her scar, and she arched when he pushed a finger into her. "Oh, *oh!*"

"I'd get jealous whenever you rolled into work late," he said from his position low on her body.

"I wasn't late!" She knew he'd been watching.

"It always made me wonder if you were coming from some other guy's bed."

Wait. He'd been jealous?

She threaded her fingers through his hair. "I just like to lounge."

His grin had a bit of the devil in it. "Good to know."

He moved and, suddenly, Everly felt his mouth between her legs.

"Devlin!"

He settled in, spreading her thighs wider as his mouth took over her world. He continued the private petting and kissed her way too intimately. Everly felt herself swelling as his tongue licked over her sensitive flesh. The familiarity made her wriggle, but he held her in place. Her thighs clenched, but the pleasure was overwhelming. He pushed another finger into her and began to rub at a spot deep inside her… One that made her shake…

His mouth zeroed in on her clit, and she twisted hard as an orgasm roared through her. He drew it out, leaving her limp before he crawled up over her.

She moaned when he thrust into her.

He'd barely seated himself before he was pulling out and pushing in again. There was no slow build-up. They'd waited too long. He leveraged himself over her and fucked her fast and deep, bracing himself on his hands to let his hips swing free. Everly found his rhythm quickly, rolling up her hips to meet his fierce thrusts. Their ragged breaths echoed off the walls of the motel room as he hammered into her, his cock hard and eager.

"Fuck," he said, his voice guttural.

She didn't want it to end, either. She scraped her

fingernails down his muscled back, but the tension and excitement building up inside her were too much. Finally, it spilled over, lighting her up from the inside. "Dev!"

He reared back his head. Her pussy clenched down tightly on his hot cock, and soon he was coming inside her.

"Ahhh. Everly, I—*Ah!*"

His weight came down upon her, and she cradled the back of his neck. Her protector. Her rescuer.

There was no way she was going on without him. She had to save him, too.

LIGHT WAS RISING when Devlin awoke in a soft bed with a warm feminine body pressed up against him. *Everly*. He ran a hand over his face, trying to clear the cobwebs from his mind. Last night had been no dream. They were together. They'd finally been able to touch.

But this would be their one and only time.

He'd already stayed with her too long. Other enforcers would be following him soon. He needed to get moving again in order to provide her cover. A twinge at the back of his neck assured him there was no other way.

He watched her sleeping, ignoring the pain, as he tried to imprint the memory in his brain forever. She was bathed in the pre-dawn light. So soft. So beautiful. So extraordinary.

He couldn't go. Not yet.

"Everly, wake up. I want to show you something."

She gave a grumble. "Lounger."

He smiled.

"Come here," he said as he rose to his knees. "Look," he said, pointing.

She rubbed her eyes in the cutest way. "At what?"

"The sun," he said, settling back on his heels.

She glanced to the window, but then scrambled up fast. Flinging a hand in front of his face, she blocked his view. "You're not supposed to look at it."

The skies were so polluted in their lifetime that looking at the sun had never been an issue, but she was a time scientist. She knew her history.

He pulled her closer. "It's okay. It's not up yet. Look."

Hesitantly, she peeked at the window. When she saw the skyline, her mouth dropped open. "Sunrise Ridge. That's what it means."

Devlin's heart filled until it was heavy. She'd never seen a sunrise.

Catching her by the waist, he lifted her over him—and onto him. She let out a soft cry when he penetrated her from behind. Slowly, he began making love to her. She was tight, hot, and so damn slick. He spread her legs so she was kneeling on his lap with her knees outside of his.

"Watch," he said, kissing her earlobe.

The light in the east was brightening as pinks and purples streaked across the sky. The silhouette of two birds crossed the panorama, the dark Vs of their bodies moving in sync.

Just like their bodies worked together on the bed.

"It's beautiful," she murmured. She lifted her hand

backwards to cup his neck as he nuzzled against the soft tangles of her hair. "The most beautiful thing I've ever seen."

"Mm-hmm," he said, watching her.

He closed his hand over her breast and squeezed possessively.

They stayed that way, moving slowly. Sensuously. Absorbed in each other and the glory of nature. A tear spilled down Everly's face, and Devlin wiped it away. He understood. The *'might have beens'*… The *'what ifs'*…

When the sun finally rose out of its hiding place, he took her down on the bed. On their sides, he pulled her top leg up to her chest and pumped into her.

"Oh, God. That's—*Yes!*"

He slammed into her, grinding deep. He came hard and long, feeling her body arch against him. He allowed himself longer than he should have inside her, but eventually, he knew he had to pull out. Rolling onto his back, he stared at the ceiling. It was time—

"Ahhhhhhhh!"

The pain that came was fast and debilitating. He reached for his head, but there was no relief. His body spasmed as it tried to get away.

"Devlin? What's wrong?"

"Ev—" He couldn't get her name out. "Go," he gasped. "Run."

"Oh, no. The chip."

He pushed her away from him when she tried to touch him. It was too much. The pain receptors had taken over even his skin. "Take the money. Have… good…life…"

"No, you have to come with me. Devlin? Devlin!"

He roused long enough to see her jump off the bed and reach for her lab coat.

Good… She was…going… He just wanted…safe…

WHEN DEVLIN CAME TO, he was lying on the bed with a pillow under his head and a blanket over his body. He braced himself for the glare, but the light wasn't too bad. His thoughts were cloudy, and he could feel his sweat on the sheets beneath him.

His saw Everly sitting at the table, wearing only his T-shirt. She was deep in thought as she studied her lab book and the mobile time travel device. So focused…

Dammit.

"What…" He had to stop to clear his throat. "What are you still doing here?"

She gave him a sharp look and put down the device.

He struggled to sit up.

"Easy." She sat down beside him on the mattress. "Not that much time has gone by. You can get steady before we move."

Temper flared inside him. "I can't go with you, Everly. Please, don't make this all for nothing."

"I've been trying to make it all *better*." She brushed her fingers through his hair. "How's your head?"

"It—" He stopped. "The pain is gone."

He frowned and rubbed his temple. He always ran a low-grade headache. Hell, his head felt calm now, but he knew it would be back. "Please. You've got to go. Make it out, for me."

"I'm going to make it out *with* you."

"The chip."

"Is no longer functioning."

He stopped, unsure he'd heard her correctly. "What?"

"All that time you were getting me chocolate and fixing my chair…?" She shrugged. "I was thinking about making things more comfortable for you, too."

She moved back to the table and showed him the crumpled tracking chip that he'd removed from her hip. "I knew the chip in your head had to be an upgraded model of mine. I'd already developed a concept on how to inactivate yours, but seeing mine helped me firm up my hypothesis."

He frowned. "Babe, my headache is gone, but those big words of yours still hurt."

She pulled something square and black out of her lab jacket pocket. Definitely not chocolate.

"What is that?" he asked.

"A high-powered magnet. The chip is still in your head, but I screwed up its magnetic fields with this."

"Where'd you get that?"

"I use it at work. I just couldn't find a way to use it on you. I couldn't exactly walk up to an enforcer and say, 'Let me press this against your head.' Especially not the big, tough, sexy enforcer."

Devlin swung his legs over the side of the bed. "That's why you rushed for my partner. You were going to use it on him."

"The blond guy? Yes—but I did the research for you."

He hauled her against him. She'd fixed the one problem he hadn't been able to get past. He'd held out

189

hope for her, but now? Could he really have hope for himself? For them? "You are scary smart."

Her touch was gentle on the back of his neck. "You figured out everything else. They can't track either of us now. We're both free. Free to be together, to do whatever we want."

He sighed. "Not quite. If my signal has gone dark, they'll send someone. All enforcers are trained to track the old-fashioned way. They'll be coming."

"But they won't find anything—not in this year."

His gaze shot to the table. She hadn't been toying with the magnet. "You fixed your mobile device?"

"We just need to figure out when to go."

Devlin could hardly believe it. He'd been planning for an opportunity like this forever, but he'd never thought she'd be with him. He didn't want to put her in danger, but what if fate had put them together for a reason...? "What do you think about going back to when this whole mess started?"

"To when time travel was invented?"

"Yeah. How about we stop that from happening? Stop the rich and powerful from changing the past to suit their own desires? Stop the butterfly effect that's dragged down the world?" He brushed a hand over her hair. "Bring back the sunrises?"

Her pretty brown eyes rounded, but then she pulled him down for a kiss. "I'd say it's about damn time."

FALLING OFF THE SINGLE TRACK

BY TRAY ELLIS

*E*mma chugged up the steep incline, her mountain bike already in its easiest gear, and gritted her teeth through the burning sensation in her calves and glutes. The top of the trail beckoned, so close and still so far. Air seared her throat as she gasped through the last dozen feet to an open spot.

She rotated her feet to unclip her shoes from the pedals and stepped down onto solid ground. After giving her body time to recover from the exertion, she chomped down on the tube snaking over her shoulder from the backpack water bladder. Resting, she spent a moment to admire the forest surrounding her.

Sunlight filtered in through green leaves. This deep into the trail system, no cars could be heard thrumming past on the highway. The absence of those sounds was a relief from the usual bustle of city life. However, the forest wasn't entirely silent. Leaves rustled as a chipmunk dashed from one branch to another. Birds chirped and hopped. An exuberant clump of men shouted vulgarities at each other, an equal mix of demeaning epithets and crude encouragement, as they climbed the steep incline Emma had just conquered.

Emma walked her bike farther off the trail to let the group pass. She preferred to ride without a rowdy group behind her, so she'd give them a head start and follow after they were gone.

The first man in the group reached the clearing and gave her a grateful look. "Thanks," he grunted. He refocused on the trail and kept going, not taking a moment to recover from the steep grade. He didn't have much leeway because other members of the group were close on his tail. They pedaled past her one by one, some giving her nods acknowledging she'd moved off trail for them and others completely ignoring her.

She admired their equipment. Most of them rode high-end bikes with full suspensions, super light frames, and gears that changed like a hot knife through butter. Emma knew that while the bikes were superb, they also took a huge bite out of one's budget. Her well-loved Hodierna Cycles "hardtail" was much less expensive, and from a woman-owned company designed in the US and made in Quebec, Canada.

Emma also admired riders' physiques. Spattered with mud and drenched in sweat, the guys pedaling past her were in prime shape. Their forearm muscles bunched as they gripped the handlebars while leaning forward against the tilt of the ground. The two strong muscles at the backs of their calves were clearly outlined as they pedaled. Their burly thighs strained in cooperation with the heft of their tight rear ends. All of them wore the mountain biker version of surfer board shorts and strapped-on backpacks with water bladder tubes snaking out. Their sophisticated bikes, impressive up-hill skills, and attire clued in Emma that these were either dedicated hobbyists, or else some flavor of professionals.

Their language cleared up as soon as each caught sight of her. Imagine that.

Emma sucked down more water as she waited for the group to move on.

She envied the group ride. She didn't often get to ride with such an exuberant bunch. Mostly, she rode with one or two friends—if the friends kept their commitments. Which they were increasingly unlikely to do lately. Like today, when Aliza had flaked on her and texted that she wouldn't make it. Emma had already been waiting at the trailhead when her phone trilled the arrival of the cancelation text. Last weekend, it had been Kaylee who'd suddenly been unable to make it, although she'd had no problem coming over later that evening for drinks and a rom-com movie.

Emma didn't love riding alone. It wasn't the safest option, but if she waited for someone to ride with her, she'd get out on the trails twice a year. So, she'd texted her sister to ask what she was doing and had ventured into the trail network.

While she chose trails that were well within her ability level, she also liked pushing herself a little bit. That was why she'd picked this particular trail. It split into three different options at the top, one of which had some really fun features. It started with hillocks for catching air, followed by a rollercoaster section of banks flowing into each other, and the bottom half had some wooden bridges. The whole thing felt more demanding than it really was and charged her full of adrenaline.

Emma unclipped her helmet and retightened her ponytail. Her hair was ridiculously thick, and she should have spent the time to braid it, but just hadn't, so it tended to droop out of its holder. She clipped her helmet back into place as the last two riders from the group pedaled past.

With a group like that, Emma wasn't surprised that the very last rider came along as the safety sweeper. Probably, the tail man could be judged as the best of the lot, considering he had to know the trail system and be able to assist anyone who developed an issue.

The penultimate rider huffed and puffed, red-faced and sweaty, and looking very displeased with his situation. He was not a chiseled figure like the earlier riders. His tummy looked soft, and his hands were pudgy. The last rider easily pedaled behind him, shouting encouragement in rude, hilarious segments.

"Drink less beer," the man suggested. "I highly recommend more planking as a way to develop core muscles, slowpoke."

The red-faced straggler groaned and looked as if he would have spat back a reply if he'd had enough oxygen to do more than grunt.

"Don't give up. If you don't stop, I won't have to tell the others that you quit. Suck it up, beer gut. You only get one shot at this hill." He winked at Emma as they rode past. "Mademoiselle," he said, obviously recognizing her bike brand. "Lovely of you to encourage us to the top with your presence."

As a reply Emma demonstrably squeezed the brake levers and lifted one shoulder noncommittally.

"We'll be out of your way as soon as we stop loitering." He aimed the last part of his comment at the distressed man in front of him, and then performed a stylish hop with his bike over a small rock in the path.

The sweaty mess had finally crested through the flat area and started downhill, but Emma could still hear his tortuous breathing as he coasted.

"Shift your weight back!" The better rider advised. "Feather the brakes! Break with your right hand first. Remember, right for rear! If you use your left, you're gonna go ass over handlebars!"

Emma shook her head. The rest of the group had chosen the most difficult single track to get down, and the inexperienced rider had gone right after them. She really hoped they wouldn't be scooping him off the trail with a spatula. It was full of steep descents, quick twists, and skinny cutaways.

As they pedaled off, Emma could see a snake tattoo coiled around the lower leg of the better rider. The snake grew thinner as it reached around the man's calf toward his ankle, but his sock obscured the snake's mouth from view. Emma wondered if the snake was about to bite the man, or if it was casually flicking its tongue out to taste the air. Emma felt a pang of regret that she'd never know the answer.

When the two men were gone from view, Emma

pushed off on her bike and clipped back in. She steered to the fun trail and started to coast down, feathering her brakes as needed. She kept her speed down on the rollers, not wanting to catch actual air while she was alone, and swooped through the banking turns.

The ride was so much fun that, when she was done, she continued to pedal up the circuit and did the whole thing all over again. Then she texted her sister she was safe and went home to settle into her ordinary routine for another week.

She didn't get to ride again on the next Saturday since she had to run errands and meet up with some friends who enjoyed cocktails more than bike trails, but on Sunday, the weather turned cool and sunny. Riding would be perfect.

Once again, Aliza texted that she couldn't make it, but at least, this time, she'd had the grace to do it before Emma even left home. Emma rode solo once again.

She texted her sister and informed her of the situation. Her sister texted back with a raised eyebrow face and the advice to, "Find better friends". Emma snorted and texted back a shrugging woman, but she couldn't disagree. Next week, she would skip inviting Aliza and send out some feelers to Neela and Jeannie. Neela had a toddler, so she wasn't often available, but Jeannie could be more reliable, if she wasn't already promised to some other activity. Jeannie did more softball, kickball, volleyball, and insert-ball-here leagues than anyone Emma knew. It kept her very social and very tied up.

Emma started in on the trail, shifting her bike into an easier gear for the uphill climb. She thought fondly of the last week's fun trail and decided to give it a go before turning her attentions to something else. Her legs felt fresh and powerful as she steadily ascended.

She reached the top in record time and began the downhill coast. Everything seemed dialed in, and the sensation of loping over the hillocks became too irresistible. Emma eased up on the brakes, letting her bike gain momentum. When the hillocks turned to banks, Emma still felt in control. She didn't slow down as she took the banks at their upper reaches before driving down again. On the third bank she saw an overturned stone, and the hole it had left behind, a moment too late to steer clear. She could either hit the stone or the gouge. She chose the stone.

"Shit," she said. In a split second of preparation time, she relaxed into an athletic pose and prepared to ride out the bump, but the stone shifted as she hit it, and her bike skittered sideways. She let herself go down with the bike, looking for a landing that seemed the least awful.

Everything happened in a blur. Her left shin and shoulder banged something, and her opposite ankle banged something else, and from nowhere a stick jumped in to tangle up her spokes. Dust flew everywhere.

The thump of the landing stunned her so that she laid there breathless, unable to gasp in any air. She could see a glimpse of blue sky through the trees as she waited for the pain to subside and her ability to breathe to return. Her shoulder and leg started to hurt, and she knew she'd have to investigate those when she could move again to see how badly she'd hurt herself.

A face came into view above her. It was the sweep rider from the previous Saturday. This close up, she could see that his eyes were a lovely dark gray, and the stubble on his chin suggested he would have light brown hair when he removed his bright blue helmet.

"You okay?" he asked.

She nodded her head because she didn't have any air for speaking, but even as she did, she thought perhaps she was already lying. Her instinct was always to brush off an injury. Maybe, this time, she should actually do an evaluation before sending assistance away.

His eyes narrowed. "Stinger?" he asked. "Or are you hurt worse?"

The pressure in Emma's chest eased, and she was able to suck in some air. "Just got the wind knocked out of me," she said, gasping between each word. "But my shoulder. And maybe my ankle...."

She twisted to release her shoes from the pedal clips, and that hurt but not too badly. Dumb. She should have managed the release prior to falling. Then she eased herself away from the bike. The guy removed the stick from the spokes before hefting her bike away. Then he returned, squatting in front of her.

Emma realized they were off to the side of the trail, and she was amazed at how far she'd skidded. That rock had really kicked her ass.

"Let me see." The guy gently touched her knee. "I'm going to help you turn your leg, okay? If it hurts, say so."

He pushed her leg a little and leaned over so he could see the damage.

Emma peered at her leg. A long, red abrasion bloomed across most of her shin, and it was just starting to bleed. But it was her ankle that throbbed the most. She reached down to pull away her sock and was relieved to see everything intact.

"It's going to be a really nasty bruise, I think," she said. She wiggled her foot. It didn't feel strained or sprained. It felt like it had gotten whacked with a rock.

"How about the shoulder?" he asked.

She thought about it and carefully moved her arm. Nothing felt torn or broken. "More bruises, I think."

"Can you stand?" the biker asked.

"Probably." Emma slowly got to her feet. She ached, and her ankle throbbed, but she was mainly okay. "I think I'm done riding today."

The guy laughed. "Good choice. I've taken falls like this and stupidly gone on riding. I paid for it later, that's for sure." His face pinched as he looked at her. "You got lucky. Your helmet is toast."

Emma unclicked her chin strap. She didn't remember hitting her head when she went down. But when she looked at her helmet, sure enough, a huge crack had appeared through the shell. "And that's why I wear a helmet." She'd seen super-machismo bikers sporting bare heads, declaring they liked the breeze or whatever nonsense they spouted to convince themselves they could go without the safety gear, but Emma knew better. Helmets did their jobs and saved skulls.

She added, "I'm going to need a new helmet before I ride again."

"Yeah, for sure." He picked up her bike and wheeled it over to her. "Can you walk down with it, or do you want me to take it down for you?"

Emma considered that seriously for a long moment. Her shoulder and ankle throbbed, and the scrape along her shin felt like a burn. For a moment, she really did want him to take care of her bike. Take care of her, somehow, because the prospect of walking out on her own seemed far too daunting. But if he took her bike, he'd have to leave his behind and come back for it later. It probably wouldn't get stolen. Maybe.

"I can manage," she said.

"I'll follow you down," he said, not even asking for permission to walk with her. "Just to make sure you get to your car. You're at the trailhead...?"

She usually fought off the attentions of some guy suddenly trying to be company, but it seemed really prudent to have someone else with her while she got out of the forest. She was grateful he had checked on her and wasn't now abandoning her. The truth was, she was shaken. Walking down and wheeling her own bike out were probably at the limit of what energy she had left, and his presence meant that, if she failed, someone was there to call for help.

"Yes. Thanks. I appreciate your stopping for me." She looked around. No other riders zoomed past or waited above or below. "Where's your group?"

The guy picked up his own bike, which he'd stashed farther off trail. "No group today. Last week was a special ride with a fitness group I'm part of. Mostly, I ride on my own."

"Me, too," Emma admitted. Her brain seemed to turn over as she remembered that she didn't know his name and he didn't know hers. "I'm Emma, by the way."

"Danny. Nice to meet you. Too bad about the circumstances."

"Did you see me fall?" Emma asked.

"Oh, yeah." Danny moved his hand to imitate a dive-bomb. "You were flying! And then you were falling. Spectacularly."

"There was a rock and a hole." Emma felt like she needed to defend herself. She wasn't such a terrible rider that she'd have fallen for no good reason.

"I saw that. You should have just jumped it," he said it insouciantly, like everyone had the skill set to hop over rocks in their path while speeding down the hill. She'd seen his skills last week. He was really good. Apparently, he was also really dense and up his own ass, if he thought everyone could just do what he did, with ease.

"Next time," Emma muttered, "I will." She thought maybe she should find the rock and lob it at his head.

"I'm impressed you could take a fall like that and get up again. I thought for sure I'd be calling an ambulance for you. Guess you're tougher than you look."

Emma narrowed her eyes at him. That was a back-handed compliment if ever she'd heard one, and she had no idea how to reply. She wanted to like this guy, he was helping her, but he kept running off at the mouth.

For a brief moment, Danny looked thoughtful. "Should probably do something about that rock." He wheeled his bike over to the spot. "Too big to try to place it back." Three solid shoves moved the rock to the side and several stomps of his heel caved in the edges of the hole until it filled with dirt. Then he looked at her. "Ready? You, first; I'll follow you down."

They'd gone barely ten feet when the whoop of riders coming along the path warned them to pull over to one side. Four men on bikes zoomed past, each one rolling directly over the spot where the rock and the hole had taken out Emma. Behind them ran a rangy dog, its tongue flopping out of its mouth as it bounded after its people.

"Good thing I fixed that," Danny said.

"Too bad they didn't go through first," Emma said.

Danny laughed.

Wending her way down the path wasn't difficult, but it was slow going. Danny called out to check on her twice, but talking back and forth was too awkward along the skinny trail so they settled into silence. Several more packs of riders spun past them, oblivious to the danger that had been fixed before their descent. Danny followed her all the way to the trailhead where Emma's parked car waited.

"Nice rack," Danny commented.

Emma opened her mouth to admonish him, but Danny had already grabbed her bike and smoothly hoisted it onto the bike rack jutting from the rear of her car. "Thank you," she ground out, "it was a gift I gave myself when I got interested in mountain biking."

"Cool," said Danny. "When was that?"

"End of last summer."

"Really?" He looked surprised. "You must be a natural. You look like you've been doing it longer."

The compliment caught Emma off guard. She'd started to get used to his stabbing way of being pleasantly mean. "Thanks. How about you? You seem really comfortable on a bike."

"Years," he said. "Got into it when I was a teenager and realized I loved it. Now, do you have a kit, or do you want me to get mine?"

"Kit?" Emma asked.

"For your abrasion. We can wash off the dirt and get a little antibiotic ointment on there. Make sure it doesn't turn into anything nasty. I've got one in my truck." He strode over to a black truck. The truck beeped when he unlocked it, and he pulled out a bag with a green and white plus sign on the side. Then he pulled down his tailgate. "Sit here, and I'll tend to your wounds."

Emma hitched herself up on the tailgate and examined her leg again. The scratches raised up like angry claw marks, but her ankle wasn't too swollen. It only looked a little puffy where contact had been made, and Emma expected the bruise to be spectacular. It didn't feel great, but she was grateful she hadn't hurt it any worse.

Danny tended to her leg, cleaning the area with water from a jug he had in the truck, and then salving on ointment. "They aren't really bleeding, so I don't think you need a bandage. You'll have some terrible scabs, though."

"Thanks," she said, giving it a full dose of sarcasm.

"Badge of honor," he replied and turned his forearm so she could see faded white lines crisscross near his elbow. "I hit a rock. Wrecked up my elbow and got two pins and an entire lost summer for my trouble. You're in good company."

For the first time, Emma smiled at him and really meant it.

He smiled back, and his entire face took on a different cast. He seemed suddenly much more handsome than he had a minute ago. "You're in the club. Hard core mountain biking is not for the faint of heart."

"Thanks," she said, and this time in earnest. Not a hint of sarcasm to be found.

"You know, I've seen you here twice and never with anyone. Do you always ride alone?"

She shrugged. "My friends keep canceling on me. This is a weekend hobby for them, so they don't think it's super important."

His eyebrows went up. "Seriously? My friends bagged on me today, too. What say we do some riding together?"

"I'd never be able to keep up with you," Emma said. She had no illusions about their different skill levels.

He laughed. "That's true. But riding the gnarliest trails all by myself isn't half so nice as when I have someone with me. And I'd rather ride with you than watch you ride alone."

It was such a romantically delivered proposal, even if the proposal itself could have used some work, that Emma leaned forward and grabbed two fistfuls of his shirt. Danny looked delighted and leaned in as she pulled him forward. They kissed over her aching ankle. The angle was awkward, and he smelled like bike grease and dirt, but when his lips touched hers, Emma felt a jolt of adrenaline, similar to when she conquered a particularly difficult trail section, and paused afterwards to admire her achievement and to shake with relief.

Danny was a challenge, and like that difficult trail, the effort would be worth the glory. She could tell.

"So, next Saturday?" Emma asked when she released him.

"Absolutely." Danny pulled his cell phone from his pocket, brought it to life, and handed it over. "Share your digits, and we can text until then."

Emma tapped in her information and returned the phone. Then she hopped down from the tailgate, checked that her bike was secure, and started to change into regular sneakers.

Danny threw a leg over his bike and gave her a salute as he headed back to the trail system. "See you soon!" He fish-tailed the rear wheel on purpose and sent up a cloud of dust before dashing away.

Emma coughed as the dust drifted over to her. *And he's back to being arrogant*, she thought. He'd made her heart race, and she'd liked that, but she hoped he wouldn't turn out to be mostly jerk.

The next Saturday, Emma waited at the trailhead. The sun had been up long enough to burn away the dew, but the air remained crisp. Two carloads of other riders had parked, prepped, and ridden off while she'd waited. She checked her phone again. No text message.

At least her girlfriends had had the decency to cancel with enough time for Emma to adequately alter her plans. Of course, she and Danny had been texting throughout the week about this ride, so Emma felt fairly confidant he wasn't bagging on her, just being annoying.

Not quite twenty minutes late, Emma finally saw Danny's truck in the distance. He pulled in three spots away, because there was no longer a free space next to Emma's car.

"Traffic," he said and gave her grin.

"As if," Emma said right back to him.

"Okay, okay. I have bad time management skills. So, sue me." Danny pulled his bike from the back of his truck.

"We'll find a way for you to make it up to me," Emma said.

Danny kept on grinning. "Oh, I can make it up to you."

Emma snorted and mounted her bike. "Let's go."

They rode for an hour, and Emma found that, once on the trail, Danny was more astute and considerate. He made sure to keep space between them, shouted encouragement as needed, and seemed agreeable to choosing exhilarating trails that were moderate enough for Emma's skill level.

At the start of a downhill, Danny stopped and waited for Emma to catch up. "Not too tired?"

"I wouldn't be upset if this was the last run." Emma panted out the words. She'd sucked down most of her water, and then sweated it out. Her ankle with the injury from last week had finally given the faintest warning twinge.

"Then let's get out of here. Last one to the bottom gets to be on top." He laughed recklessly then scooted forward. "Nobody loses that bet!" he called as he sailed down the trail.

Emma shoved her bike forward. She was far too tired to catch him, and she wasn't sure she cared to win the bet anyway.

The trailhead was full of people and cars when they careened down. Two drivers' eyes lit up at the prospect of snagging parking. Emma and Danny ironed out that she would go to his place, then loaded their bikes, and squeezed past the waiting vehicles trying to find a spot.

She followed him to his apartment, which was ten minutes away. His place was sparse, but well put together in an ascetic way. One couch, a coffee table, a large screen television, and an actual living potted plant. A terrarium with a warming light and a big rock rested on a stand against one wall, but she couldn't see what he kept in there. The dishes were drying in the rack and not piled in the sink. Also, a black-and-white cat with amber eyes looked super comfortable in its cat basket. It uncurled when they entered and came to the door for a greeting.

"This is Bracket. She's a good kitty." Danny rubbed her ears. She blinked at him, politely sniffed Emma's shoe, and slowly rolled away again, back to her bed.

"She's adorable," Emma said and turned back to see his face crease into a devil-may-care look.

"Have you hurt your ankle terribly?" he asked and scooped his arms around her.

Emma gave an oomph of surprise as her feet left the floor and Danny cradled her in his arms.

"I wanted to be able to do this last week," he told her as he carried her toward the bedroom. "But you were actually injured, and it seemed like a bad idea. Plus, it was only our second date."

"Second date?" Emma raised her eyebrows. She would have considered today their actual first date. Well, maybe one and a half dates. Men counted things differently. And wrongly.

"Technically, we'd seen each other the previous Saturday when I rode past you. First date." He pushed the door open with his foot and set her down gently on the bed. "If you'll have me, I would love to worship your body." He pulled open a drawer next to his bed.

Emma looked in. There was a box with condoms and other accoutrements.

"Fully stocked for your pleasure and mine."

"By all means," Emma said, "let's get on with the pleasure. You owe me at least fifteen minutes since you were late this morning." She laughed. "And I won the bet." Danny had strangely gotten himself stuck on a tree root on their last ride down until Emma had passed him, and then suddenly he'd been able to free himself and ride behind her all the rest of the way. Highly suspicious.

"That's right," he said. "Bad luck on my part, getting stuck like that." His fingers danced up the inside of her legs. "Time to get naked?"

"You first," Emma said.

He peeled off his shirt, exposing his chest, and Emma could see the accumulation of many mountain biking hours. Muscles bunched at his shoulders and corded in his forearms. Danny's biceps pushed up like mountains when he flexed to pull off his pants. His torso trimmed down into his waist. His butt was an artistic testament to pumping up steep trails. He pushed each sock off with the toes of the opposite foot, and Emma dragged her attention down to his thighs. She caught sight again of the snake tattoo. It started high up on his thigh, the tail of the snake in his groin before flowing and curling all around his leg to bite at his ankle. A little mystery solved. From what she could see, and now she could see everything else in all its promising glory, there wasn't another tattoo on him.

She traced one finger along his calf while he plucked at her socks.

"This is amazing art," she said. "Why did you choose this?"

He cupped his hands around her breasts through her clothes, just warming and holding her. Except for her now discarded socks, she still had on all her clothes, and he was entirely naked.

"Accidentally stepped on a snake and got bit when I was a kid. Scariest thing I remember ever going through."

"A venomous snake?" Emma asked.

"We believe it was a copperhead. And it was a dry bite. Which means, I didn't get any venom, or a really little amount, anyway. Which was incredibly lucky. Still hurt. The whole thing sucked, really." He glanced down to his own leg. "But I swear, I had one of those fever dreams that kids sometimes get, and I felt like that snake sparing me meant something. I've been interested in snakes ever since. When I got older, I got this tattoo." He rubbed the length of his body against hers. "Why are we talking about snakes? Why are we talking about anything other than you telling me what you like and what makes you feel good?"

"Oh," said Emma, losing concentration for a reply. His body against hers felt amazing. A flood of warmth and the enticing promise of possibilities raced through her, tightening some parts of her and making other parts feel incredibly loose. "Ah," she said, again struggling to form words. With one hand massaging her breast in a slow, sinuous way, his other hand had circumnavigated the layers of her shorts and underwear and was mirroring that mesmerizing movement.

"That's a good start," he said. "Now, tell me exactly what you'd like the most."

Everything after that was a complete haze of lust and satisfaction. Emma found her words and they tumbled out of her. Danny followed and expanded on everything. As he stroked her, the pressure built within her core. She kept that energy sequestered, letting it grow and grow, but some of it leaked out through her voice. Her words slurred together and merged until she spoke a language all of her own making. All of it urging. All of it demanding. Incredibly, Danny seemed to fathom her desperate utterings because he kept touching her, kept moving in unison with her.

She could feel the effort in his lovemaking. His skin became slick with sweat, the sliding stickiness of it apparent when their bodies moved together and then apart, and still he persevered. His rhythm remained as steady and sure as a constant pedaling up a steep mountainside. That great reserve of athleticism from biking was now all being spent for her, depleted for her benefit.

She writhed with the sensation of the pent-up energy building. Energy that had to go somewhere. She was nearly bursting, and it could not be contained forever.

The bed squeaked and creaked beneath them as they moved and Danny grunted, echoing her nonsense language from before. The bed complained repeatedly and vociferously. Emma absorbed the building pressure until finally it escaped in a rush, cascading across her every fiber.

For a few moments longer Danny kept moving, still on those final last revolutions before he reached the top of his own, personal mountain. The whoosh of air from his lungs told her he'd succeeded.

Emma popped open one eye to check her partner and watched as a look of rapture spread across his features, and Emma felt assured that it wasn't just her own satiety that had been reached.

After a few moments of awkward cleanup and attention to mundane details, Emma snuggled in against Danny. It seemed like a long languorous time that they rested there. The afternoon sun glowed golden against the shades in the windows. Her stomach rumbled.

"We haven't eaten yet, have we?" Danny stretched and checked the time. "Hours until sunset. How about we go out for some food, and then head back to the trail? Get another tour in…?"

Emma raised her eyebrows. "Back to the trail, and then back to here?"

His gaze locked with hers. "I can't think of anything better, can you?"

Emma thought briefly about her girlfriends, who she would probably not be counting on for trail companionship anymore. She'd exchanged their no-shows for a guy who wanted to go at least twice a day, and if she could manage to keep up, it was all going to be fantastic.

"Nope, I can't think of anything better," she said and meant it.

THE $5.00 KISS OF LIFE

BY MICHAL SCOTT

oose lips sink ships, Bev. Now it's 1946, and they still do.

Beverly Reynolds understood a big city investigative reporter like her brother John had to suspect everyone and everything. His work had him engaged in many a dangerous situation. The latest was reporting on equal rights work in the South.

He had written to her about the war being waged in states from Virginia to Mississippi.

Loose lips sunk ships during the war, Bev. And still do. Only now, the ships are voter registration drives and lawsuits and attempts at economic self-sufficiency. It's not Nazi spies listening and betraying, but law enforcement officers who first tip-off Klansmen, and other night riding types, then stand by as they target the Negro lawyers, teachers, and ministers who educate and encourage the folk of color to claim their rights. It's not Tokyo Rose undermining Negro pride and confidence, but those among our own people who choose the safety of their present limitations to the risks of a future determined by the freedom of true independence. Loose lips sink ships, Bev...and they still do.

You'd expect the ones oppressing you to do all they could to keep you down. But for members of the race to sow envy and fear and suspicion, so as to undermine efforts to uplift the race, was most distressing.

And most familiar.

Where she lived, a good reputation was the battleship in need of protection. To keep it afloat, peer pressure, tradition, and societal expectation waged a constant battle against the loose lips of gossip and scorn and lies.

As the daughter of the town's minister, she'd experienced the looks and the whispers and the dressing downs that kept her in her place. The freedom garnered by her one small rebellion—becoming the town librarian rather than the dutiful wife of her father's associate pastor—had turned out to be as limiting as the choice she'd rejected.

Around her, children screamed with delight as they won at games of chance in Vernon's annual winter carnival and craft fair—the first fete her small upstate New York Black community had been able to enjoy, now that they were free of the restrictions and rationings they'd had to endure during the war. She should be smiling. She would be smiling, except for the letter she'd received from John almost a month ago.

Damn, Beverly. You'd think from the attitudes of Blacks and Whites alike down here we'd just fought the Civil War, not a world war. Reporting on the work of the NAACP is as hazardous as any battlefield I served on in Europe. Not a day goes by without someone going missing or being found dead. The resentment of the White community and the fear of the Black makes me despair there'll ever be racial equality in the US. Keep me and these folk in your prayers. Give dad a hug for me. Hope to see you soon.

Since then, no one had word from him.

"This isn't the longest we haven't heard from him," her father cautioned. "He's used many an unorthodox approach to get information for his stories in the past."

Beverly prayed every day her father was right. She pushed her concerns away and distracted herself with preparing for the library's Christmas giveaway booth at the carnival.

Even in his letters from the Army, John had stated over and over he'd take the danger of combat over the safety of civilian life in Vernon. He wanted to live before he died. Her younger brother had come back but soon left Vernon, choosing the risk of striking out on his own to retain the independence he'd tasted in the military.

She yearned for that same independence but settled for safety then and now. Admiration for John's choice warred with an equal amount of dread every time she read his articles and received his letters. Now as she helped restock the baskets and shelves, her unease returned. Was John all right?

She handed a copy of *The Wonderful Year* to a grateful parent then turned to her library assistant. "Lydia, I'm going for a walk. I'll relieve you in an hour."

"Don't rush," Lydia answered. "Your hard work has made our booth one of the most popular around. You deserve to take as much time as you want. As a matter of fact…why don't you check this out?" She pressed a business card into Beverly's hand. "Go have some fun."

Beverly blanched at the words on the card.

$5.00 and this card will get you a 10-second what-you-will kiss of your life from Firefighter Rob Williams.

"Where did you get this?" Beverly asked, her eyes wide.

"From a friend of a friend…" Lydia laughed and waggled her eyebrows à la Groucho. "Of a very good friend."

Beverly stared at the card, her spirit doing a little secret dance. She'd be a liar if she denied she'd never fantasized about a Rob Williams kiss.

Even in 1946, after all the changes wrought by a world war, reputations in small Black communities like Vernon, deserved or not, never died. In the church circles Beverly lived and moved, there was still contempt for being from the wrong side of the tracks; and even more, for being born on the wrong side of the blanket. Both applied to Rob. Never mind that he had served his country with honor in a medical unit or how, now, his willingness to be among the first to respond in any number of community calls for help proved him to be a credit to the race. The adjectives of his youth still followed him.

Promiscuous.

Rebellious.

Insubordinate.

Arrogant.

To her way of thinking, those very adjectives made

him the perfect mentor for many a troubled young person in Vernon. And each time Rob had confirmed he was just that: perfect. But while she had the courage to thank him for helping troubled youth, that courage didn't extend to being seen with him socially. Preachers' kids, like her, carried reputations deserved and undeserved, too. Reputations they couldn't escape, even as adults. John had escaped by leaving Vernon and reporting news stories on the NAACP and the Civil Rights struggles in the South for the Amsterdam News in Harlem. She'd stayed upstate in Vernon, resigned to her role as the respectful spinster preacher's daughter.

"I dare you," Lydia challenged.

Beverly shook her head but didn't hand back the card. She shoved it into her skirt pocket then walked off. A half hour of meandering through the crowds filling the small town's downtown park decorated with candy canes and black Santas and red-nosed Rudolphs and breathing in the happy scents of cotton candy and corn dogs, she hadn't escaped the dread engendered by her brother's disappearance.

She shuddered and closed her eyes. Her brother's voice, full of bravado and good-natured chiding, surfaced in her thoughts.

Remember what it says in Matthew: Which of you by taking thought can add one cubit unto his stature? Answer: No one. So, stop worrying. Worry lines don't suit you. You know my bottom line. The unexamined life isn't worth living, Bev.

But was the examined life worth dying for?

She sighed and opened her eyes. Loudspeakers

placed on lampposts around the park filled the air with the fun-filled song "Let it Snow! Let it Snow! Let it Snow!" Beverly buttoned the top button on her sweater, grateful the song was the only sign of snow in a surprisingly warm December. She looked around at all the fun going on.

She firmed her lips and gave herself a gentle chiding. "Think positive, Beverly. Find something in all of this holiday cheer to rescue you from your worrying."

She reached into her pocket, withdrew Lydia's card, and read its invitation again.

$5.00 and this card will get you a 10-second what-you-will kiss of life from Firefighter Rob Williams.

Well, no one could find fault with her if she did. After all it was for a worthy cause.

She headed toward the First Baptist's Kiss for A Cause booth and Rob Williams' lips.

FIREFIGHTER ROB WILLIAMS glanced at the kissing booth's fee chart and smiled.

1 second shy – $0.50

3 second air-kiss chaste – $0.75

5 second pucker up – $1.00

He'd laughed when Reverend Reynolds had approached him with the idea.

What better way to take the tarnish off your bad boy image than volunteering to pucker up for a good cause?

Rob couldn't disagree. Plus, he liked the irony of being someone whose job often had him administering the "kiss of life" to now offering kisses that had nothing to do with resuscitation.

All proceeds from the Kiss for A Cause booth would be split equally between First Baptist's Women's Stork's Next ministry for impoverished mothers and their newborns and the Sunday Soup Kitchen. Both he and Emily Tyson, the wife of another firefighter, had agreed to work the booth. They also had a side bet going as to whose kisses would raise the most money. On the sly, Rob had had members of the firehouse secretly pass out cards with a level of kiss the church would never promote. What Reverend Reynolds and the church didn't know wouldn't hurt them.

Young and old, male and female, plopped their coins in the jar. Smiles, winks, and all-around laughter accompanied each of the lower level pecks and lip locks for which Emily was in the lead.

No one had yet presented him with the "10-second kiss card."

"My lips need a rest," Emily declared. She waved to her husband. "I'm taking a break, Rob."

Rob gestured her on her way. "Never fear. My lips will be here."

Up ahead, he caught sight of Beverly Reynolds, standing off to one side and looking at him as she fingered a small piece of paper. He stared at her, pleasantly surprised and secretly aroused that the minister's daughter might be his first $5.00 kiss.

He'd admired the way she used the library to help teens express themselves in non-destructive ways. One would never know she was shy by the way she took on town council members and their reform school mentality, a mentality he'd come up against often enough as a kid. A number of boys and girls had found a place to belong and contribute because she'd gotten the council to offer community service instead of juvenile detention for wayward behavior. Even more, he appreciated how Beverly trusted him to mentor several youths despite the rumors of his well-deserved reputation.

But that was as far as her trust went. Any attempt on his part to express his gratitude through a possible date had been met with a smile and a chiding wag of a finger.

"I'm too square for you, Rob."

He'd only smiled, his mind on the numerous upright uptight "square" women of First Baptist, who'd let him round off their edges when no one was looking.

He sucked in a breath at the sight of her perfect white teeth gnawing her lower lip, shuddered at the possibility gleaming in the gaze she shot his way. He shifted right then left to ease the bulge between his legs.

Aw, come on, Beverly, he thought to himself. *You know you want to.*

LORD HAVE MERCY, when had she become such a coward? It was just a kiss, for goodness sake. And in the name of a good cause. It would be fun. Besides, she didn't have to present him with the card. She could just as easily pick one of the official kisses she'd written for her father on the Kiss for A Cause booth's sign.

Beverly firmed her lips, took a deep breath, and stepped up to the booth.

"Come to pucker up for a good cause, Beverly?"

The mischievous glint in Rob's smile and equally mischievous lilt in his tone did nothing to still the throb between her legs.

"You're a good sport to do this," she said. "Given the way people talk about you and all."

Rob chuckled. "Hey, if a bad reputation can't do a good turn once in a while, what's the point of having it?"

"You saved lives in the war. You've saved lives here in town. It's time you make people acknowledge that for a change."

"Pigs'll sprout wings and fly before that happens." Rob snorted. "Let them think what they want. I've lived with too much space around me to be hemmed in by their small minds."

Beverly sighed. "I've always admired that about you, Rob. You don't care what people say about you."

He waved that off. "Sure, I care. I'm just very good at handling the slights."

"No, really," she insisted. "You don't seek anyone's approval. You live by what you're for, not what you're against." She looked at the rates on the booth kissing chart, and then considered the card in her pocket. "I admire you." She cast her gaze down. "I wish I were more courageous, like you."

"No time like the present," he teased.

Beverly looked up and saw him thumb toward the kissing rate chart.

"Do you have the courage to be seen getting a kiss before God and everybody from the town bad boy?"

His cheeky tone stirred amusement in her troubled breast. "I have been toying with buying one or more of these kisses," she said.

"So, what'll be? One of these on the chart?" Rob leaned forward, an eyebrow raised, his manner sly. "Or the one on that card in your pocket?"

A LOVELY RED blush flushed across Beverly's face. Even her dark skin couldn't hide the glow of embarrassment.

"Hello, Beverly."

"Hi, Miss Reynolds."

Rob watched Beverly blanch and then acknowledge each greeting with a nod or a smile. Several other people stood away from the booth but milled around within earshot. The stiffening of her body proved she'd suddenly become aware gazes were on her.

And on her reputation.

Her hand fisted around the card in her pocket. Her face took on a wary, thoughtful expression. Once again, those perfect teeth captured her quivering lower lip. What would those teeth feel like nipping on his anatomy? He huffed out a breath to tamp down the pulsing in his cock.

Rob sucked in a deep breath. Whatever courage had brought her to the booth for a kiss was slipping away, as was his chance to taste this shy, desirable woman.

However much she might think she lacked courage, he knew her well enough to know she wouldn't back down from a challenge.

"You're right to hesitate." Rob stepped back and

crossed his arms. "Perhaps a $5 what-you-will kiss of your life wouldn't be a good place to start."

Her eyes sparked with indignation. She withdrew the card, laid it down on the booth's table, then placed a five-dollar bill beside it.

MORE THAN A CARD and a five-dollar bill lay on the table. Her goody-goody reputation lay there, too.

Quite a few of the people who had greeted her, and now lingered at nearby booths, numbered among her father's congregants. The more senior of them had watched her and her brother grow up. More times than she could count, she'd allowed the approval or possible censure of these people direct her actions.

Around her, astonished murmurings flitted through her hearing.

"She gave him five dollars!"

"She paid for five dollar's-worth of kissing?" A whistle rent the air. "That's a whole lot of smooching."

Out of the corner of her eye, Beverly caught expressions of surprise on the faces of women her age, scorn on those of the older ones, amusement on the faces of the men her age, and envy on those of the older men.

Heat rose up her neck as she waited to see what Rob would do next.

He placed her five-dollar bill into the jar then crooked a finger, beckoning her closer.

Beverly squared her shoulders and leaned in. He placed his hands palms down on the narrow table separating them.

"What-you-will means you're in charge of the kiss, Beverly," he said. "It's up to you to make it what you want it to be."

She blinked, her mouth gaping in an O of surprise.

I'm in charge.

She was in charge to choose between the danger of losing her goody-goody dutiful pastor's daughter reputation or the danger of losing a chance to be who she'd always dreamed but never dared to be. In this kiss lay the freedom she envied John for, the freedom she admired Rob for, the freedom she told herself she longed for.

Slowly, quietly, she moved closer, cupped his face, then pulled his mouth to hers. He responded in kind. Despite the table separating them, he was able to reach around and press his palms against her back, securing her to him. She shifted so neither of them had to lean forward too far.

The press of her lips to his was careful but full of impatience. A moan from him signaled he was as excited as she was. The sound sent a jolt of delight throughout her body. Her nipples tightened and strained against her blouse. Her stomach muscles fluttered, and the beat of her heart matched the throb between her legs.

He moaned again.

Like a cape waved before a bull, the sound sent her charging ahead.

Her tongue lined the seam between his lips until they parted, and she slipped her tongue into his mouth.

She hummed at the delicious pressure of his lips, at

the teasing tussle of his tongue with hers. Their tongues danced in time to the growing swirl of arousal. Joy rose at what she happily realized was a shared eagerness to explore and be explored.

Moments ago, she'd been dying under the possible opprobrium of the onlookers who attended her church. Now, she was dying with delight.

The examined life was indeed worth dying for.

Somewhere a ding pierced her consciousness. The pressure on her mouth lessened. She blinked, confused a little, disappointed a lot. He had pulled back and was now studying her with a mischievous smile.

"My ten seconds is up?" she asked.

"Yep." He nodded and pointed to the little white chicken-shaped egg timer.

He pulled a five-dollar bill out of his pocket and put it in the jar.

"My turn," he cooed, moving his pursed lips toward hers. "Pucker up."

She did as he ordered. Once more, his tongue pushed past her lips. This time, a quick burst of air followed, puffing her cheeks, pushing its way down her throat. Surprised, she laughed, opening her mouth and being rewarded with several more spurts of air.

What on earth was he doing? She couldn't figure it out, but she didn't care. It was fun.

He angled his head right. She angled hers left. He angled left. She angled right. Right, left, left, right. The blowing intensified until she couldn't take it any longer, pulled away, and laughed until she cried.

"What—?" She gasped and took a deep breath. "What was that?"

"The kiss of life." He winked. "Surely you didn't expect anything less from someone who has had to administer the kiss of life as part of his job."

She feathered her fingers over her still-tingling lips. "If I'm ever in need of artificial respiration I hope you'll be the one providing the life-giving kisses."

He laughed. "Me, too."

Someone cleared a throat. Both she and Rob looked to their right and laughed. A line of twenty women had formed, each waving five-dollar bills in his direction.

She looked at him. He shrugged.

"It is for a good cause." He leaned in so his mouth graced her ear. "But I'd love a chance to make you my personal cause. Maybe later tonight?"

She turned so her breath tickled his ear. "You know where I live."

Head high and spirit soaring, she strode through a clutch of church mothers, glaring and tsk-tsking in her wake. The rest of her time she spent behind the library's giveaway booth literally flew. Not a few disapproving matrons turned their noses up as they passed by.

"What's that all about?" Lydia asked.

Beverly grinned. "Take five dollars over to the kissing booth and find out for yourself."

Lydia whooped, gave her a big hug, and raced away.

At the close of the carnival, Beverly and Lydia broke down the library's booth and packed the remaining books into Beverly's car.

"You know, you're going to be the talk of the town,"

Lydia warned. "Lots of girls had those $5.00 cards, but by being first, you gave them permission to use it."

Beverly chuckled. "Yep. I'm sure my father's telephone line is already clogged with their complaints about the bad example I set."

She drove home, hoping she had the backbone to explain, but not apologize, when her father confronted her tomorrow. Thank God, she had her own place so she wouldn't have that conversation tonight.

Take therefore no thought for the morrow: for the morrow shall take thought for the things of itself. Sufficient unto the day is the evil thereof.

The scripture pressed a smile into her heart. Tomorrow had its own evils she'd have to deal with.

But so did tonight… evils she anticipated with delight. She focused her thoughts on Rob and what pleasurable wickedness being his personal cause would bring.

She stepped inside her foyer and spied a single letter lying on the floor. Her address in her brother's hand caused her heart to seize. Inside, an article from the Amsterdam News dated last week with John's byline brought tears to her eyes. A three-line note made her laugh.

Best piece I've ever written.

See you and dad for Christmas.

You brave enough to give Harlem a try yet?

She clutched the note to her chest and swiped away a tear.

"Thank you, Lord," she said.

A knock on the door had her giving thanks once

more. Through the door's curtained window, she could see Rob waiting to be let inside.

She didn't keep him waiting long.

"The kissing booth did way more business than we anticipated," he said.

"Do tell?" She tilted her head and smiled. "Hope you made a bundle for First Baptist's charities."

He beamed, his grin almost unbearably handsome. "Two hundred dollars for each." He produced two bottles from behind his back. Sparkling cider in one hand, champagne in the other.

"I didn't know if you drank," he explained. "I don't want to be accused of corrupting you where alcohol is concerned as well."

She laughed and pulled him inside.

"I'm no teetotaler. I'm also not a virgin."

"Whew," Rob sighed. Mock relief bowed in his smile. "Two less sins to confess."

He wrapped his arms around her and swayed in the hug. "I can't tell you how long I've waited for this."

She wrapped her arms around his waist and hugged him just as fiercely. "Possibly as long as I have."

She hurried to the kitchen and collected two champagne flutes. She rejoined him in the foyer, motioned for him to leave the sparkling cider on the hall tree's seat then follow her upstairs. Once inside her bedroom, they set the champagne and the glasses on the nearest nightstand.

She laced her fingers against the back of his head and pulled him backwards toward the bed then down on top of her. She'd lost her virginity to her father's seminary intern when she'd been eighteen in a wham-bam-thank-you-ma'am humping during a youth group camping trip.

She was twenty-five now. There'd be no hurrying or humping tonight. Not if Rob's kiss of life at the carnival was anything to go by. Not if she stayed in charge.

And she would.

The scents of their arousals perfumed the air. She sucked in lungful after lungful, committing their unique odor to memory. Tonight, the urge to hurry would yield to patience and produce genuine satisfaction. Slowly and deliberately, she executed her plan of attack.

Her mouth on his mouth, on his cockhead, on his shaft. She took him to the hilt and made him come, thrilled at his unbridled shout of delight. She gazed at the satisfaction showering up at her from his eyes.

He rolled over so she was now under him where he lavished her with his attention. His mouth on her mouth, on her nipples, on her labia. He licked and nipped and sucked between her legs until her chest was heaving, until her sex was slick with expectancy. He produced a condom and rolled it on with practiced ease. She guided him deep inside her. Her vagina clenched, wet and welcoming, around his penis. Moans of delight and appreciation accompanied each squeeze. Gratitude swelled her chest then zinged her clit. Her shout of "Thank you!" rent the air as her orgasm hit with lightning speed.

She exhaled, sated, her limbs trembling, her mind reeling around those two words.

Thank you.

Her fantasies about sex with Rob paled by comparison to the reality of sex with Rob.

"Thank you," she whispered.

"You're thanking me? God," he gasped. "I was the one on fire. Thanks for putting me out."

She laughed out loud, happier than she'd ever thought possible. "Glad I could come to your rescue as you came to mine."

He blinked, his expression clearly showing he had no idea what she was talking about. "I rescued you?"

How could she explain? She lay her head on his chest and listened to his heart beat, enjoying the rise and fall of his abdomen. Equally, she'd enjoyed what they'd shared, and what she now claimed: freedom from the displeasure of others. Yes, there'd be her father's disapproval as the gossip mill churned. She wouldn't give them the chance to grind for long. Reverend Reynolds would hear the truth from her over his morning coffee tomorrow. The examined life was worth leaving for. She had no doubt she was more than ready to live in Harlem, that glittering mecca of Negro pride and accomplishment in New York City.

And she had this man in her bed to thank for it.

"You really don't know?" she asked, wrapping the used sheath into a tissue and tossing it toward the nearby wastebasket.

"Honestly," he confessed, "I don't."

She grasped his shaft, savoring the sound of his hiss of gratitude. With equal gratitude she snagged the new condom he held in shaky fingers. After a few more strokes, she had him hard again. She covered his penis then took him inside her in one greedy thrust.

"Why," she answered, blessing his lips with hers, determined to remain his personal cause until she left Vernon, "you rescued me with a $5.00 what-you-will kiss of life, of course."

DRIVE

BY M. JAYNE

In the world of the Novus Pack...

I sat my butt down on the top step, looping my arms around my bent legs, and dropped my forehead against my knees. *Decision time.* I'd packed my duffle bag an hour ago. It now rested against the back door, mocking me. During my shower, I'd almost talked myself out of leaving. So what if something so bad had happened at my neighbor's that crime scene tape was still up when I'd gotten home from work? That had nothing to do with me. This identity had been good enough to get a driver's license and work credentials. My stomach started to ache. I had a job and was settled into my rental. I didn't want to run again. *Fuck!*

My enhanced hearing detected a car in my driveway, and within a minute, my doorbell chimed, followed by an aggressive knock. I stood and leaped to the bottom of the stairs. I could see a man flashing a badge through the peephole. *Terrific.*

"Who is it?" My voice sounded a little higher than usual as I spoke through the door.

"Detective Graham Vincent, Perryville Police Department."

I slid back the deadbolt and tried to paste a calm yet curious look on my face. As I pulled the door toward me, his scent filled my nose.

Acting on pure instinct, I used all my strength to try to slam the door in his face even though the wood would not stop a Lycan male, even in human form.

"No, No, No," I screamed as his hands gripped my upper arms and slammed me against the wall. My head connected with the plaster with so much impact that I saw streaks of light.

His body trapped me against the wall. "Who are you?" he rasped.

I struggled against his hold while trying to figure out what was happening. If he was here to kill me, why wasn't I already dead? Was he going to make me suffer first? Was his plan to capture me then send me back to my former pack, the Burkes'? That thought terrified me most.

The male leaned his face close to my neck and inhaled deeply. "Tell me your name." His voice was low and rough.

Suddenly, I wanted to hear him say more. Heat rushed through my veins, as I felt the need to touch and taste this stranger. What was happening? I was no longer fighting. It was more like I was rubbing against him, and it felt…good. He was over six feet and thickly muscled. His body hard where I was soft. His golden hair had a little bit of curl. Insanely, I wondered if it was soft to the touch. What was wrong with me? I was never an aggressive female.

"Your name, Wolf," he demanded in a growl.

"O...Olivia." My name came out as a sigh when his tongue ran along the sensitive skin under my jaw. My body was so aware, my breasts felt heavy and my nipples were so hard that they ached.

"Mmmmm," he hummed, and I realized that his body was hard...everywhere. His penis was pressing against me.

I pulled my head away from him. "Tickles." My giggle was throaty as I studied his face. His sculpted cheekbones were complimented by a strong, stubble-covered jaw.

"Olivia, where did you come from?" His full lips parted to show strong white teeth as he smiled.

Dear Goddess, he was striking.

"Olivia?" He was waiting for my answer. His blue eyes turned hard

"Wha...who?" My hands should have been pushing him away, but instead, they were stroking his firm chest under his suit coat. His body's warmth made me feel comforted which made no sense. This male scrambled my instincts.

"Graham," he leaned in again and as his lips brushed mine, "your mate."

"My what?" I hadn't met any other wolves in this area. "How did you find me. Who sent you?" My voice held a hint of hysteria.

"I was next door working that case when my wolf got curious about this house's owner."

How could this be happening? I called to my wolf. She would know if he spoke the truth.

"What says your wolf?" He flashed another charming smile.

She was resolute, pleased with The Lady's match, as she urged me to taste this male again.

His knowing chuckle was pitched low and made my body pulse with need.

I kissed him back, opening my mouth to him. I needed this. My hands moved upward to loop around his neck to pull him closer. All my concerns about the Burkes' vanished. I only wanted this.

His rough palms were under my shirt, teasing my back and belly. "Arms up."

I reacted without a thought, and my shirt was gone.

His hands cupped my breasts through my bra.

I dropped my head back, so I could take in oxygen. Somehow his shirt was pulled from his slacks, and I could feel his warm skin under my palms. My nails lightly scored the strong muscles along his back.

My bra was ripped from my body, and his mouth covered my aching nipple. His strong pulls made my pussy ache as I rocked against him.

"Oh…Oh, yes." This felt so good.

He plumped my other breast, and then he switched to suck the tip.

My hand moved to the front of his pants, stroking the outline of his cock through the material. The other moved to his belt and started to pull the leather free.

What the hell was I doing? My hands froze as my body went stiff. "Stop," I mumbled, and then more strongly, "We must stop."

He slowly straightened, and our gazes met. He tilted his head to the left silently asking, *Why?*

I didn't know where to start. I felt confused, aroused, and for the first time in over a year, safe. *How could this be happening?*

Ours. My wolf announced with a contented sigh.

"Hello, Mate." He grinned, acknowledging my inner wolf.

"We can't. I mean, you can't...*this* can't be happening." I ducked under his arm and started to pace. "It's not safe for you." I began wringing my hands like an idiot.

He leaned casually against the cracked wall. "Olivia, I think I can take care of myself...and you."

I shook my head, feeling a little out of control. "You don't understand. They will kill you...along with me."

"What?" His dark eyes sharpened, and it was as if his frame grew larger.

"It's true." I ran out of air, and quickly nodded my head.

He held out his hand. "Tell me what's going on."

I took his hand and immediately felt more centered. Leading him to my sofa, we sat side by side. "I'm the one who told Novus...about the Seer."

His eyebrows drew together. "I'm not affiliated with a pack, so I have little to do with the Lycan world."

That caught me off guard. I turned my body toward him. "Really?" Lycans could live on their own, but most chose to live on pack land or nearby. I'd never met a true lone wolf.

"My parents left their packs to mate, so I've never seen the need."

I licked my dry lips as I pondered this information and his phrasing. Lycans, especially older ones, were tricky about word choices. "I was born into the Burke Pack in Texas. Our Leader…he acquired a Marked." I paused to see if he knew what I was talking about.

His eyebrows rose. "One who is touched by The Lady? I thought that was a myth."

"She, Theodora, is a Seer and the Packleader's son he…he almost killed her." Remembering how damaged she'd been, my eyes filled with tears.

"He injured a gift from our Goddess?" His eyebrows drew together as he considered the ramifications. "That's a crime against our species."

"I was…I'm a nurse, and she was alone. What he did was wrong. I called her friend, who was a part of The Novus Pack, and they took her away."

"Does she live?"

"I don't know." I swallowed roughly. "Novus gave me a reward, and I took off." I closed my eyes for a moment. "Their Second, he told me I could come to Novus land for safety."

"But you chose to run." It wasn't a condemnation, more of a statement.

"I was in panic mode. I drove to Little Rock and found a place to stay but soon realized I had no idea what I was doing." I was meant to have a home and a family, to care for others, not to constantly be looking over my shoulder in fear.

"How old *are* you?"

I sat up straighter. "Seventy-one."

One side of his mouth tipped upward. "So young."

"I bought a burner phone and called my father." I had to take in several breaths before I could continue. "I sent half of the money to him, so he could pack up my brothers and sisters and leave."

Graham looked around my living room. "I assume they didn't."

"I turned on the phone once a day to check for an update. There were photos of what…" I had to pause because it hurt to think about. "What they did to my family." I started to sob.

"Oh, baby," he pulled me into his chest and hugged me.

"My fault," I choked out the words.

"No. They should have left." His chest rumbled as he spoke. "You did the right thing, but it put your people in jeopardy."

I pushed back, away from him. "The woman across the street…was it…do you think…they were looking for me?"

He shook his head. "It was her boyfriend."

I used my nose to verify that he was telling the truth. Wolves could sense emotions.

"But you have had a visitor," he said, his voice deepening. "I caught his scent near your front porch."

"What?" I jumped to my feet and tugged on his hand. "You have to go."

He got to his feet slowly. "Olivia, I can handle anything that comes our way."

"They will kill you."

"They can try." He flashed a confident grin, once again showing his teeth.

Graham stood tall and strong, resolute. I wanted to believe him so damn much.

"Assuming the wolf I scented is an assassin, you need to leave this place." He walked into the kitchen.

I followed. "Bag's already packed."

He glanced out the window. "Here's the plan: we go through your backyard, cross through the pond, and keep going to the park. I'll double back to get my car and meet you."

"But…" I started. So much could go wrong.

"Trust me."

I did and more importantly, so did my wolf.

SOMETHING WAS WRONG. Too much time had passed, and Graham hadn't returned. My wolf wanted to go back to the house to check on our mate, but I knew that if he couldn't handle the problem, we didn't have a chance.

Mate. I had a mate, and he was…very determined. I shook my head to clear the memory of how his hard cock had pressed into me. What kind of lover would Graham be? Focused? Demanding? Amazing?

His black sedan pulled into the parking lot.

I ran to it.

Graham leaned across to seat to open the door. "Get in." He now wore a white T-shirt and jeans.

My stomach dropped. "What happened?"

"Got jumped." He drove toward the street.

Giving his body a quick scan, I noted he looked unharmed and I didn't detect the scent of blood. I clamped my lips together so I wouldn't ask any more questions. Some Lycans were dangerous after an adrenaline rush.

He drove over the speed limit but was in control. I got the impression this was his usual style. We traveled to a side of town I was unfamiliar with. He pulled into a driveway, and we paused while the garage door opened.

"My place."

I wasn't sure how to respond to his short sentences. After he shut off the car, I followed him into his kitchen.

"Want a drink?" he asked as he tossed his keys onto the counter.

"What I want is to know what happened." I was proud of myself, my voice sounded calm, not demanding.

He stalked to the stainless refrigerator and returned with two bottles of beer. "Let's sit."

I followed him into a living room that held a huge sofa.

Graham sat at the far end, and I took the cushion next to him.

I yearned to touch him, but I was unsure. What did I really know about this male? Some Lycans were unpredictable as they came down from an adrenaline high.

Trust him, my wolf urged.

He took two long draws then dropped his arm around my shoulders. "It happened fast. He was on me before I knew he was near. He must have used a masking agent for his scent."

"But you survived."

He smirked. "Yeah."

"Was it only one?"

"Only one attacked. He was on me, and then it was over." He finished the bottle.

I waited for more, but he added nothing. "What does that mean?"

"He's dead."

My eyes widened. "So, uh...the evidence?" I had never heard another speak so easily about killing...not that I had experience with those who did.

"I dumped him by the railroad tracks near Jenkins Road."

"I'm sorry." I'd ruined his career and his life.

"I'm not." His scent registered as sincere. "One less to worry about."

I slowly scooted away from him until my back was against the corner of the sofa. "There will be more." I dropped my head back and stared at the ceiling.

He finished the second bottle and placed it on the end table. "Olivia, what you did was courageous, but it made you an enemy of your birth pack."

My eyes burned with unshed tears. "It's okay. I do understand." I felt like I couldn't breathe. "I release you." It wasn't fair for him to be tied to me.

"Not going to happen." He crawled toward me, and

in three moves he was on me. He slid my body down to the cushions so that I was under him. "We'll figure this thing out. I promise."

I wanted that to be true. "But…"

He kissed me. It wasn't gentle. His lips were hard and possessive.

I wrapped my arms around his shoulders as I curled a leg around his muscular thigh.

"Ready?" he asked, his voice low and rough.

"For what?" I loosened my hold because, with him, it could be anything.

"To reward your hero." He pushed up and stood, and then pulled me to my feet.

He led me down the short hallway to his bedroom. Letting go of my hand, he pulled his shirt over his head.

I undressed quickly then stood by the chest of drawers feeling unsure. What if I didn't please him? I was small for a Lycan female. What curves I once possessed were gone, being scared all the time wreaked havoc on my appetite. I'd always worn my dark hair long and kept it pulled back in a braid or a ponytail. Now I wished that I had taken better care of myself. My mother had warned me that once you recognize your mate that the attraction was strong but this was moving fast. We were both acting on hormones stirred with adrenaline. There was no way to slow the physical pull that I felt toward this male. Need clawed at my core, the stories were true, our attraction was imprinted on our DNA.

As he studied my body, I tried not to squirm. I felt

my wolf awaken, and she was aware. "Olivia," he said softly, "I'll try to be gentle."

I moved without thinking. "Don't." I wanted all of him. "No holding back."

He threw me onto the bed and landed next to me, rolling me onto my belly. Hot kisses rained down my back as I tried to get to my knees so that I could turn to touch him.

His body covered mine, pinning me to the bed. "Mine," he growled.

"Yes," I panted as I tried to rub my ass against him. We both could smell my arousal.

His arm encircled my waist and lifted me to my knees.

"Please," I begged as I widened my stance, so I'd have better balance.

His warm palm swept over my ass a moment before I felt the head of his cock at my entrance.

Desperate, I pushed back to meet him.

His hips surged forward, and he filled me.

Overcome by a rush of emotions I couldn't yet identify, I had to catch my chest on my forearms.

His mouth was on my shoulder, and I felt a sting as his teeth broke skin a moment before he growled, "Mine."

"Graham," I moaned. I needed…so much at that moment. I started to squirm under his weight, begging him to fuck me.

He slowly pulled back his hips.

I felt every inch of his cock glide from my body followed the returning pressure as he entered me again.

He did this several times, and it was driving me insane. My nails shredded the sheet under my hands. "Please…I…want…. Mate, I need…"

He snarled, and I felt his teeth again on my skin as his hips moved faster, driving into my body.

I was making almost incomprehensible sounds that were words of urging and satisfied cries. This felt so good. My wolf let out a pleasure-filled howl that rumbled deep in my chest.

He gave me more of his weight as his hands wrapped around mine. Our fingers entwined.

It felt like my body was on fire, and I wondered if I would survive the burn. I wished this to never end. Every muscle tightened in a spasm as I shouted my release.

Graham's deep growl was deafening as he came, his hand tightening on mine.

A few moments later, he pulled out and rolled off.

I turned to face him. My fingers were shaking as I brushed them over his cheeks. I wanted to remember this moment forever. "You are mine, Graham Vincent."

"Glad to hear it." He kissed me, and we began again.

"Mate, you need to eat more." He had cooked for us.

"I haven't had much of an appetite." Fearing for your life will do that to you.

He took my hand and gave it a squeeze. "That will change."

I blushed. This felt nice.

"We should go for a run." He pushed his chair back.

"I think we need to discuss what we are going to do." He would have to give up this life, everything that he'd built to be with me.

"I do my best thinking while I run." He flashed a charming smile I was sure got him his way often. He was difficult to resist.

I needed for him to come up with options because I could think of only one.

"Come, Olivia, let us enjoy the night."

We'd been out for several hours covering miles, playing and enjoying the early hours of the morning. We had crossed his property line when two wolves attacked.

They went after Graham, who managed to bark, "House."

I was torn between running to safety and staying with my mate. I'd never seen a wolf fight like he did. He went for the kill immediately. One attacker was sent flying through the air, and then he turned his attention to the other. The action was so fast that, even with my superior vision, their motions were a blur.

Suddenly, a head flipped into the air, and a cry tore from my throat. I wasn't used to seeing such violence. The other wasted no time leaping onto Graham's back, his jaws tearing into his vulnerable shoulder.

Graham somersaulted his body so quickly, that the wolf was torn free, and my mate was on him. He clawed into his chest, ripping out his heart then tossing it toward me.

I didn't hesitate shifting into my human form, I

stomped on the organ, flattening it into the ground. After I finished my task, I started to move to my mate.

Graham grunted something that sounded like, "Run."

I felt a stinging sensation in my thigh, and then another in my side. Suddenly, I could no longer stand. I tried to crawl toward him. My brain became clouded with pain.

"Shift."

"Wha...?" My head felt heavy as I tried to turn it toward the sound of the voice.

"Olivia, Baby, please, please shift," the voice urged.

I had to use all of my strength to open my eyes. "Graham?" He was in his human form, and I saw fear in his dark eyes. Graham afraid? That didn't make any sense. Nothing scared my brave mate.

"Shift, now."

His command called to my wolf, and I felt the tingle of magic spread throughout my body.

"Thank The Lady..."

His voice seemed very far away.

I WOKE SLOWLY, which was odd for me. Typically, the second I became aware, I was up and ready to face the next crisis. My body felt heavy, and my mouth was very dry.

"Olivia?" Graham said quietly.

"Water," I croaked.

"Be right back."

I rolled over, which seemed to take a great deal of

effort and reached for the side of the bed. I slowly sat up, and the room spun.

"Whoa, hang on." He grasped my upper arm to help balance me.

"That was weird." I blinked several times quickly as I tried to recall what had happened.

"You almost died." He sat beside me.

"I did?" I searched my memory. "What happened?"

He opened the bottle of water for me before answering. "We got back from our run, and they were waiting for us. You were shot six times and almost bled out."

I sipped the water and thought about what he'd said. "You…you fought them." I turned to him as the memories returned. "Are you all right?"

"Except for having the shit scared out of me, I'm fine. I've been in worse fights."

I nodded, storing that information away for a later time. "Where are we?" I didn't recognize this room. It was smaller than his bedroom and shabbier.

"One of my safe houses."

I finished the water. My brain felt slow. He kept safe houses?

"You should eat. I'll make you something."

I needed a shower and a moment to think.

Graham had brought my duffle bag, so I had clean clothes. When I shifted into my human form, I would envision "clothes" and the magic would make sure I was covered, but those clothes were usually very basic. I liked my own things, and specifically, I liked my panties.

I followed my nose down a narrow hall to a kitchen that looked as if it had not been touched since the seventies. Graham was punching the buttons on a rounded pot. "How do you have food?"

"Freezer and an air fryer." He glanced over his shoulder. "You don't look as pale."

"The shower helped." The sluggishness had disappeared. "What's to eat, babe?" The endearment felt natural.

He smiled. "A little of this and a little of that."

I leaned my hip against the counter on the other side of the sink. "Anything sounds good." I was starving.

We'd started with meatballs, which I ate the majority of while he cooked more meat. Next came a turkey breast that was so moist that, if I wasn't so busy shoveling it into my mouth, I would have complimented the chef.

I leaned back in my chair. My stomach was full. "I'm sorry. I didn't mean to be such a pig." I placed my napkin on top of my plate. "I thank you for preparing the meal."

"Olivia, I'm happy to cook for you and to see you eat. In fact, I'm glad that you are still breathing." He reached across the table and rested his hand on top of mine.

"I was no help," I said, dropping gaze. "I'm not much of a fighter."

"I handled the two that attacked. The sniper...well, if I'd had the time, I would have found him." Graham didn't sound angry or disappointed.

I lifted my gaze. "You saved my life."

"I could do nothing less."

What could I do for him? "How did you learn to fight like that?"

"My father worked with me, and then being on my own…there have been a few scuffles."

"I don't think I can ever learn to…to do that." I wouldn't be able to provide back-up.

"I'm sure you have other skills that will be …helpful" He looked resigned as if he had accepted that I was a burden.

My stomach dropped and, suddenly, I felt nauseous. He was going to ask to be released. "Just say what is on your mind." I pulled my hand free.

"I don't know if we can ever be safe."

It was hard to breathe. "You've had time to think about this. What is your decision?" *Please don't say we go our separate ways. I need you.*

"We go where you will be safe."

"What?" My jaw sagged as I tried to understand his decision. "But…" I felt like I might start to cry. He was doing this for me.

"A life filled with constantly looking over my shoulder, worrying about you when I am away…that is no way to live."

"But for me to be safe, I would have to live on Novus land, and they'd probably require you to make promises and take an oath to join their pack." How could he want me? We had been together for two days, and I was making him sacrifice so much.

"Olivia, I will do whatever is needed to keep you safe. You are my life." He took my tightly fisted hand then peeled back each finger to place a kiss in the middle of my palm.

"What if you hate it there?"

"We won't, because we cannot," he said, his tone sure. "It and you are my destiny."

I pushed back my chair then walked around the small table to slide onto his lap. "I am very lucky to have you."

He placed my hand on his cock. "You are going to get lucky."

I giggled like a teenager as I pushed his sweatpants down and stroked his cock. I shimmied out of my jeans and panties, climbed over him, then slowly lowered myself onto his cock.

"You feel so good." He nuzzled my neck.

I rode him, while resting my hands on his thick shoulders. "I've never seen anything like what you did to those wolves."

He lifted his head and looked at me through heavily lidded eyes. "Liked that, did you?"

I paused my motions. "I don't like that I put you in danger. I don't like that at all."

He gripped my hips, signaling he wanted me to keep moving. "I would fight a thousand more for you."

"Shh." I silenced him with a kiss.

He pulled my shirt over my head and expertly unhooked my bra with one hand.

I increased my speed, lost in how good it felt to be filled.

His grip tightened. "More."

I chuckled, and then almost bit my tongue as his finger found my clit. "Oh...oh yes." My orgasm came hard and fast.

. . .

LATER, I sat wrapped in a blanket on the sofa, staring at my purse, which Graham had placed on the coffee table in front of me.

He wore sweats with no shirt and looked amazing. "Just do it. I'm right here with you."

My chest was so tight that I felt like I couldn't take a breath. "I'm scared."

He stroked my back.

I cleared my throat. "Before all of this, my dad or our leader told me what to do. I had never made any real decisions. It has been hard…being on my own. I've made mistakes."

"We all do."

"What if…" I didn't even know where to begin with my list of concerns.

"Want me to make the call?"

Relief washed over me. "Please."

"That wasn't so hard, was it?" He grinned as if I'd given him a gift.

I had a feeling this was going to be our life. Me working myself up over something silly, and Graham swooping in to take care of it without any drama. I didn't deserve him. But then, we were fated to be together. I should stop questioning why I had been given such an amazing mate. "His card is in my wallet."

He waited for me to nod once, giving him permission to dig inside my purse. Pulling out the card, he examined it. His finger traced the worn edges. "Looks like you've spent time thinking about this."

"I have, but I wanted…I wanted to try to do it on my

own. It was my chance to be independent." I shrugged once, feeling disappointed in myself.

"Being alone is one way to live, but it isn't for everyone." He sat back on the sofa. "I know that you need others to watch over and to love."

"I have you."

"And we will have sons and daughters."

I smiled at the idea.

He touched the screen on his cell and typed the number. "I'm going to put it on speaker."

One ring, two, and then, "Conal MacGregor," boomed through the device.

"This is Detective Graham Vincent from Perryville, Pennsylvania."

"What can I do for you, Detective?" Novus's Second didn't sound concerned.

"I'm with Olivia Stern," he began.

"What about Olivia?" he said quickly.

"The Burke Pack is sending assassins after her."

"Is she safe?"

I leaned a little closer to the phone. "Yes, Second, I am here."

"Are you unharmed?"

"For now," I answered truthfully.

"Where did you say? Pennsylvania?" Conal demanded.

"Middle Pennsylvania," Graham said.

"What is the closest airport? I'll send a plane."

"No, no flying," Graham told him decisively.

I wanted to smirk. My hero was afraid of something.

"Noted," the Second replied smoothly.

"We'll drive," Graham told him with certainty.

"We?" Conal inquired.

"Graham is my ma...mate." I sounded a little unsure as I stumbled over the word.

"I'll send an escort. They can meet you somewhere in Illinois, let's say?" Conal suggested.

I liked that the Second was being considerate, offering to work with us.

"How about we see how the drive goes, and I'll call you if we need help?" Graham countered.

The Second's laugh sounded through the speaker.

I glanced at Graham. I didn't understand.

"She is mine to see to," Graham explained more for my benefit than Conal's.

"I wish you every happiness."

"Thank you, Second."

"Please, call me Conal."

I liked how this call was going, but I needed to know what would be expected of us. "I have some questions."

Conal took over smoothly. "I'm sure both of you will have many."

Graham didn't look upset. If anything, his expression was serene.

Conal continued, "Once you are here and settled, we will discuss your future with Novus. I am very happy you called. I've worried. Keep me updated, and we await your arrival Graham Vincent and Olivia Stern."

"Thank you, Conal." Graham and I said at the same time.

. . .

I GLANCED at the cell phone's screen. In two miles, we would be on Novus land. It had taken me hours to convince Graham to let me help with the driving. A Lycan, even my strong mate, can only go so long without sleep. I slowed to pull onto the shoulder of the highway.

He woke immediately and reached for the gun resting between his thighs. "What's wrong?"

"It's okay." I put the car in park and turned to face him.

"Are you tiring?"

"No. We are almost on Novus land, and I wanted to give you one last chance to change your mind."

"Honey." He grasped my hand and placed it over his heart.

I hated feeling this way, as though I created drama everywhere I went. I had to know if he was sure about this decision. "I feel like I came into your life and changed everything."

"For the better, Olivia," he said, his dark gaze locking with mine.

"The reality is that once I enter Novus Land, I may never be able to leave."

He cupped one side of my face. "You don't know that."

"It might mean forever, Graham. Are you sure that is what you want?"

He dropped his other hand onto my shoulder and pulled me closer so that our foreheads touched. "My beautiful Mate, I will go anywhere, do anything, to be with you."

"I love you." I kissed him.

"Always."

I kissed him again.

He placed his hand on my thigh and squeezed lightly, "Drive."

BLACKOUT

BY JANUARY GEORGE

"*H*old it, please!" Ruby Ramirez yelled across the dim foyer toward the closing elevator door. Her arms ached from the heavy canvas bags, and the loop of an umbrella strap cut into her wrist. She usually wasn't so winded by the three-block walk to Trader Joe's, but the oppressive August humidity was like a smothering electric blanket. Couple that with the fact she'd broken into a jog when it had started raining, and she was left panting.

"Thanks," Ruby gasped as she slipped into the elevator, glancing up to see her savior.

Of course, it was *him.*

All six-feet-three inches of him. Six-feet-three inches of drool-worthy muscles and chiseled features, blond hair, and eyes the color of the North Sea. Six-feet-three inches of grade A asshole.

She'd managed to avoid Liam Rygaard for three weeks. She'd dove into doorways at the sound of his voice, peeked into the hallway before leaving her apartment; she'd even kept track of his schedule to prevent the most minuscule chance of running into him.

And yet, she'd sprinted, soaking wet and in a white tank top, right into a tiny enclosed space with him. She sank back against the wall, wishing it would absorb her.

"No problem." Liam's dark blue gaze clung to her; the weight so intense she almost squirmed. He looked about as happy to see her as she was him, but it was a short elevator ride, and there was no reason to say another word.

She kept her gaze forward, but some magnetic force pulled it back to glance quickly at him. A navy T-shirt, the one with his ladder company logo, molded to his broad shoulders and the smooth muscles of his chest, highlighting every hard ridge before disappearing into his fire-resistant pants.

Three weeks ago, she'd expected to strip that shirt off his body, trace her lips and tongue along those ridges and hollows, and feel his big hands on her hips, on the breasts that were aching from just the thought. She'd spent more nights than she cared to admit imagining the sensation of his skin against hers, and it hadn't been so easy to shut off those fantasies when the entire thing had exploded into a fireball of awfulness.

Liam stared straight ahead, giving her a view of his profile—the aquiline nose and full lips lending his features an ancient, aristocratic air that the faint dusting of black soot did nothing to diminish. The scent of woodsmoke clung to him, mingling with the aroma of clean sweat and soap to create an intoxicating cologne.

Ruby let out a breath, her vision partially obscured

by the long bangs she'd been trying to grow out for three years. Liam had already pressed the button for their floor, and she resisted the urge to reach over to punch it again. The doors finally hissed closed, and she felt the smallest whisper of relief.

"Haven't see you around."

His deep voice made her jump.

"How you been?"

She wouldn't look at him because she didn't want him to see that her cheeks were on fire. "Fine." Her ribs were clamped around her lungs so tight the single word came out taut and strangled.

Why was this stupid elevator so slow? And why was the heat from his gaze dripping down her traitorous body like lava, igniting every nerve pathway and every cell until she was engulfed with flames? She could almost feel the air quivering with his presence, expanding and swelling. She should've been grateful that she'd learned who he really was before they'd crossed that line, but some primitive part of her still felt like she'd missed out. However, whatever she'd missed out on didn't matter, because in four more seconds she'd be out of the elevator and away from him.

As if on cue in a nightmare, the elevator shuddered then jerked to a stop. Ruby instinctively reached out to grab the rail, her bags banging into her thighs. There was a long groan, and then the lights flickered and went out, leaving them in complete darkness.

A second passed in total silence. Ruby held her breath, waiting for something to happen. Her hands tightened around the canvas straps. But when time stretched with no change, self-preservation trumped her stubbornness. "Uh…what just happened?"

"Don't know," Liam muttered. The sound of something heavy hit the ground. From the accompanying whoosh of air, she figured it was the gear bag that had been hanging on his shoulder. He moved, not touching her, but she could hear the brush of his pants, feel the way the air bent, making way for him.

Her heart, which was already beating too fast, thundered into overdrive. She shifted, pulled toward the empty space he'd occupied, telling herself she was scared and wanted the reassurance of someone else, even if it was only the lingering residue of his presence.

Plus, he was a fireman. He knew how to handle dangerous situations. It was only natural to gravitate toward him. "Liam?"

"Hang on." A second later, his cellphone flashlight came on. He'd moved to the doors and was kneeling in front of the panel. He withdrew a large flashlight from his bag and flipped it on, setting it on its square base. The odd diffusion of light sharpened the tension in his strong jaw and the edge of his cheekbones, making her think of campfire stories and s'mores.

He pressed the emergency button, but nothing happened. "Elevator lost power."

"So, we're stuck?" Ruby finally let the bags slide down her arms and onto the floor, along with the umbrella she'd borrowed. Blood rushed back into her hands bringing a painful numbness.

"For the time being." He hit a number on his phone and stuck it against his ear. He looked up, his gaze quickly scanning her. "You okay?"

"Just dandy." She didn't want his pity or concern; she wanted out of this elevator. He seemed so *calm*, and she...wasn't.

"Hey, Pete. It's Ry. We lost power to the elevator in my building. I'm trapped." There was a pause, and she could hear the voice on the other side but couldn't make out the words. "No shit."

The elevator, like the building, was old, and Liam was shaking his head as he inspected the panel. "I don't see one. Yeah, well, as soon as I get out of the goddamn elevator, I'll be sure to tell them. I don't know, Pete. Well, it's nice to be able to afford to live in newer buildings, but not everyone has rich parents. Uh-huh. Can you just send someone over to get us out?" He listened for a few more minutes, rolling his eyes, and then said goodbye. He cleared his throat and shot her a glance. "Apparently, our elevator isn't up to code."

"What the hell does that mean?" At his nonchalant shrug, her voice skittered into the beginning of hysteria. "Can't you just pry it open? Aren't you trained to rescue people?"

"From outside the elevator," he said, his voice dry.

"Can't you wedge the doors open or climb up the elevator shaft or something?" she asked, her voice jumping an octave.

His arms, which were dusted with blond hair that glowed in the flashlight, flexed as he rooted through his bag. He appeared to be taking stock of what he had, barely reacting to the operatic crescendo she'd built to.

Liam frowned. "Both of those are terrible ideas. Pete said there's a blackout for a couple blocks. They'll be here when they can. Storm knocked out some power lines."

The air, thick and stagnant, was suffocating with the scent of him. She plucked at her tank top, which was damp from rain and sweat. "How long 'til they get here?"

He shrugged. "Don't know. A while."

She sank down, dread and defeat crashing over her.

Liam, having completed his examination of his bag, seemed at a loss and sat opposite her.

Ruby pulled her phone from her purse and scrolled through it, trying to think of something she could do, but her eyes didn't register anything. She noted her low battery and shut it off. When she looked up, Liam was watching her.

She looked everywhere except at him, shifting and repositioning herself under the prickly and not altogether unpleasant weight of his gaze.

"What?" she finally asked, turning toward him.

He didn't say anything.

All the oxygen burned out of the air. She couldn't make out the color of his eyes in the dimness, but she knew exactly how blue they were, how they darkened when he looked at her. How they crinkled at the edges when he laughed.

She jumped to her feet and paced the tiny space. "I

can't take this anymore. I can't be trapped in here."
With you.

"It's going to be okay." He reached out to touch her, his fingers brushing her wrist.

She snatched back her hand as if he'd burned her. "Nope, nope, nope."

Fuck no, she wasn't staying in this elevator. Not with him. Not with his fake concern and reassurance. Because he still made her insides turn to jelly, made smoke and fire smell like heaven, made her forget how to breathe, and she knew she wasn't going to survive being trapped in here with him for another minute.

"Oh, I'm sorry it's so unbearable to be stuck in this elevator with me." Liam rolled his eyes, the implication painfully clear.

"You know what? It *is* unbearable." But not for the reasons he thought. The situation was untenable because she still wanted him, and she couldn't reconcile wanting someone who had done what he had. She grabbed the umbrella, the one she'd taken from the stand on her way out when she'd seen the dark clouds outside. She'd been dumb enough to hook it inside her arm with all the bags on top, and when it had actually started raining, it had been too much trouble to try to untangle it, so she'd run. If she'd bothered to stop to use it, Liam Rygaard would've been stuck in this elevator alone, and she'd have been huffing and puffing up nine flights of stairs.

It was the goddamn umbrella's fault.

She jammed the plastic tip between the doors,

wedging it back and forth in what she knew was a completely fruitless effort to pry them open.

Liam raised an eyebrow, but his expression remained impassive. He pulled his phone out and used his thumb to navigate the screen, glancing up at her. "That's going to—"

The rod snapped.

"Break," he finished unnecessarily, frowning at the phone against his ear. "Missy, call me when you get this. I'm trapped in an elevator. Not kidding." He hung up.

Ruby looked down at the dangling piece of metal, feeling sorry for whoever's umbrella she'd broken. "Why can't you just pry it open with the jaws of life?"

"We don't just carry those around." He turned his head, and his eyes widened. "Isn't that Mr. Fletcher's umbrella?"

Ruby looked down at the dangling, broken rod. Mr. Fletcher lived on the floor below hers and was one of the sweetest men in the world. "I just grabbed it from the stand. I don't know."

"I think that's his umbrella, the one his wife gave him."

His deeply loved wife, who had died last year. "Seriously?"

Liam's face split into a grin. "Naw, I'm just fucking with you. I don't know whose that is."

She whacked him with the dangling umbrella. "Why would you do that?"

His hands shot up to defend himself. "You're freaking out. I'm trying to get you to calm down. Laughing is a great way to relieve tension."

The moment reminded her of how they used to be. How she'd playfully push him when they sat on the folding table in the basement; how her heart would speed up just a little at that simple contact. "You are an asshole."

His smile faded. "Apparently."

She and Liam Rygaard had gone on a date three weeks ago. A really, really great date. A date that Ruby had fully expected would end with them both naked. They'd been flirting for weeks, doing laundry in the basement together, laughing, talking about politics, and exchanging playlists and restaurant recommendations. Nights when they'd run into each other on the elevator would end with them standing in the hall talking, minutes stretching with each soft laugh and subtle shift closer. And she'd had a crush. An embarrassing smile-at-the-thought-of-him, crimson cheeked, inability to speak near him, crush. When he'd asked her out, she'd felt as though it was almost too good to be true.

Guys are dicks, her best friend always said. And Ruby was grudgingly starting to believe it.

"I just wish I knew what I did."

He sounded so genuinely confused she almost believed him. No, she wanted to believe him. Big difference.

Ruby crossed her arms. "I just wish you would get us out of this elevator."

Sure, he'd called and texted her after she'd left the restaurant. He'd tried to talk to her. And she'd intended to talk to him—she really had—as soon as she figured out what to say.

Liam's phone rang, and a picture flashed on the screen. A stunning blonde. Something knotted in her stomach as he answered. "Missy, I swear I'm not fucking with you. The power is out, and I'm trapped in my elevator. No, I'm off-duty. I told you I was leaving early. In my building!" She heard some high-pitched shrieking, and Liam held out the phone. "Ruby, tell my sister I'm not lying to get out of her stupid party."

It was getting warm in the elevator. Hot, almost. Sweat ran down her back, between her shoulder blades. She fanned the air in front of her with her open palm.

Wait. "Your sister?"

He shook the phone, and the picture flashed again, along with the name *Melissa Rygaard*, taunting her.

Ruby's stomach twisted as she took the phone. "Hi," she said in a small voice, "yes, we are stuck in an elevator. He's not lying." *Had he not been lying to her?*

"Ruby?" a woman's voice asked. "Like the Ruby my brother went on a date with? The one who ghosted him? What was the deal with that?"

Ruby's mouth twisted with the sour taste of regret as she handed back the phone without answering, pretending she hadn't heard his sister's question.

Liam took it. "They're working on getting the power back on. The guys'll come get us, but they have to attend to life-threatening situations first. No, this isn't life-threatening. I'll get there if I can. I'm covered in soot and need to shower. Okay, is it really the end of the world if I miss *one* of the thirty-seven pre-wedding events? Maybe you should have scaled it back a little. Well, you can take it up with the building manager.

Okay, other people exist. Yes, I know. Goodbye, Melissa."

Ruby slid to the floor across from him, her off-white canvas shoes almost touching his big black boots. She stared down at her bare knees then stole a glance at him.

Liam followed her to the floor and ran a hand through his blond brush cut.

Unable to meet his gaze, she turned her face toward the elevator door. She swallowed a painful lump in her throat. She'd put off feeling anything except anger, but the earnest way he stared at her, now, made her feel prickly all over. Made her wish she hadn't fucked up so monumentally.

Ruby pulled her knees to her chest, even though her entire body was slick with sweat. "Did you meet your sister before our date?" Ruby forced her gaze up to Liam's face, expecting to catch a wave of guilt, of alarm, something other than his curiously perplexed stare.

He stilled, his gaze holding hers, making her squirm. "Why?"

She drew in a breath and blew it out. "When we were getting ready to leave," she paused, as a flash of memory rolled over her—the way that night had been filled with longing stares, how he'd leaned in to brush back her bangs and found any excuse to touch her, how her body, fully charged with anticipation, had been fueled by every glance, every touch. She ran her tongue over her lower lip. "You went to pay, and I went to the bathroom."

He didn't speak. His gaze just stayed on her.

"The waitress pulled me aside and said I should know that you'd been there on another date, before I arrived. With a *stunning* blonde."

"And you believed I would do that?" His voice almost broke her, a mix of disappointment and frustration, tempered by an ominous softness.

Ruby sat back, letting her head fall against the wall. She stared at the ceiling, wondering if she could escape through the vent. "I didn't know what to believe."

He snorted. "Well, you could have fucking asked."

She tightened her arms around her knees. The self-righteous anger she'd cloaked herself inside because he'd wronged her lay in a puddle, and she grappled with the idea that she'd been the one who'd been wrong. Now, she was desperate for anything she could use to deflect her guilt. "Why would you meet your sister before a date?"

He shook his head like he didn't owe her an explanation but was going to grudgingly give her one anyway. "She's getting married. Everyone was fighting. She wanted to come over and bitch, but I told her I had a date I couldn't miss. So, she met me at the restaurant before our date for a drink." His eyebrows lowered. "I liked *you*, Ruby. I always looked forward to running into you in the hallway. I used to wait until I saw you going down to do laundry to do mine, just so we could hang out. I never gave you a reason to think I'm a dick and, honestly, it pisses me off that you wrecked a pretty incredible date because you thought I was an asshole."

Ruby looked down at the floor. They were so close, their feet and knees almost touching. If she just moved her foot slightly, they could be joined. But the relief she expected to feel had only cracked open wider to expose something else.

She looked away, at anything except the searing blue of his eyes. "I'm sorry. I feel like a jerk now."

He leaned forward, resting his arms on his knees. The scent of smoke, of him, filled her lungs. "Why didn't you just ask me?"

She shook her head, hating the sting of tears blurring her vision and lowered her gaze before he saw them. "I don't know...when she said that...I just sort of panicked. And then I thought...I just thought maybe I'd been wrong about you."

Liam's finger nudged her chin, lifting her face. "That's not it."

His gaze burned through whatever flimsy wall she was trying to erect, exposing the painful truth she'd been trying so hard to hide. "You're...you. You're the kind of guy... You're gorgeous, a firefighter, you literally save lives... And I..." she stopped. "I'm me. I'm just...me. My thighs touch, and I only wear makeup if it's a really special occasion. So, I guess, maybe, I just worried..." *I wasn't good enough.*

Liam pushed up from where he sat and moved closer, so the heavy canvas of his pants brushed against her bare skin. "I still remember the first time I saw you, downstairs in the laundry room. You asked if you could borrow two quarters for the dryer. You weren't wearing any makeup, and you had on these tiny gym shorts, and, yes, your thighs were definitely touching. You also wore a Michael Kiwanuka T-shirt, tied in a knot..."

He remembered that? The air around them was scorching, but all she wanted was to feel his skin against hers. To finish what they'd started three weeks ago. "I was impressed you even knew who Michael Kiwanuka was." Her words, softly muffled, were an afterthought as she stared at his mouth.

"I mean, he sings the theme song to *Big Little Lies*. He's not that obscure." His tone was teasing, but his eyes were filled with hunger. "I wanted you then." He scanned her face.

They were close, but not close enough. Her head swam, her heart fluttered against her ribs, drowning out everything but his voice and the sound of her breathing.

"And I've wanted you every damn day since."

She drew in a breath that scorched her throat. If she leaned forward, she could touch her lips to his. "I'm sorry that I doubted y—"

He didn't let her finish. He leaned in, brushing his mouth against hers in a chaste kiss that silenced her. But he didn't push. If anything, he pulled back, giving her space to decide.

She swallowed. The hot, sticky air crackled around them. The strange, dim lighting gave the experience a surreal quality, and she fought against the back-peddling her brain was doing. This wasn't the time to find another excuse for her paralysis.

This moment was everything she wanted, and yet, she stood on the edge of the precipice, terrified to jump. And was it really her own insecurity? Her own belief that she wouldn't measure up? She looked up, held his gaze, held her breath, held onto some stupid fear that made her hesitate. Did she want the fantasy, her empty bed and carefully protected heart, or did she want him?

She drew in a breath and let go.

Her hands came up to clutch his head, and she pulled his mouth down to hers. There was nothing tentative about the kiss as raw hunger spread through her.

And he *wanted* her. She could feel it in the urgency of his hands as they tugged her closer, cupped her cheeks, and tilted her face to savor her lips. His tongue swirled against hers—deep, hungry strokes that erased her insecurity with every bold plunge. Their bodies collided, sweaty limbs bumping together as he lifted her, his hands capturing her waist as she rose to her knees.

He drew back, just enough to see her face. "If you want to wait—"

"No, I'm done waiting." She dragged his face back to hers, her hands scraping the short hair at the nape of his neck.

He laughed against her mouth. "I was going to say— until we're out of the elevator."

She fingered the suspenders on his shoulders. "You said that could be hours."

Liam grinned, and in a smooth motion, rolled her so she was straddling him. His hands settled at her hips, pushing aside her thin tank top so his palms sat flush against her skin. Their weight felt so right that the battle that had been raging inside her for weeks calmed. She leaned forward, looping her arms around his neck. This was where she was supposed to be. Exactly where.

"Damn, I've wanted you," he muttered.

Ruby rocked against his pelvis, feeling the hardened length of him even through his thick pants. She glided her fingers along his jaw then followed with her mouth. His skin was subtly salty, and the soft moan he gave, and the way his hands tightened at her hips, encouraged her.

Liam drew her up so he could look at her, and the moment stretched between them, as heavy as the humidity. The air changed. Gone was the frantic need, replaced by a languid, aching desire. While his gaze remained locked with hers, he dropped his hands and slid them up her thighs until they reached the frayed hem of her shorts. His eyes were filled with all the same emotions bubbling up in her heart. Desire, but something more, something nameless, a recognition that formed a tether between them, and which bound tightly to the ribs surrounding her heart.

She bent to touch her lips to his, pressing kisses to the corners of his mouth. His hands continued their leisurely path up and down her thighs, stopping at the point where the denim pressed into her skin. She spread her fingers over his jaw, kissing the edge of bone, the faintest scrape of stubble burning her lips.

"Beautiful." His voice was a whisper against her ear.

And she believed him. His fingers fumbled with the brass buttons on her shorts, loosening them just enough that he could slip his hands down the back of the tight fabric. She pressed her throbbing sex against the hard ridge of his, the sharp edge of the seam of her jeans only pouring gasoline on the flames. His hands tightened on her ass, and he grunted, drawing her deeper against him.

"It's so hot in here," she said, grasping the bottom of her tank top and pulling it over her head. She wore a plain white bra, but his sigh as the cups became visible filled her with confidence. "Isn't there some survival thing, where we should both get naked?" She freed his suspenders then pulled up his shirt, exposing the hard dissection of his abdomen.

His mouth twitched. "As a first responder, I can assure you this elevator is reaching a dangerously hot temperature, and disrobing is potentially lifesaving in this situation." He reached behind his back, thrusting his pelvis into hers as he moved and yanked his shirt over his head.

She ran her hands over the carved lines of his chest. Under his skin, his muscles were firm, tensing in reaction to her touch. "Aren't we supposed to huddle together?"

His lips formed a crooked grin. "I think I do remember hearing something like that."

She raised up onto her knees, enough that he could slide off her shorts and underwear, and she kicked them free, leaving her in only her bra. Liam tugged his pants down to his thighs, his thick erection springing free.

His hands stilled on her shoulders as she scooted back and bent to dip her head. She swirled her tongue around the head of his cock, encircling the base with her thumb and forefinger. There was a hiss as she took more of him into her mouth, sucking until her cheeks hollowed. His fingers tightened in her scalp, tugging at the strands loosely bound with an elastic. Ruby turned her wrist, moving her hand to meet her mouth as she sucked. His hips rose to meet her, and he let out a growl.

"My turn," he said, his voice tight between his clenched teeth.

Liam pulled her up, his body tense, and held her arms for a moment, as if he just needed to be nearer. Then he reached around her back to unclasp her bra. Her breasts fell free, and he leaned into her, his hands cradling their weight. Her skin was on fire, slick with sweat, but he didn't seem to mind. Liam drew one nipple deep into his mouth, sucking hard enough to run the border between pleasure and pain. Her head fell back, and her hair tumbled loose from the tie, tickling her spine. Liam's hands tangled in it, gathered it in handfuls as her arching back thrust her breast further into his mouth.

Her eyes drifted close as she was lost on a sea of pleasure while his mouth tugged on her breast and his hands explored. His right hand skimmed along her hip until it settled between her thighs, nudging open her sex. She tightened her grasp on his shoulders, and he sucked hard on a nipple as he spread her, using her moisture to coat his fingers. He moved slowly, circling the point where she ached to be touched, torturing her with each swipe. The muscles in her thighs tightened, begging for release.

"Liam," she whispered.

He bent her back, moving his mouth down her stomach. Her shoulders settled on his knees and he propped her up, using his height advantage to tug her knees apart and hook them over his shoulders. Some part of her thought she should be embarrassed that she was spread out, draped across him, her bones turned to jelly. But that voice was quickly silenced when he touched her. He kissed her as deeply as if it were her mouth. His tongue swirled and caressed that tight, hard bud between her legs until her body trembled with its need for release.

Ruby came hard, her back arching and muscles spasming. A deep cry erupted from her throat. Liam held tightly to support her, sucking relentlessly as her body shook and contracted.

Without missing a beat, he reached over to his bag, fumbling with a condom he'd pulled from his wallet. A minute later, he pulled her down, straddling his lap. She sank onto him, feeling the stretch of him as he entered her, filling her. His fingers moved against her, rubbing as he began to move. She used the tight muscles in his shoulders as an anchor, steadying herself as he thrust. They moved together, frantic and needy, clumsily in the small space, as Liam increased speed. His boots thudded against the walls and his hands settled on her hips, tightening as he lost control. She clung to him, her eyes shut as she rode him, her ass slapping against his thighs. She let out a muffled scream against his shoulder she came again, just seconds before he exploded inside her.

"Jesus," she gasped.

His thighs twitched, and he tightened his hold as he spasmed. "Fuck, Ruby."

They sat like that for a long moment, neither

moving. Just holding each other. She pulled back first, and he tilted his face up to hers.

His flushed face was sweaty, his eyes glassy. "You, ah, want to go to a cocktail party if we ever get out of here?"

She grinned, running her finger along the path of a drop of sweat along his hairline. "I think we're doing this backwards. Aren't you supposed to ask me out before we have sex?"

"Just say you'll come." He snorted. "I didn't mean it like that."

"I already did," she said with a wink.

The lights flickered on above them. Ruby scrambled up, grabbing for her clothes as the elevator started to move.

Liam reached over to slam his palm on the emergency stop button, and for the second time, the car came to an abrupt stop.

Ruby looked up in a panic. "What if the power goes out again?"

He tugged on his shirt right side out, grinning. "Get dressed fast."

They both pulled on enough clothes to be decent, and Liam pressed the button for the elevator to start again. Ruby didn't let out her breath until the door slide open on the ninth floor. Despite being dressed, she was still grateful no one was there when the doors opened. They both hurried out, the stuffy hallway feeling like an open field after the stagnant elevator air.

As she neared her door, she turned to face Liam. Her body still tingled, and she didn't want to say goodbye.

Not yet. "I think there's a thing about conserving water in emergency situations..." she said, then bit her lip, hoping he was as eager as she was to continue.

A slow grin spread across his face. His bluer than blue eyes sparkled. "Yeah, I think there is."

HANDCUFFS AND G-STRINGS

BY MARGAY LEAH JUSTICE

*P*ierce

        "Rogan! My office. Now."

The words cut through the noise of the squad room like a machete through butter, mostly due to the sharp edge of the voice delivering them. Everyone jumps to attention at their sound—we're all Pavlov's dogs where the Chief's concerned—but that doesn't stop one of the smartasses surrounding me from calling out, "Which one, sir?"

And I'd know that voice anywhere. I should—I grew up with it. That's my baby brother, Keith. New to the force this year, after taking a longer route to getting here than the rest of us, via college, getting his master's degree in criminal justice. For a while there, we thought he'd go the lawyer route, but baby bro has other aspirations. Let's just say, the Chief better watch out for his job. Keith Rogan has it in his sights. But for all his seriousness when it comes to his job, he's still the happy-go-lucky member of the extensive Rogan clan, and it shows in his fearlessness in addressing the Chief just now.

Fucking great. *Better not get us all in trouble, little brother.*

The Chief gives his more-salt-than-peppered head a hard shake. Like he's silently cursing himself. "Dammit, I forgot there's more than one of you," he grumbles, more to himself than to us.

"How could you, Chief?" Keith asks, adopting a hurt expression, hand to his heart and everything. Should've been a damn actor, this one. "I think I can speak for all my brothers"—–uh, no, you can't; don't you dare speak for me, little bro—"when I say that I'm hurt. How could you forget there's more than one of us here, sir? We come from the illustrious Rogan clan, after all—*everyone* remembers us." See what I mean about that fearlessness?

Chief gives Keith a hard glare. "Well, in that case, you *all* can come in."

All around me, my brothers groan. Well, *three* of them do. The fourth one—and the youngest—is pretty damn proud of himself for getting the Chief riled. He and I are going to have some words. After shift. Or sooner, if I can manage it. Maybe I can switch things up so I can ride patrol with him, then he'd be stuck with me and my lectures all day. I smile inwardly at the thought. That might just be the perfect revenge.

Although he doesn't need to, the Chief does a roll call, just so we know he means business, I'm sure. "Pierce, Adam, Michael, Jesse, Keith." And he does so in the order of our births. Impressive. "My office. Now. *All* of you."

With that, the Chief ducks out of the squad room with the confidence that we'll follow him like the faithful, well-trained dogs we are. Well, *some* of us—Keith still needs some lessons in obedience and respect, that one. Before we do, though, we give him a little hell for getting us all called into the Chief's office.

"What the hell, K?" That's Jesse, closest in age and birth order to the little shit-starter. "We weren't even on the Chief's radar 'til you opened your mouth—that was all Pierce."

"How do you know it was *me* he wanted?" I challenge, leading the way out of the squad room. "As baby bro pointed out, there's more than one Rogan here. Could've been any one of us."

"Hey! Please don't call me 'baby bro' at work," Keith said. "It's demeaning."

We all ignore him.

"He was looking right at you," Michael says, ever the helpful brother.

"Until big mouth *opened* his mouth," Adam gripes.

And Keith is the unlucky recipient of death glares from all of his brothers. Looks like I'm not the only one who's going to have words with him after work. Stand in line, boys. As the oldest, I get first dibs on the little shit-starter.

"Come on," I say, moving this forward. "Let's go see what the Chief wants so we can get out on patrol in a timely manner."

"Yes, Daddy," Keith chirps, totally unaffected by anything his antics have wrought.

Well, we'll just have to see about that, won't we?

With a shake of my head, I set my own plans aside as I lead the way into the Chief's office—plenty of time for that later.

The Chief doesn't waste a second getting to the purpose of our visit to his office. I usually admire that about him. But now, not so much. "So, here's the deal, boys. As you know, we've got that fundraiser coming up for the Fallen Heroes fund, and I want to do better than we did last year."

We all groan at the reminder of our dismal showing last year against the fire department assholes, against whom we always measure ourselves. It's kind of hard *not* to when they're the ones pushing it in our faces all the time. It doesn't help that a good portion of those assholes are our cousins, so we hear about it all the damn time at family functions.

"So, I'm putting it on you five to come up with something better this year," the Chief continues, eliciting more groans from us. "Something that'll put our friends in the fire department on notice that they're not the top dogs anymore."

As one, my brothers turn their glares on Keith, who gives them an innocent *"Who me?"* look with raised shoulders and everything. *Little punk.*

"Don't disappoint me." With that, the Chief sends us on our way.

Michael barely waits until we clear the threshold of his office before he slaps Keith upside the head.

The little runt actually has the audacity to look affronted. "What?" he splutters. "What'd *I* do?"

"He was only gonna call in P, you little shit," Michael says.

"Yeah, now, thanks to you, we're all responsible for coming up with a gimmick for the fundraiser," Adam, the more solemn of the bunch, adds his piece to the conversation.

"And it has to be something better than what the fire guys do every year with their bare-chested calendars." Thanks for the reminder, Jesse. Not.

Yeah, I still can't scrub my mind of the images of my cousins in sexy poses without their shirts on. Thank fuck everyone insisted Layla keep *hers* on—but she did wear a way-too-damn-tight tank top, so I don't know how effective *that* was.

"Okay, so everyone, give it some thought, and let's pitch some ideas tonight," I say, trying my best to wrangle these miscreants I call brothers.

"Drinks and a show at the Suite?" Keith asks with a hopeful look.

"What is it with you and strippers?" I ask.

"*Exotic dancers*," he corrects. "They don't like to be called 'strippers' anymore."

Same difference, if you ask me.

SOMEHOW, little brother gets his way, and we end up at The Executive Suite after dinner with our parents. Weird as hell going from a home-cooked meal with your folks to a gentleman's club with your brothers to talk strategy about a fundraiser. But if it gets the job done, I'm all in. Anything to come out on top of the fire-holes at the FD. Last year, we made a little side-bet with them, and we ended up cleaning the firehouse for months after we lost it.

Not this year.

Not if I can help it.

All I have to do is make sure my brothers aren't so distracted by the talent onstage they can't contribute to the brainstorming session. Talk about a fucking challenge. It doesn't help that Adam got waylaid by Browning, a fellow officer who moonlights as a bouncer, apparently, and they disappeared outside together and haven't come back yet. Don't know what that shit's all about, but I'll be asking. Later. For now, though, we have *this* shit to deal with. I consider waiting for Adam, but I just want to get this over with, so I get it going with, "So, any of you wunderkinds got any ideas yet?"

Michael and Jesse immediately respond in the negative, and I'm just about to add my two cents when Adam reemerges from wherever he was and joins us at our table, two back from the stage. I narrow my eyes, giving him a critical once-over as he slides into the booth next to Michael. It might be my imagination, but the dude looks like he just came back from a mad make-out session, his lips kind of swollen and his usually neat hair mussed up at the sides, like someone ran their hands through it. But he was just with—wait. Him and *Browning*? Is that why he's been so secretive about his hookups lately? Because they're with a dude? I didn't even know he swung that way, not that it makes a difference in how I feel about him. He's my brother and nothing will ever shake that bond, sure as shit not his orientation. He doesn't give me shit for *mine*, so I won't give him shit for his.

He lifts his gaze to mine just as I have that thought, and I can tell by the look in his eyes, he knows I figured it out. And it bothers him, because he quickly looks away, toward our other brothers. Yeah, we'll be clearing that shit up real soon—after we nail down a gimmick for the fundraiser. I've never been one to let things go and fester.

But for now, I let him have his secret as he says, "So what'd I miss?"

"Nothing," I say, keeping my tone neutral. "Nobody has any ideas."

"I do," Keith argues. "And it's something that'll put the fire boys to shame." He pauses here so we can all soak in the brilliance that is him (we don't), but then he smiles broadly and with a dramatic motion, points to the stage—where a dude wearing a Zorro mask is currently dancing.

Did I forget to mention that? He brought us here on ladies' night, but hey, at least the dude's good, mesmerizing all the women—and some of the men, too—with the undulations of his hips. Hell, if I swung that way, I'd want a piece of that.

"What's better than the fire boys taking their shirts off for a stupid calendar? How about the boys in blue taking it *all* off Magic Mike-style?"

He's got to be fucking kidding.

"*That's* your idea?" I balk. Sure, I gave a silent nod to

the talent of the guy onstage, but that's *his* thing, not ours. "You want us to *strip for charity?*"

There's some squawking from my other brothers until Jesse pipes up, "It's actually kind of a good idea." When we all—well, Adam, Michael and I—start to turn on him, he holds up a hand and says, "No, think about it for a minute. Who do the ladies always go crazy for at these strip shows—who do they ask for when they hire one for private parties?"

And he's got us there. Everyone knows the answer to that is cops.

"So, why not give them the real thing?" Jesse says.

Keith shoots us a challenging look. "Can any of you think of anything better?"

Unfortunately, we can't. So, it looks like we're all going to be bumping and grinding for charity. This could be the best thing ever—or the worst. And if it's an epic fail, our cousins will never let us live it down.

I look toward the stage, watch for a beat as the dude —who was introduced as Rocco Starr (not his real name, I'll bet) —finishes his dance with a fuck lot of hip action. Is that what *we'll* be doing? No pressure there. "Better make sure this works, K," I warn, swinging my gaze back to him. "Since it's your idea, it's on you if it tanks."

"It won't," he assures us.

I wish I had his confidence about it.

Everly

I can't believe he talked me into this. I'm what you

284

might call socially awkward, so things that involve dealing with people in a social sense are a challenge for me. Give me a glass of wine, a good book, and a quiet place to read; that's all I need to make me happy. Unfortunately, my well-meaning, meddling older brother doesn't agree. No, *he* thinks what I need is a raucous night out at a glorified strip club where I can get drunk off fruity drinks and hook up with a one-and-done I'll surely regret in the morning.

Let me repeat that.

Strip. Club.

That's my brother's idea of a good time. But then, I think he might be interested in someone who works there (I don't know, he's very mum about his relationships lately), so of course that's his idea of fun these days.

Needless to say, I tried to get out of it. Countless times. I only relented when he told me this was an event for charity (kind of a strange gimmick for a fundraiser), he knows how I feel about that. Yeah, no matter how bad off I might be doing, I always try to give back in some way or another, if not by a monetary donation, then by one of time. Yeah, I'm always volunteering for things like this—well, not *this*, but fundraisers. And Dakota played on that when he coerced me into coming tonight. I still have no idea why it's so important to him that I be here tonight, but I really hope it has something to do with whoever he's been seeing lately. Maybe he's going to introduce us tonight. I hope so. Even if it's a stripper. I don't care about that as long as he's happy. I just really wish we could've met anywhere else. Like my place, over a home-cooked meal. Or at least a restaurant, restaurants are fine. But this—a strip club filled with loud, booming music, flashing lights, and all these people making all this noise—this is definitely not fine.

But here I am, anyway.

Even if I *did* drag my heels so much, I'm forty minutes late for our meet-up, and the show has already started.

With another nervous look toward the stage, to the far right of the entrance, I once again scan the rowdy crowd for my brother. But there are so many people crammed in here (seriously, isn't that a fire hazard?), it's almost impossible to find him. Why couldn't he have bright red hair, so I could easily pick him out of the crowd? Why did it have to be a light brown, like mine? Can't pick that out of a crowd like this very easily.

Oh, God, *why* did I let him talk me into this? I like my life just as it is, with my books and my cat, and yeah, I realize that makes me a stereotypical single girl. Or cat-lady-in-the-making, as my bestie, Cam, would say. But I'm strangely okay with that. I've done the dating-to-mating ritual with not so great results, which is kinda why I'm single now. And in no rush to repeat myself. If only my family would be as fine with that as I am. But every time one of them finds a partner, they jump on the Everly-must-find-Mr. Right bandwagon and try to set me up on a date. Or worse, drag me out in public to some club—like I'm going to find the love of my life in a place everyone goes to get drunk and laid, not necessarily in that order. Yeah, I kinda gave up on that a long time ago. The love-of-my-life thing, not necessarily the get-drunk-and-laid one. It's been so long I'd actually welcome that. *If* I could find someone to interest me. Yeah, I haven't had much luck in *that* department lately, either.

Giving up on finding my brother this way (seriously, where *is* he?), I opt for finding a quiet spot at the bar, so I can call him. Or text him. Yeah, with the noise in here, maybe texting would be the better option. I just hope he has his phone on vibrate so he gets the message. I barely hit SEND when my attention is drawn to the stage where they've just announced the next act, and oh, damn, it's my Kryptonite. A gorgeous guy in a police uniform. Yeah, I have a thing for cops. So, he's doing a rather awkward rendition of Magic Mike to "Pony", and he doesn't have the smoothness of Channing Tatum—then again, who does? —but he *can* rival the guy in the looks department.

I'm not even close to the stage, and I can see how striking he is with his dark spiked hair and incredibly fit body, which he reveals piece by piece as he shimmies around the stage—much to the screaming delight of the other ladies here. Geez, where's your pride, ladies? Must've gone out the window with their inhibitions. Seriously, I think I can see that one's nipples through her gauzy shirt. Glancing down at my white Henley and jeans, I suddenly feel under-dressed. Or is that *over*-dressed since all things are covered?

I don't know how long I stand here re-assessing my life decisions, when I'm startled out of my thoughts by the gorgeous "cop" dancer. Oh, lord, he's even more stunning up close with his full mouth and sapphire eyes and the uniform shirt he didn't bother re-buttoning. And are those handcuffs real? I'd like to have them clamped around my wrists, chaining me to his bed while he—whoa, where did *that* come from? It really has been a long time, if I'm already fantasizing about a guy I haven't officially met, yet.

"Yes, they are." Well, that's an odd opener. I give him a blank look. "The handcuffs," he clarifies, sending a bolt of dread through me. *Please don't say I did, please don't say I did.* "You asked if they were real." Of course, I did. "They are."

"Good to know."

Good to know. Really? What a brilliant conversationalist.

"Anything else you'd like to know before we do this?"

Okay, now I'm really stumped. "Do what?"

He gives me a cocky smile as he leans in to say in my ear, "I saw you watching me." Of course, he did. My embarrassment wouldn't be complete if he didn't. "I was watching you, too."

"Y-you were?"

"I was."

"What now?"

"How about I show you what I can do with my cuffs?"

"Okay."

And I follow him as he leads me away. Without hesitation. Or even asking his name. I clear that up when we reach the privacy of a storage room. "I don't even know your name."

"Rogan."

"Everly."

"Nice to meet you, Everly," he murmurs, right before he cuffs me to some sort of rack, my arms over my head. I have no time to protest the move as his mouth dives for mine. And I'm gone. It's a quick descent into mindless passion now. Oh, lord, he kisses like a god. He must have a similar thought as he says, "Fuck, you're a goddess. I have to have you."

"I don't usually do this," I whisper into his mouth. And when he gives me a *that's what everyone says* look, I rush to clarify, "No, really. I don't. I'm the stay at home with a good book kind of girl—not the one in the story that gets banged against the wall." I flick a glance behind me at the metal fixture at my back. "Or whatever that is."

"Full disclosure?" he murmurs into my neck, which he can't stop kissing. "Neither do I. Do this kind of shit, I mean. I'm the guy at home with a beer and *Game of Thrones* on TV."

"I find that hard to believe, given your profession."

He gives me an odd look but doesn't comment on that. Instead, he says, "Enough talking," and dives for my mouth again.

PIERCE

I find that hard to believe, given your profession.

What a fucking odd thing to say. What, does she think? That just because I'm a cop, I can't enjoy a little epic fantasy about dragons and shit? Hey, when the uniform comes off, I like to relax and unwind just like any other guy, so it makes no sense, her saying that. But she's cute in a young, Jennifer Aniston kind of way, so I'll give her a pass on that. Plus, she's really fucking responsive to my touch, so she's got that going for her, too.

I can't keep my hands off her.

My touch is eager, bordering on frantic, as I slip my fingers under the hem of her shirt and sweep them up to cup her tits. She moans when I rub her nipples through the lace of her bra, so I do it again, getting the same response. Wonder how she'll react when I touch her clit?

Not one for dicking around, I go for it, making quick work of the button and zipper on her jeans so I can get to the prize. Fuck, she's wet—so wet, she practically soaks my hand in one go. "You like that, don't you?" I murmur into her neck, but I don't need a verbal answer; it's already coating my hand.

Still, she whimpers as she nods, so I say, "How about this?" as I sink a finger deep inside her, giving it a pump or two as I swirl my thumb over her clit. And that's all it takes to send her shooting off like a fucking rocket, the jolts of her body making the metal rack clang noisily against the wall. Hope no one heard that over the noise in the club because I'm not done with her yet—not by a fucking long shot.

I don't even wait for her to come down from her high before I sheath my dick and plunge inside her. Fucking. Heaven. That's the last cognizant thought I have as I go at her with a vigor I haven't managed in a damn long time—since my fiancée left me for a dickhead suit four years ago. This. *This* is what sex is all about. Or should be. Just mindless fucking. And that's what I am right now. Mindless.

Maybe that's why I don't hear the commotion until it's almost too damn fucking late.

EVERLY

I can't believe I'm doing this.

I don't *ever* do stuff like this. I'm the good girl who does everything just so, by the book, just like her parents raised her to. Which could account for why I've never had sex like this. Sure, I've had sex. I've just never.... *Had. Sex.* You know, the kind that happens up against a wall with a total stranger. And sure as heck not while handcuffed to a rack. You know, the animalistic kind with the grunts and pants, and the *oh, my, god, I can't take anymore, don't ever stop* pleas. I've never been this into it before, and the guy's never been this into me. But here we are, two strangers, who barely met before we started going at it. And it's the best sex I've ever had. So good, I swear I hear fireworks when I come. For the *second* time. Yeah, ladies, he's *that* good. Eat your hearts out.

Wait. There it is again. Is it possible to still hear the fireworks minutes after you already came? I've heard of post-coital bliss, but isn't that a bit much?

Hang on a second, that's not fireworks, that's—

"Is that gunfire?" I start to whisper-shout, my question muffled by his hand over my mouth before the last word is fully out. I'd be annoyed at that, and the way he shushes me, if I weren't so certain of the answer to my own question. My dad's a cop, and I've been to the range numerous times, so I know what a gun being fired sounds like. That was more for *his* benefit. Rogan's.

"Stay here," he barks the order like every cop I've ever known, hastily readjusting his clothes in the process. "Find a place to hide"—–this while he quickly uncuffs me—"until I come back and tell you it's safe."

After delivering that directive, he dashes out the door and down the long hallway, back into the thick of things in the main club area. He doesn't even look back to see if I comply. He just assumes that I will.

Like every other guy in my life, my well-meaning brother included.

Not this time.

PIERCE

The scene that greets me as I sneak back into the main room is every cop's nightmare. A couple of thugs with semi-automatic guns holding everyone hostage. How the fuck did they get in here with them? Where the fuck is the bouncer? Which one was it? Brand, the big dude with the military background (yeah, I checked him out while we were planning this) or was it Browning? If it was Browning, I'll be having words with him when this shit is done—and not just because he's been dicking my brother around with his secretive nature.

But that's a problem for another day. Right now, there's this.

I'm guessing the shots we heard were a warning to prove their threats weren't idle; a way to ensure complicity with their demands. And from the looks of it, it's working, as the attendees of the fundraiser start dropping to their knees with their hands behind their heads at the gunmen's orders. Little did they know what they just walked into, but they're about to. Once I find my brothers and devise a way to take them down.

The thought's still in my head when Adam materializes beside me, as if I summoned him. "You think these clowns realize they're in a room full of real cops?"

"How about we show them?" I spare a glance at him; he's focused on the scene before us, as he should be. "Where are the boys?"

"Where they need to be, waiting for my signal."

"Let's do this."

He doesn't have to be told twice.

And neither do our brothers. The second he gives them the signal—one we instituted at a young age when we used to play at being cops—they converge on the gunmen from various spots in the room.

And I'd be right there with them, if I wasn't distracted by Everly slipping into the room like she's going to take on the gunmen herself. Is she fucking *crazy*? Or maybe she has a death wish, putting herself in the line of fire like this. If the nearest gunman sees her. Fuck, too late.

I dive for her, bringing her down with the force of my body as a bullet whizzes by us, embedding itself in the wall above our heads. Chipped plaster rains down on us as I growl at her, "Didn't I tell you to stay put? Don't listen well, do you?"

"I thought I could help—"

"How? By making yourself a target?"

Whatever she might say is lost in the chaos that ensues as my brothers—the blood ones and the brotherhood ones—take down the fools who made the mistake of holding up a charity event put on by cops. What? Did they think we were actually *strippers*?

Well, shit. Now, it makes sense—*given your profession*. She thought I was a stripper.

At least I won't have to see her again after tonight.

EVERLY

Of all the ways you could possibly be embarrassed, mistaking a real cop for a stripper has got to be the worst. At least for someone who comes from a family of cops, as I do. But in my defense, he had been up on a stage, in cop uniform (a favorite stripper persona, or so I've heard), and dancing. Well, kind of. He had looked awkward doing it. I should've known it wasn't his true profession based solely on that. But I'd been so caught up in the moment, under a spell of insta-lust, that I'd let myself get carried away by it. So carried away, I'd had sex in a public place with him. Cuffed to a damn rack like I was recreating a scene from *Fifty Shades of Gray*. Cue the mortification.

Oh, well, at least I never have to see him again. Yeah, once the night was done, so was I. Well, after I gave my statement to the responding officers, that is—yeah, the ones who all seemed to know *Officer* Rogan (his last name, apparently). Tell me that wasn't a shock to realize the guy I'd had such wild sex with in that storeroom was an *actual* police officer. No wonder his handcuffs were real. Crap, that should've been a clue right there, Sherlock. Who else carries around real handcuffs? I can see I'm going to be so good at my new job. Hope I don't embarrass my dad.

As to that, I inhale a deep breath, bracing myself for my new future, and then step into the squad room for the first time as a newly minted officer.

The first thing I notice is there are only two other people in the room right now: my dad and an officer with his back to me. My dad sees me first and greets me with a proud smile. To the officer, he says, "Rogan, meet your new partner, my daughter, Everly Browning." And to me, "Ev, this is Pierce Rogan. He'll be showing you the ropes."

Please, don't let it be him; *please*, don't let it be him.

But do you think karma would listen?

Oh, no, she has a good laugh, when *he* turns around.

Officer *Pierce* Rogan.

So much for never seeing him again.

CROSSING THE LINE

BY A.C. DAWN

ire station romances never end well, Jeff reminded himself while forcing his gaze away from Kat's shapely backside. For five long months, he'd been telling himself that with increasing regularity. When she'd been assigned to his station at the academy graduation ceremony, he'd known he was in big trouble.

As if she could feel him looking, Kat straightened and peeked over her shoulder. He gave her a grin, unrepentant for being caught. She smiled back, showing off her dimples, and then lowered her eyes in that sultry way that made him crazy.

He cleared his throat and forced himself to say, in what he hoped was a normal voice, "You and the rookie are on the rescue. Are you good with that? Do you think he's ready?"

Kat closed the distance between them to stand just out of arm's reach and glanced quickly around. They were alone in the bunk room. "Derek will be fine. He just needs some experience." She tucked a stray lock of hair behind her ear, and then let her hand trail down her neck to make a lazy trek to her chest.

Jeff couldn't contain a low rumble of desire as he watched her blatant flirting. In a blink, all his well-intentioned objections about why he shouldn't act on his attraction flew out the window. With a quick step that made her gasp in surprise, he crowded her back against the wall. "I can think of some experience I need," he whispered in a low, husky tone.

She looked up at him and, in a voice that was a little breathless, quipped, "Captain, you know that fraternization among the crew is a no-no." She clucked her tongue disapprovingly but put her hand on his chest and curled her fingers gently into his uniform shirt.

"Kat," her rookie's voice called from just outside the door, "we've gotta go to logistics and get a new med box," he continued as he walked into the bunk room.

At the sound of Derek's voice, Jeff abruptly turned and put some distance between him and Kat. He kept right on walking into the locker room, as if he'd been heading that way all along. He needed a moment to collect himself. Otherwise, everyone would see how badly he burned for her. Through the door, he heard her muffled reply and flipped on the faucets. As he splashed cold water on his face, he waited for his throbbing cock to stand down. *Good God*, he thought, *she's going to be the death of me.*

KAT STARED out the window as the familiar disheveled neighborhoods of Station 10's territory slid past. Dusk was closing in, and they hadn't been back to the station since they'd left that morning. Her stomach gave a pleasant lurch as she thought about the interlude in the bunk room. Keeping her hands-off Jeff had become an endless fight. She wanted to touch him, to run her hands all over his broad chest and muscled arms. His lips had brushed her cheek today when he'd pinned her against the wall, and the thrill of that action had made her breathless. If Derek hadn't interrupted them, they might have finally crossed the line they'd been dancing around for months.

"Medic 10, Engine 10, respond with PD to shots fired." The dispatcher's voice interrupted her daydreams and went on to rattle off the address.

Kat sighed. It didn't look like they were destined to see the station anytime soon. "Medic 10, we're clear and responding," she replied after she heard Jeff acknowledge the summons for the engine.

Derek flipped the lights on and made a U-turn at the next light. They'd just passed the location and would be on the scene in less than a minute.

"This is Medic 10. We'll be staging on Maple Street until PD secures the scene," Kat informed dispatch and pulled on a pair of gloves. To Derek, she said, "Never go into an unsecured scene. It doesn't matter how bad it sounds. Things will only get worse if you get shot, too."

"Yes, ma'am," Derek said and shifted in his seat.

Kat suppressed a smile. He hadn't been on a major scene yet and was anxious to see some "action." All the rookies craved their chance to see if they had what it took when it really counted. She'd been a medic for almost 8 years, and though she was new to this depart-ment, she no longer got excited when the big calls came in. She loved helping people. Saving lives, or just making someone feel better, filled her with satisfaction and joy. But somewhere along the line, she'd realized that the big calls usually meant someone's life had been permanently altered. At first, man's ability to be cruel and disregard human life had shocked her, but now, it just left her feeling sad.

It was almost fully dark, and the decaying neighbor-hood seemed quiet as Derek stopped the truck at the corner of Maple and Oak Street. The address was at the end of Oak Street where several duplexes that were plagued with violence sat, slowly sinking further into squalor. They waited and listened to the police sirens growing louder and louder.

Movement in the shadows of the dark street caught Kat's eye. The street lights had been shot out and not replaced too long ago to remember, and their emer-gency lights threw light in chaotic patterns all around them. She stared at the spot, trying to decide if she had just imagined the movement when a child stumbled into their headlights.

The boy looked to be about ten, all lanky arms and legs. He clutched something to his chest. He ran toward them, his eyes wide with terror. He shot a frightened glance behind him as his skinny legs sprinted as fast as they could.

Kat flung open her door and jumped down to hurry toward the child. As she rounded the front of the ambu-lance, gunshots shattered the night. The boy pelted toward her, and she opened her arms to him, crouching low.

"Keep down," she yelled, and then cringed as gunfire continued.

The impact of a bullet as it struck the young boy in the back propelled him the last couple of feet into her embrace. Kat caught him and his bundle, and they fell in a heap in front of the ambulance. More gunshots filled the air, and Kat curled around the boy.

"It's ok. We're all right," she whispered frantically as the boy shook in her arms. Shouting and more shots sounded in the darkness. Kat squeezed her eyes shut and murmured nonsense to the terrified child as she ran her hands along his back, searching for the wound. In her mind, she prayed fervently to anyone who might be listening, *Please, let me save this child. Please.*

DEREK'S hysterical voice came across the radio. "Medic 10, shots fired at the corner of Oak and Maple. Medic down!"

Jeff's heart stopped beating. The siren wailed, and everyone in the truck froze for a beat. Levi, Jeff's driver and second in command, began to swear and put his foot to the floor. Tyrone, who was riding third, scrambled to pull on gloves and grabbed a flashlight.

Jeff fumbled with the key to his headset. His mouth had gone dry, and he had to swallow hard before he could respond. "Engine 10 to Rescue 10—we're two minutes out. Derek..." Jeff threw proper etiquette to wind. The rookie needed some clear direction before he did something stupid. "Stay down until PD gets there."

Derek's panicky voice came back, "Yes, sir. I can't see Kat anymore. She stepped out just as some kid came running and the shooting started. I can't see her! Fuck, they're still shooting—"

"Radio to Engine 10; PD is on scene," the dispatcher said in a clipped, urgent tone.

"Take it easy, Derek. Keep your head down," Jeff soothed, though his hand was about to crush the button for the microphone. "Hurry up, Levi," he growled as they turned into the neighborhood. Cop cars swarmed in with them, and the night was ablaze with red and blue lights. "Engine 10's on scene," Jeff told dispatch. To Levi, he ordered, "Don't block the rescue. We're going to load and go. Leave the engine. I need you to drive the ambulance. Come on, T-Bird. Stay low." Jeff barked the orders and bailed out his door, dropping into a low crouch as he ran toward the rescue.

PD hadn't secured the scene, and he was disobeying every protocol they had. He knew there would be hell to pay, but he had to get to Kat. He rushed forward, using the back of the rescue for cover. Police were every-where, shouting and running. Derek threw open the driver's door as they came alongside. In the dancing light, the rookie's face held no color, and his eyes were wild with fear.

"She's just over there," he shouted and started around the front of the rescue. Jeff grabbed the back of his uniform and yanked him back.

"You and T-bird get the stretcher and stay behind

the rescue." Jeff glanced over his shoulder and saw Tyrone's nod as he grabbed Derek's elbow. It was one thing to risk his own neck in an unsecured scene, but he could minimize the risk to the rest of the crew. Without another thought, he sprinted around the front of the ambulance and fell to his knees next to Kat.

KAT WAITED until she didn't hear any shots for at least the count of ten before she cautiously loosened her hold on the child and pushed up from the ground. She heard footsteps running toward her, and suddenly, Jeff was there. He pulled her to him with one fierce heave, but she fought against him. He needed to grab the child, not her.

"Jeff, I'm fine. Get the kid," she shouted and pushed against his hold. He froze for a moment, and their gazes locked. "I'm fine. I'm not hit. It's the boy!" Kat squirmed against his iron grip on her shoulders. She had lost her hold on the child when Jeff had picked her up. The boy lay on the street, curled in the fetal position, and lay utterly still. With something close to a sob, Kat reached toward the injured child.

Jeff swore under his breath. He let her go and scooped up the child, who much to Kat's relief, moaned and held his grip on his bundle. Kat scrambled to her feet as Jeff grabbed her hand and towed her along behind him. They all dove behind the rescue as PD started a fresh wave of shouting and running. Two more rapid shots sounded, and for a moment, the night seemed to hold its breath.

"Engine 10, status update," came dispatch over the radio. "PD states they have two more patients in critical condition. The scene is now secure."

"Engine 10 to radio. Start another full response and two additional rescues. Medic and Engine 10 personnel are fine, but we have a critical patient. I'll send someone to triage," Jeff told dispatch as Kat pulled the child away from him.

Kat placed the child gently on the stretcher. Derek steadied it on the other side. His eyes were as big as saucers, and his trembling hands fumbled the stretcher straps.

"I'm ok, Derek. Let's get the kid in the back the truck," Kat snapped at the rookie. She needed him to concentrate on her. His gaze flicked to hers, and he took a deep breath. With a nod, he pushed the stretcher toward the rear of the ambulance. She turned to Jeff. "I'm gonna need Levi to drive because I have to have Derek with me. Send Tyrone to triage. Let's load and go," Kat told Jeff as they hurried behind the stretcher.

"You got it," Jeff replied and turned to issue the orders. Kat felt the same wave of gratitude she always felt when he backed her without question. He never pulled rank, and in medical situations, always deferred to her higher training.

Kat hopped into the truck. "Derek, get on the radio and alert Mercy we've got at least three critical gunshot wounds coming their way." With the rookie occupied, she turned her attention to her patient. His big brown eyes stared wildly around him, bright with pain and fear. "What's your name, kiddo?" she asked.

"My name's Calvin," the boy gasped as a violent shiver ran through his small body.

"Calvin, you're all right now," she reassured and grabbed a blanket to cover him, fearing he was going into shock. "Let me have what you're holding, so I can see where you're hurt." She talked low and soothingly to the child as she tried to pull the bundle away from his chest. "I won't take it away, Calvin. We'll keep it right here. Just relax," she urged as the boy fought against her. When the bundle gave a squirm and a yelp, she stopped. Carefully, she pulled back the blanket to see the black button nose of a puppy.

Her eyes filled with tears as she realized the boy had fled to save his puppy only to wander right into the middle of the shoot-out. Anger at the needless violence surged through her. Little boys should be able to play with their puppies without fear of being shot.

Kat blinked back tears as she reminded herself that she couldn't save the world, but she could save this little boy. "Jeff, I need you," she yelled out the back of the truck and bit her lip when her voice cracked. *Get your shit together*, she told herself sternly. *Focus on Calvin. Can't fall to pieces now.*

Jeff's head snapped toward Kat's voice. He left the police officer who was updating him on the situation in midsentence and pulled himself into the back of the rescue.

"What's wrong?" Jeff asked, looking her up and down.

Kat swiped the back of her hand across her eyes and squared her shoulders. There was a time to cry, but at this moment, the little boy on the stretcher needed her to be a soldier. So, instead of huddling against his chest like she longed to do, she began firing off orders.

"Help me get the dog away from him so I can figure out where he's hit," she said with a gesture at the child's bundle as she started grabbing supplies off the self. "Let's roll, Levi. Derek, get an oxygen mask on him, and get me a set of vitals, please." Her voice held the tone of command, and everyone set to work.

JEFF SAT down on the stretcher at the boy's feet and began to coax the little bundle away from the frightened child. The ambulance started rolling, and for the next ten minutes, the world shrunk to the back of the truck. Kat worked furiously, and Jeff and Derek did what they could to help. None of them took an easy breath until they rolled the stretcher into the trauma bay.

Calvin had been hit high in the shoulder, and the bullet had nicked his lung. The puppy had been uninjured and was currently being fussed over by the ER techs. The kid was already on his way to surgery and was going to be fine.

Jeff wasn't so sure he could say the same about Kat. She was more rattled than he'd ever seen her. She was always one of those who could walk away from the worst scenes and soon after be scarfing down a burger and joking with the guys. The calls never seemed to get to her, but Jeff thought that this one might have slipped past her defenses. He watched her as she finished up her hand-off report with the nurses and followed her as she walked toward the medic's breakroom.

"Derek and Levi, awesome job back there. We'll debrief later. Tyrone's taking the engine back to the station. Why don't you guys get started on putting the truck back together," Jeff said as he and Kat walked into the break room and found their crew members drinking cans of soda at the small table. Levi gave him a look, but thankfully, didn't argue.

Jeff locked the door behind them and dropped into a chair. Kat didn't say anything. She just went to the sink to wash up. He could see her hands shaking from across the room. He leaned the chair back on two legs and tried to pretend he wasn't shaking just as badly. Those kinds of scenes got under your skin. You had to get it all out, or it would eat you alive. He'd never before seen Kat pushed this far. He wasn't sure how she would handle it. Hell, he wasn't sure how he was handling it. It took every ounce of his restraint to sit and wait. Later, he'd deal with his own baggage, but for now, if Kat needed to fall to pieces, he wanted to be sure she had a soft place to land.

KAT WASHED her hands in the sink and forced slow deep breaths in and out of her lungs. Her body felt like a car with the accelerator stuck to the floor. She wanted to scream, run, dance, and cry—all at the same time. It was like having a caged tiger crashing around inside her. She hated this part. Usually, she'd take a walk or get something big and chocolaty from the cafeteria. But this time was different. This time, she'd been in the line of fire, not just dealing with the aftermath. Her guts churned as she replayed the bullet slamming into Calvin's tiny body, and the night suddenly exploding with chaos and noise.

She leaned on the sink and looked down at her uniform shirt that was smeared with blood. She unbuttoned it, yanked it off, and let it fall to the floor. The white tank top she wore beneath it was similarly stained. She swore and tugged it over her head. She thought about rinsing it out but knew it would never come clean. Moving on autopilot, she tossed it in the garbage and stood there for moment, unable to think of what to do next.

Finally, she noticed him. Jeff sat there kicked back in a chair, lounging like he had all the time in the world, and he was watching her.

Kat's gaze locked with his. The tiger raging inside her roared. A rush of heat ran through her as she looked at Jeff with his long legs spread wide, balancing the chair on its back legs. His hands rested lightly on his thighs, but they curled into fists in a testament to the tension he was working hard to hide. She crossed the room in a couple of quick strides.

He let the chair fall with a sharp crack against the tiled floor and opened his arms to her as she straddled his lap.

Kat wrapped herself around Jeff's hard body. Hungrily, she pulled his willing mouth to hers for a searing kiss. God, she had wanted to feel this for so long. His arms tightened, pulling her hard against him.

Her heart thundered in her ears as her hands moved restlessly through his hair. A frenzy of desire and energy clawed at her, wanting to be set free, and with a moan, she gave herself over to it.

Jeff tried to soothe her, to hold her, but she couldn't relax. Desire whipped inside her like an inferno. Kat rocked her hips impatiently against his as her fingers worked the buttons of his uniform shirt. His tongue darted in her mouth, hot, hard, and insistent, answering her passion. Distantly, her last vestige of reason warned that they should stop this before it went too far, but even as that thought blossomed, it was snuffed out under a tidal wave of lust. This was no place for reason. Need, hunger, and passion ruled the moment.

Jeff trapped her hands against his chest, where she still struggled with his buttons. He shifted so he could pull his shirt and T-shirt over his head in one swift motion. Kat rained hot, hungry kisses across his bare chest and took delicious, delicate bites down his neck and shoulders. He let his head fall back inviting her to taste and touch him. Eventually, she made her way back to his mouth, and he kissed her greedily again, until they both had to come up for air.

Kat felt like every fiber of her body burned as they broke apart from a kiss that left her mind devastated and her heart pounding. She wanted more. She needed more. Her breasts ached with need as her nipples drew painfully tight within the confines of her bra. She freed herself of the garment, and with a whimper that was both plea and demand, she pulled him to her. One strong arm snaked behind her to support her while the other hand answered her by cupping and squeezing her breast. His mouth traveled a slow, torturous route down her chest. Kat thought her heart might explode. It hammered so hard as expectation and desire built. When he drew her nipple slowly between his lips with exquisite gentleness, she ground her teeth together and fisted his hair in her hands.

"Harder," she growled and arched against him.

Jeff's ragged moan as he claimed her nipple stoked the already raging inferno inside her. She could feel the tension in him, and she realized he was working hard not to lose control. This was no time for control. Recklessly, she pulled him tighter to her, offering herself like a feast before a king. He kissed and licked one nipple, and then the other. He tasted the hollow of her throat and ever so gently nipped the sensitive skin there. Every brush of his lips sent jolts of pleasure through her. Kat jerked and moaned, and her hips rocked against him in response.

Abruptly, he stood, carrying her with him. Kat dropped her feet and met his hot urgent kiss as her hands began to work on his belt. Jeff tried to help, but she batted his hands away. Finally, she conquered the belt and zipper, and his erection sprang free. She growled a moan born of hunger that had been too long ignored. He echoed her when she wrapped her hand firmly around his shaft and stroked slowly up and down. With a commanding push, she urged him back in the chair.

Kat looked at Jeff sprawled in the chair with his huge, hard cock standing at attention. She felt high and euphoric like she was outside of herself as her body hummed with energy and excitement. She dropped to her knees and took him in her mouth.

Jeff groaned his pleasure, and the sound of it fed her passion. Greedily, she took more of him, sliding slowly down his shaft until he filled her mouth. She closed her eyes and began to slowly work him up and down, losing herself in the rhythm. She felt him growing harder and heard his breathing hitch. He mumbled something that she ignored. Her hand joined her mouth, and she quickened her pace. He was like smooth steel under her touch, and she knew she had him on edge.

His hand wrapped in her ponytail and pulled. She opened her eyes, surprised, and looked up to see Jeff watching her with eyes dark with lust. He looked primal. With deliberate slowness, she made one more pass up and down his hard length with her mouth and released him with a wicked grin. She knew what they both needed.

"Tell me you're the kind of guy who always has a condom in his wallet for times that you need to fuck a girl in the breakroom," Kat said as she pushed to her feet and began to unbuckle her belt.

Jeff smiled. "Not until you joined the crew," he said, watching her hungrily as he worked to free his wallet from his uniform pants that were crumpled around his ankles.

Kat kicked one boot off and wiggled out of a leg of her uniform pants. She let them drop and pool around her other leg. In another place and time, the whole thing would have been ludicrous, but here and now, it was the only thing that was right. She snatched the condom from him and took her time rolling it over his erection.

Kat's stomach flipped as she stood and saw Jeff's tightly clenched fists. Her body ached and throbbed with need. He looked like he was as desperate as she was. A fresh wave of heat seared her as that frantic feeling overtook her again. She needed him buried deep inside her. She needed him to slake this desperate hunger that clawed at her, demanding release.

She drew the tip of his cock first over her pulsing clit. She shivered with pleasure, and her nipples puckered in response. Jeff rolled one between his fingers as she pleasured herself against him. Desire beat at her. She couldn't wait any longer. Kat guided him to her slick entrance. His hands closed on her hips and urged her down. She lowered herself on to him and dropped her head to rest against his shoulder with a small sigh of relief. It felt so right for him to be there, filling her, completing her.

Jeff's arms locked around her. Kat reveled in his strength as she rocked her hips in slow, sensual strokes. No man had ever made her feel so hopelessly out of control, but so safe and treasured at the same time. Jeff slipped a hand between them and found the tiny, hard bud of her clit. Another, hotter wave of desire swamped her, and she whimpered in desire and desperation. She was unraveling and powerless to stop it. His groan of pleasure spurred her on. She kissed him, hot and hard, as she moved faster, driving them both toward the release they craved.

Kat's hips slammed down against Jeff as he rose to meet her. His hands clamped around her waist, pulling her firmly against him with every thrust. His gaze locked with hers, and it burned with primal urgency. She dug her nails into his shoulders as she rode him hard, blindly seeking her climax. Nothing else mattered but the spiraling pleasure growing within her. She shook with her effort and excitement. Her body tightened and she buried her face in his shoulder as she came. Kat shuddered, and her back arched as she clung to him. Jeff drove his hips upward, thrusting hard as he exploded inside her. Kat ground her hips into him as his body jerked and trembled.

In the aftermath, Kat pressed herself against Jeff's muscled chest. She held on to him as the waves of tension washed through her, leaving her breathless and limp. Images of the night flooded her brain, and finally, she let herself think about it. Finally, she acknowledged just how close the danger had been. Finally, she let the tears spill over.

Jeff's arms held her steady, and his hands ran soothingly up and down her back. It took several long moments before she realized, he was shaking, too. With a sniffle, she pulled back and looked at him. Gone was the desire that had raged in his eyes moments before. The tenderness and relief she saw there made her heart squeeze.

"I thought you were dead when I saw you lying there," he whispered and pulled her back to his chest again. "Don't ever do that again. That's an order," he said in a shaky voice.

A fresh round of tears flooded her eyes as she huddled against him. He was still inside her, and she felt like nothing in the world could hurt her when he held her like this. She straightened and kissed him tenderly. "Yes, sir," she whispered against his lips and kissed him again.

"Company 10, Battalion 4 is requesting a status update." The dispatcher's voice yanked them back to reality.

"Shit," Jeff said and began to fumble through the discarded clothing for the radio. They had been so lost in each other. God only knew how long dispatch had been trying to reach them. "Company 10, we'll be headed back to the station in 15 minutes," he growled, betraying his displeasure.

Kat couldn't contain her giggles. He tossed the radio back down amid their clothes and gave her one of his heart-stopping smiles. It didn't last long. He sobered as reality reestablished itself. Things had just changed in a big way.

KAT'S AMUSEMENT evaporated as Jeff's smile faded, and a pang of loss lanced through her as the moment slipped away. How had she let herself get so carried away? She had to get herself together. She still had paperwork to do—and then there was the fact that she'd just fucked her captain like an out of control sex-crazed maniac. Pushing that firmly from her mind, she started to lift away from him. His arms tightened and held her in place. Jeff leaned back and looked at her.

She held her breath as she met his gaze. Here it came. The "this was a mistake" speech.

"We'll have to talk about this, but Kat, I don't regret this. I've wanted you from the moment I first saw you, and now that I've had a taste, you better believe I want more."

Kat's breath caught. The ragged edge in Jeff's voice betrayed his emotion and made her stomach do another one of those pleasurable flips. She smiled and brushed a kiss across his lips.

"Whatever you say, Captain," she murmured as she pushed herself off his lap. "I look forward to it." She couldn't help the grin that tugged at her lips as she started to get her clothing sorted.

Kat knew there were a lot of emotions she was going to need to sort through, but for this moment in time, her heart was full. The jagged edges of her soul had been soothed. She'd deal with the rest of it later. She didn't know what was going to happen in the long run, but she felt like, for the first time, she had someone at her back.

JEFF LET OUT a long sigh as he watched for a moment. His heart squeezed as he thought about the roller coaster of the last several hours. He couldn't get into that just yet. He firmly shut that door in his mind and stood to get himself put back together. Her wicked little grin made her dimples stand out. He wished he could pull her back down onto his lap and show her exactly how much more of her he wanted.

As he scooped his shirt off the floor, he realized that he would probably never get enough of her. He shook his head. It was official, he decided. Kat, with her quick wit, saucy temperament, and luscious body, was sure to be the death of him. *Oh well*, he thought ruefully, *I'll die a happy man.*

IN THE WILD

BY DELILAH DEVLIN

*J*f not for her GPS device, Martika Mills wouldn't have had a clue where she was. All she knew was that she was soaked to the skin, mud sucked at her boots, and two days into this hunt, she was no closer to finding Marlon Oats.

Earlier that morning, after sliding a twenty to a gas station attendant on the Montana border, she'd thought she was getting close. She'd gotten a description of the car Marlon had "borrowed" on his flight into the wilderness and had found it parked in a narrow roadside viewing point, just inside Yellowstone National Park.

After that, she'd followed the narrow stream into a deep gully off the road, knowing Marlon considered himself quite the fisherman, or so his mother had said. No doubt he intended to live off the land until the heat died down after he'd failed to make his date with the judge in Helena, where he was due to be tried for robbing a pawn shop in Springdale at gunpoint. His mother had been very helpful, liking the fact that Marti seemed like "a nice girl" who might "ask" her son to let her put him in handcuffs rather than shooting him. His mother didn't want Marlon hurt, even though his skip might cost her the home she'd lived in since she'd married Marlon's no-account, long-dead father.

Marti was just about to call it a day, figuring she had just enough daylight left to get back to her SUV parked behind Marlon's at the roadside park, when she spotted a puff of dark smoke rising over the gully. Noting its direction, she climbed up a steep embankment, seeking footholds in mud and rock and grabbing vines along the sides of the rocky face until she stood at the top and realized the land on this side of the stream was flatter and filled with tall spring grass—and a herd of buffalo that didn't seem to pay her any mind as she bent over and dragged in deep breaths. She glanced at her hands braced on her knees and grimaced, because they were covered in mud, which she shouldn't give a shit about because her jeans were streaked with dirt as well.

Marlon had a lot to answer for, but thoughts of the rich bounty she'd score kept her from throwing in the towel. Her mother liked to say that stubborn was her middle name, which was a quality that worked well in her line of work. She always got her man because she never, ever gave up. She'd been bounty hunting for nearly three years now, the last one going solo because she didn't like sharing her bounty with a partner or an agency, although she was considering working for one again. Agencies often served as bail bondsmen, too, and therefore had the downlow first on the richer bounties.

Fetch Winter from Montana Bounty Hunters had been working on recruiting her to join a new satellite office he was trying to get off the ground in Dead Horse, Montana, to service southwest Montana and into Wyoming. He needed hunters with experience, and he'd heard good things about her.

She'd heard good things about the agency, too, if a you discounted the cable TV show that followed his hunters out of Bear Lodge. Fetch gave his crews a higher percentage of the bounty than most agencies did, and he'd assured her that he wouldn't be looking to do any spin-off series featuring his other offices, but he had admitted that the bonuses for the hunters who permitted the production crews to accompany them were very generous. The job was hers, if she wanted it. But first, she had to find Marlon Oats.

Trying her best not to draw the herd's attention, she walked along the edge of the ravine, keeping within the narrow line of trees standing along the edge of the ravine as she made her way toward the place she believed a campfire had been lit.

As she drew closer, she stayed hidden and peered into a clearing. A small tent had been pitched, one that had seen better days. One of the screen windows was torn, and one of the poles that held up the tarp over the door was missing. But she couldn't make out whether anyone was presently occupying the campsite.

Just then, she heard movement coming from the stream below and a soft off-key whistling. Hunkering down, she waited patiently until the person climbed over the edge of the embankment and stood.

"Marlon, you sweet idiot," she said under her breath. Her heartbeats quickened, and she drew slow breaths. She needed calm, not adrenaline, to get closer to her target.

Marlon strolled toward his campsite holding a string of four fish, which he lowered into a pot beside the fire. As he began taking them out, one at time, gutting and filleting them, and then tossing the pieces into a pan he'd filled with oil, she moved closer, choosing her footsteps carefully, grateful for the chorus of gargling grunts from the buffalo nearby that masked the sounds her feet made in the suctioning mud.

She studied Marlon to see what challenges he might present. A rifle leaned against the tent, and he held a knife in his hand. Slowly, she dropped her backpack to the ground and drew her own 10mm Remington from the holster on her thigh, and then began to work her way toward the edge of the tree line, knowing she'd eventually have to expose her position to prevent him from making a move toward the rifle.

Soft chuffing grunts sounded from the herd, but she ignored the animals, keeping her gaze fixed on the more dangerous game in front of her.

Then she stepped on a twig, and it snapped.

Marlon's gaze swung toward her position, and his eyes widened. His gaze shot to the rifle, but she shook her head.

"I'm a Fugitive Recovery Agent, so you know why I'm here," she said, keeping her tone low and hard.

Eyes still wide, his body tensed as though he was preparing to bolt upwards and make a run for it.

"Don't even think about running," she bit out.

He blinked, and his gaze went to something behind her. "Bitch, *you* might want to think about making a run for it." Then a smile stretched across his face as he slowly stood and waved his arms.

What the fuck...?

Then she heard it. A deep, gargling grunt. With her handgun still held in both hands in front of her, she darted a glance behind her.

A large bison bull faced her from about twenty feet away, his head lowered toward the ground, his gaze fixed on her.

Marlon laughed then darted toward the tent.

No way was she letting him get anywhere near that rifle, even if he promised to shoot the bull. As big as the fucker was, Marlon's peashooter wouldn't do anything more than piss the animal off. "Marlon!" she rasped as loudly as she dared as she weighed her rapidly dwindling options. "Stay clear of that rifle, or buffalo or not, I'll shoot your ass."

"Your choice," he said, raising a hand to his mouth and issuing an ear-piercing whistle. Then he turned and ran toward the gully.

Another grunt, this one louder and harsher, sounded, and she knew she couldn't just stand there; she broke into a run, following Marlon as he ran parallel to the gully, keeping twenty yards ahead of her.

Behind her, she heard the heavy thud of hooves striking damp earth, coming closer and closer.

Any second now, she'd have to veer toward the gully

and jump, and hope like hell that she didn't break something on the way down.

Then another sound came from a distance. An engine. Something small. She dared to glance back and saw an ATV running parallel but slightly behind the bull. The person driving it wore a green Park Service uniform.

Oh, thank God! But was he too late to distract the angry animal from trampling or goring her to death?

Ahead of her, Marlon gave a gleeful laugh and ran toward the naked edge of the gully, took one last glance behind him, then slid down the side on his ass, disappearing from sight.

Time for her to do the same, although with the way her hiking boots were gliding in the muck, she thought she'd be a lot less graceful and likely pitch headfirst over the rocky ledge.

The ATV's motor revved, bringing it closer by the sound behind her. But she didn't dare glance backward. The bull's hooves were shaking the ground beneath her feet.

With her lungs and legs burning, she veered right, just as the ATV pulled into the path of the bison.

She peeked behind her again. The buffalo slowed then gave a loud chuffing grunt, trotting now behind the ATV. The ranger slowed, too, coming alongside her and reaching out an arm.

No way could she swing onto the back. She wasn't particularly graceful, would miss by a mile, and get trampled for her efforts. She waved him away and veered toward the ravine.

Glancing backward, she watched the idiot ranger stop his ATV and begin waving his arms high over his head as he walked backward towards her.

"Get on the ATV," he said, his voice calm as the buffalo ran several steps forward then made a little circle, which left him a few feet farther away when he halted, still grunting his warnings.

How like a man.

"I'll take my chances in the ravine," she snapped. "Besides, that's where my skip went."

"Get on the goddamn ATV! I'm trying to rescue your ass."

"They teach you how to talk like that at ranger school?"

"Jesus Fucking Christ."

He walked toward her, giving her Remington a hard glare.

She holstered it quickly but backed away, holding out her hands. "We're good. The bull's more interested in your Tonka toy than me now."

Just then, the bull proved her right when he ducked his head and butted against the ATV, flipping it onto its side.

The ranger cursed and turned to look.

The motor sputtered out.

"I'm sure you can push it over again," she said, trying to sound like she gave a shit. "They make 'em pretty sturdy these days."

Then the bull backed away, lowered his head and ran at the 4-wheeler again, shoving it over, then sliding it in the mud until it teetered on the edge of the gully.

"Fuck!" the man standing next to her said just as the ATV rocked toward the gully and slid down the side, metal clanging, and then a loud thud and splash sounding below them.

They both turned to stare at the bull that looked pleased with himself as he trotted off to rejoin the herd —cows protected. She bet he'd get plenty the next time mating season rolled around.

Remembering Marlon, she went to the edge and peered deep into the gully in both directions, but there was no sign of her target. Shadows were gathering inside the ravine. She'd lost another damn day and was no closer to apprehending him. "Dammit."

When she turned back to her would-be rescuer, she found him glaring at her, his hands fisted on his hips. "I should take you in."

She arched an eyebrow. "On what charges? I'm just doin' my job."

"You didn't notify authorities you'd be hunting inside the park."

"I didn't know I'd be heading into the park. I was on his damn trail. I didn't have time to break off and come fill out the proper forms." She tapped the badge on her web belt. "I have the right to follow a skip damn near anywhere in this great state."

He shook his finger at her. "Well…you had no right to agitate the bison."

She cocked a fist on her hip. "Is that even a thing?"

He stepped closer and narrowed his eyes. "Try me."

This close, she realized for the first time that he was young—maybe thirty—and built like a bull himself—all muscle from his big shoulders down to his huge-ass thighs. "You play football?" she muttered as she raised her gaze to meet his. His eyes were sky blue, and his buzz cut glinted like gold. Aside from a nose that looked like it had slid a little to the side of his face after meeting a fist, he was pretty darn cute.

His gaze bored into her. "Through checking me out?" he said, his voice deepening in warning.

"Just looking for your nameplate, uh, Ranger McKay." A flush began to rise up the back of her neck, but before it could reach her face, she turned abruptly toward the ravine. "Think if we turn it over again, it might run?"

They both turned toward the ravine and glanced downward. The ATV was bobbing in the middle of the stream.

Ranger McKay let go a deep sigh. "Guess we're heading back on foot." His glance went toward the sky. It was dusk. Lightning flashed like a jagged fork across the sky. "Or not," he muttered under his breath.

Marti blew out a breath that filled her cheeks. "Took me all day to get this far in."

He shook his head. "Not if you know where you're going."

"It does if you aren't half damn mountain goat."

He gave her a sideways glance. "Didn't your mama ever wash out your mouth with soap?"

She frowned. No one dissed her mama. "She had to catch me first."

Ranger McKay pressed his lips tightly together then turned back to stare down at his vehicle, which was half submerged and jammed between two rocks in the center of the stream.

Her stomach rumbling, Marti glanced toward the campsite a football field's distance away. "I wonder if the fish was burned."

CALEB McKAY SAT across the campfire from the bounty hunter, pulling off another charred bit of fish to eat. Even smoke-flavored, it was better than what he'd had for lunch—which was nothing.

Her name was Marti she'd said, after she'd rescued the fish from the fire. And she was a bounty hunter. She seemed pretty proud of that fact, although in his experience, bounty hunters tended to be loners with few social skills. Thinking about it, he guessed she was perfect for the job.

She'd slid down to the stream to wash up before she ate, but her jeans were muddy up to her thighs. She wasn't anything like the women he usually gravitated toward. Still, there was something about her that pulled him in. She was gruff, had a potty-mouth, and didn't wear a bit of makeup, but when she wasn't scowling, she was almost pretty.

Her long hair was the color of leaves in Fall—brown, red, golden—all at once. Her eyes were brown, almost as soft as a doe's—again, when her brows weren't lowered, darkening them. Her mouth—he was pretty sure that was what had him hooked. It was soft and plump, especially the well-formed bottom half…

He gave an internal shake of his head to rid himself

of thoughts of where he'd like those lips to travel on his body.

Taking another bite, he gave her frame a surreptitious glance. She was lean, hardly a curve—small breasts, a trim waist, but when she turned, her bottom was nicely rounded—not lush, and certainly not soft, but curved just the way he liked a woman's bottom.

"You can get those thoughts right out of your head."

He blinked and returned his gaze to her face, glad the darkness hid the flush heating his own face. "What thoughts, Marti?" he drawled.

"We might be stuck here all night, but that doesn't mean we're getting busy." She glanced up at the sky. The storm that had set back their plans to hike out had moved farther toward the east side of the park. "Tell me again why no one could come give us a ride out?" she said, her voice nearly snarling.

He thought about the radio conversation he'd had with his boss. "Not a priority. You yourself said you didn't need any rescuing. Yeager took you at your word when I promised I'd see you safely to your car first thing in the morning."

She glanced across the grassland at the herd grazing in the distance. "What were you doing out here on an ATV, anyway? I thought you all had trucks and SUVs."

He shrugged. "I trucked in my ATV on a trailer. Not a lot of roads or trails out this way. An ATV gets me around when I want to do things like check on the herds."

She shivered and rubbed her arms. "Thought that big bull was going to toss me."

"So did I," he said grinning.

Her gaze went to his mouth, and she glanced quickly away. "Guess I better toss what's left of the fish over the side of the ravine, or we'll have a different kind of company."

He glanced at the tent. "You can have the tent in case it starts raining."

She wrinkled her nose. "No thanks. Marlon didn't look as though he made use of the stream even though he's been parked beside it for a day or two. I'm sure his tent is pretty ripe." She patted her backpack, which she'd retrieved from where she'd hidden it in the woods. "I have a couple of space blankets. You can have one."

"I had a rucksack. It's floating downriver."

Her lips thinned, like she was trying to suppress a smile.

"It's okay. You can laugh. I have to see the funny side or I'll cry."

She barked a laugh then sat grinning across the fire. "Wish I'd had my phone out. A video of a buffalo pushing your 4-wheeler into the stream would've gone viral."

"Glad you didn't. The hazing I'm going to get will be hard enough to take for the next few weeks." He stood and stretched his arms over his head, watching her out of the corner of his eye as she gave him another once-over, her glance snagging on his hips and thighs. Feeling like she deserved a bit of discomfort for all the hassle she'd caused, he moved around the campsite, gathering trash and bagging it, tossing tinder and broken branches into the fire so that it would burn long into the night to discourage any predators from coming too near. Bears weren't anything to play around with.

She tossed the charred fish over the edge of the ravine.

When he'd finished, he gave her a hard glare because she'd sat on her ass most of the time he'd worked.

"What?" she asked. "You didn't ask for any help."

"You could have just pitched in a little more. It would've been the polite thing to do."

"Polite isn't something I've ever been accused of."

Caleb grunted and shook his head. "Are you always this grumpy?"

She frowned. "Seeing as I'll have to start from square one tomorrow to find Marlon, I'm entitled to be grumpy."

He walked over to her and held out his hand.

She stared at it for a second then placed hers inside his.

He waited a second then raised his eyebrows. "The space blanket, sweetheart. You said you'd lend me one of yours."

She jerked back her hand then ducked her head as she dug into her pack, but not before he noted a deep flush the firelight revealed. He felt bad about embarrassing her, but she'd shocked him a little, giving him her hand. And he'd noted that her hand was slender, if a little callused. He'd liked the way her palm had felt against his.

When she pulled out the blanket, he took it, not saying a word as he walked behind her and laid the blanket out on the ground.

"What are you doing?" she asked, her voice softer than before.

"My job."

Her eyebrows lowered. "Um, okay. So, I'll move."

"No, you won't. I'll sleep beside you, away from the fire. If a bear or a cougar comes nosing around, they'll have to get past me first."

Her mouth opened but quickly closed again. She pulled out her blanket and placed her lumpy backpack on the ground to use as a pillow. After she unfolded her blanket, she removed her vest, web belt, and holster. Then she sat on the blanket and separated her thick braid until her hair fell around her shoulders in a thick, curly mass.

Damn, she really was pretty, and he liked the fact she probably didn't have a clue what she was doing to him.

Next, she removed her boots and socks, setting them away. "God, I hope they'll dry by morning. The leather's soaked through."

"Don't count on it," Caleb said, sitting on his blanket and removing his boots and socks as well, while trying not to admire her figure, silhouetted against the firelight.

When she lay looking up at the sky, he did the same, placing an arm beneath his head to look up at the moon which was blurred by clouds.

"So, did you play football in school?"

"Yup."

"Thought so," she murmured.

He smiled and pulled the edge of the blanket over him before closing his eyes.

. . .

A LOUD HOWL woke Marti from the best dream she'd had in…well, ever. She'd been snuggled against a broad chest, cocooned in warmth. A hand swept up and down her back. She sighed and moved her hips, liking the solidity of the form she moved against. The howl sounded again, and her eyes popped open.

"Just a wolf," a deep voice said beside her ear.

She pushed up and stared around her. The fire had burned to coals. And somehow, during the night, she'd managed to gravitate toward the park ranger. His hard chest was what she'd rested against. His warm hand had soothed her back. "Sorry," she muttered. "Didn't mean to crowd you."

"Got a little chilly," he drawled. "Makes sense to share body heat."

His hand pressed against her back, nudging her to lie down again. She settled, but now, she was wide awake. Her right thigh was between his legs, and her hip was resting on something hard.

She knew exactly what was hard and, for some reason, she felt a little disgruntled by the fact his cock was prominent and he didn't seem to mind that she'd been grinding against it in her sleep.

"It's been that way for a while. Haven't jumped you yet," he said, his voice a rough rumble.

"I wasn't worried."

"Then why are you holding your breath?"

"I'm n—"

He tsked. "It's only natural. Pretty girl sleeping on me."

"I'm sure any old girl would do."

"But you're not old. And you look sweet when you aren't scowling at me."

"Do not."

He chuckled, and his chest moved beneath her cheek. She couldn't help smiling at the sound.

They both went quiet for a while. In the distance, she could hear the soft grunts from the herd, the occasional howl of a distant wolf, and the ribbeting of frogs from the ravine. Without thinking, she nestled deeper against his body, her hips curving, naturally seeking anchor.

"Stop," he muttered.

"Thought it was only natural," she said slyly, feeling emboldened in the darkness.

"It's natural when he's not being strangled by layers of clothing."

"Then why haven't you gotten rid of those layers?" she asked, then wanted to bite her own tongue. *Why did I say that? Do I really want him to get more "comfortable"?*

"I'm being a gentleman," he said, his voice sounding pinched. When she moved her hips again, hoping to take off some pressure so he wasn't so…strained, he placed his hand on her ass. "Don't move."

She couldn't help but notice how big it was. Her belly pressed hard against it from just above her belly button to the top of her thigh. "That can't be healthy. You're pretty…"

"Hard?"

"I was going to say...*erect*."

He groaned. "You think that's a better word?"

His fingers bit into her ass cheek, and she gave a very muffled moan.

"Like that?" he whispered. "Or do I need to move away? I could head to the woods for a few minutes... take care of the problem."

She grinned against his chest. "But a bear might get you, being that far away from the fire and all..."

His chest shook. "It might. Don't think I'd notice."

"To keep on the safe side," she said, lifting her hips and sliding a hand between their bodies, "I'll let him out, just to let him stretch a bit."

"Fuck me," he said under his breath.

"Don't go getting ahead of yourself. This is just a mission of mercy," she said, flicked open the button at his waistband, and slowly dragged down his zipper.

With his chest rising and falling, she lifted her head to keep from getting motion sickness and eased most of her weight to the side so he could slide down his pants.

His cock bounded outward, a large enough shadow she gulped a little at the sight.

"That's better," he said, giving an exaggerated sigh. "You can go back to sleep now."

"As if!" she said then scooted downward to have a better look. Unable to restrain her curiosity, she wrapped her fingers around his shaft, discovering there was a wide gap between her fingertips and her thumb. "I can see why you weren't worried about the bears," she muttered.

"Uh, Marti…" he said, reaching down to move away her hand.

She gripped him tighter. "Not so quick." She moved her hand up then down, measuring his length. "That's…unnatural."

Soft, chopped laughter sounded in the darkness. "Seriously, if you don't stop, I can't promise not to…"

Realizing she was arousing him, she quickly ringed the base of his cock, thinking fast because she knew her brain was about to disengage the longer she held onto his steamy hot rod. All this could be hers…

She glanced up at his face. "Seeing as neither of us can sleep…"

He drew a sharp inward breath. The shared a long, intense stare. Then, "I have a condom or two in my wallet. That is, if…that was where this conversation was heading…"

She gave a brief bobbing nod. "I'm holding onto this. Find that condom."

He reached down for his pants, cursing as he dug into a pocket for his wallet. When he found it, he nearly spilled the contents on the ground until he held up a small square packet. Then he ripped it open and smoothed the sheath down his length.

When he finished, it was his turn to hold his breath. "You sure about this? I didn't think you liked me all that much," he said, his tone dry.

"I don't…dislike you," she said. "You spoiled my takedown."

"Then I owe you, don't I?"

She glanced upward, a half-smile stretching her

mouth. "Clothes off," she said, releasing his cock and rolling to the side.

Then it was a free-for-all as they both stripped, tossing away their clothes.

"Hope nothing's in the fire," he said. "Would hate to walk out of here in my birthday suit."

"I'm handy with a needle. I could sew you a skirt from his nasty tent."

He laughed and laid back, both hands cradling the back of his head, his cock pointing toward the dark, cloudy sky. "You don't have to do anything you don't want to. No pressure," he said. But his narrowed eyes held a hint of challenge she as incapable of ignoring.

"I can't believe I'm doing this," Marti said, sliding a knee over his thighs then scooting upward, letting his cock ride the center of her folds until she felt the tip at her entrance. Her pussy clenched. Moisture flooded her channel.

He reached down to hold his cock as she took her first, tentative downward glide. The pressure against her entrance was...substantial.

"I'll fit," he reassured her.

"Not worried. Not much," she amended then pushed downward, taking more of him inside.

He released his cock and placed his hands on her breasts, molding them and pinching the tips until they grew hard. Then he pushed up on his elbows and nosed at her breasts, flicking the tips with his tongue before sucking one inside his mouth.

As he drew on her flesh, she tossed back her hair and began to move in earnest, up and down, long glides that forced his thick cock through her channel. More fluid eased his passage while friction built heat, and soon, she was pumping faster, pushing on his shoulders for leverage as she bounced.

She'd never felt this full, this aroused. Already she was nearing the precipice, but she wanted more, wanted to savor this first ride. She halted her movements and cupped his cheeks, pulling him off her breast.

He raised his face, his eyes gleaming in the flickering light through half-closed lids. "Need me to take over?"

Breathing heavily, she could only nod.

With a move so fast she let out a gasp, he had her under him and his cock slid back inside her, going so deep she felt him bump her cervix.

"Sorry, don't want to hurt you," he murmured, coming closer to kiss her.

His lips claimed hers, his tongue thrusting straight inside her mouth as he began to move. Their faces aligned, hers to the left, then to the right, as they devoured each other's mouths.

Marti couldn't hold back the sounds scraping at her throat. She moaned and whimpered as he stroked faster and faster. She raised her legs, opening them as wide as she could so that their groins slapped noisily with each hard jerk of his hips.

When he circled his hips, she arched her back. His mouth glided along her neck. His teeth nipped her bottom lip. She dug her fingernails into his ass and forced him against her, holding him deep inside her as she ground against him. When she came, she felt as though she was shattering into a million little pieces.

Streaks of gold light shimmered behind her closed eyelids. When he pulled out and thrust forward again, she shouted as he trembled and jerked against her.

Together, they fell back against the earth. She hugged him with her arms and legs. He nuzzled into the corner of her neck. Gradually, their breathing slowed.

The ranger raised his head and smoothed her hair from where it stuck to her cheeks. "That was incredible."

Still connected, she felt vulnerable, exposed. She licked her dry lips and offered him a soft smile. "I think I can sleep now," she whispered.

He pressed a kiss against her forehead then slowly withdrew, taking care to hold his condom in place. He turned away and disposed of it, then rolled back toward her to gather inside his embrace.

She reached for the edge of one of the blankets and drew it over both of their cooling bodies then turned and let him spoon against her back. Lying surrounded by his warmth, she couldn't remember ever feeling this at peace with herself and the world.

"Sleep," he said and kissed her ear.

She liked that he held her, that he was openly affectionate when she really didn't expect it. It gave her hope that, after they left the woods, there might be a chance they'd see each other again. She was surprised at that thought and the fact she hoped it was true, because she really wasn't into relationships—been there, had the scars.

But just in case this was their one and only night

together, she pretended to yawn and wiggled her hips, pushing against his cock.

"I'm guessing you're not all that tired," he said in a soft growl.

"The fire's almost out. Don't we need to make some noise to keep the critters away?"

His chest shook against her back. His hands cupped her breasts. "If I'd known bounty hunters were this horny..." His cock poked against her backside.

"Don't you know? Be warned, I always get my man..."

ABOUT THE AUTHORS

A.C. Dawn is an active and enthusiastic author and reader of short stories, novellas, and novels. She enjoys bringing her characters to life and strives to stir the imagination of her readers. She believes the best writing touches the reader in ways they hadn't expected and will never forget!

Ava Cuvay writes out of this world romance featuring sass and sex set in a galaxy far, far away. She resides in central Indiana with her own scruffy-looking nerfherder and teen kiddos. When not writing, Ava is thinking about writing. Or wine. And she's always thinking about bacon.

Elle James spent twenty years livin' and lovin' in South Texas, ranching horses, cattle, goats, ostriches and emus. A former IT professional, Elle happily writes full-time, penning adventures that keep her readers begging for more. When she's not writing, she's traveling, snow-skiing, boating, or riding her ATV, concocting new stories.

Jaap Boekestein (1968) is an award-winning Dutch writer of science fiction, fantasy, horror, thrillers and whatever takes his fancy. He usually writes his stories in the coffeehouses of his native The Hague, the Netherlands. Over the years he has made his living as a bouncer, working for a detective agency, and the Justice Department.

January George has been writing since she was a child and has always had a special love for happily ever after stories. She lives in upstate New York with her husband, children and two cats.

Kimberly Dean is an award-winning romance author. She's known for creating strong emotional connections and sizzling chemistry between her characters. She's a 2019 RITA Finalist, and the author of forty published books. In her mind, a beach, some rock 'n' roll, and a good book make for a perfect day.

M. Jayne spends her days waking up to sexy men and chatting with feisty females. Her books predominantly feature characters over the age of thirty-five, facing life head-on. She shares an old farmhouse with a patient husband and mastiff, Duncan Keith on a grain farm in Indiana.

Margay Leah Justice is the author of the paranormal romance *Sloane Wolf* and the MM romance *Strip Me*, winner of the Hot Books, Cold Nights contest and is published by Pocket Books. She considers herself a multi-genre writer, writing whatever story hits her—you never know what comes next!

Megan Ryder discovered romances while sneaking around the "forbidden" section of the library. Ever since then, she's been voraciously devouring romance novels. Now, Megan pens sexy contemporary novels all about family and hot lovin' with the boy next door. She lives in Connecticut, spending her days as a technical writer and her spare time divided between her addiction to knitting and reading.

Michal Scott is the erotic romance pen name of retired minister, Anna Taylor Sweringen, who also writes inspirational and gothic romance. She writes African-American erotic historical novellas for The Wild Rose Press.

N.J. Walters has always been a voracious reader, and now she spends her days writing novels of her own. Vampires, werewolves, dragons, time-travelers, seductive handymen, and next-door neighbors with smoldering good looks—all vie for her attention. It's a tough life, but someone's got to live it.

Payton Harlie is a writer. Who knew? After a lifetime of other unrelated work involving computers and offices without windows, Payton discovered she loves writing happy endings. Especially when they happen later in life. Now, she spends her time crafting romances full of heat, heart, and a bit of grit.

Reina Torres is an author for whom reading was always a way to escape, dream, and travel to different times and places. Writing was a way to discover new adventures and share those stories with others. Reina writes across a number of different romance sub-genres, remembering that those who wander aren't always lost.

Tray Ellis should be culling through her home full of chaos, but she'd rather hide in her writing nook and spend time creating something out of nothing. It takes a lot of effort not take on too many responsibilities, but she's not giving up.

ABOUT THE EDITOR

Delilah Devlin is a *New York Times* and *USA Today* best-selling author of romance and erotic romance. She has published nearly two hundred stories in multiple genres and lengths, and has been published by Atria/Strebor, Avon, Berkley, Black Lace, Cleis Press, Ellora's Cave, Entangled, Grand Central, Harlequin Spice, Harper-Collins: Mischief, Kensington, Montlake, Running Press, and Samhain Publishing.

Her short stories have appeared in multiple Cleis Press collections, including *Lesbian Cowboys, Girl Crush, Fairy Tale Lust, Lesbian Lust, Passion, Lesbian Cops, Dream Lover, Carnal Machines, Best Erotic Romance (2012), Suite Encounters, Girl Fever, Girls Who Score, Duty and Desire, Best Lesbian Romance of 2013,* and *On Fire.* For Cleis Press, she edited *Girls Who Bite, She Shifters, Cowboy Lust, Smokin' Hot Firemen, High Octane Heroes, Cowboy Heat, Hot Highlanders and Wild Warriors,* and *Sex Objects.* She also edited *Conquests: An Anthology of Smoldering Viking Romance, Rogues: A Boys Behaving Badly Anthology, Blue Collar: A Boys Behaving Badly Anthology, Pirates: A Boys Behaving Badly Anthology,* and *Stranded: A Boys Behaving Badly Anthology.*

www.ingramcontent.com/pod-product-compliance
Lightning Source LLC
Chambersburg PA
CBHW062013170626
46813CB00001B/141